RHYANNON BYRD

RUSH OF
PLEASURE

Recycling programs
for this product may
not exist in your area.

ISBN-13: 978-0-373-77577-4

RUSH OF PLEASURE

Dear Reader,

I can't believe this is it—with the release of *Rush of Pleasure,* we've reached the final chapter in the Primal Instinct series. I just wanted to take this moment to thank you for your incredible support. I've been looking forward to writing Noah's book and loved seeing his relationship with Willow unfold. Forced to fight for his very survival, Noah needed a woman who was strong but tender. One who could stand up to him but who could also understand him and help him find happiness. Theirs is a story full of dark passions, and one I hope will hold a place in your heart.

Wishing you all much love and happiness!

Rhy

For my three little sisters—Nikki, Amy and Crystall.

Here's to the memories that always make me smile:
The Three Amigos, 4th of July parties at Dave and
Lisa's, *The Princess Bride, South Park,* the infamous
buttered popcorn incident in Carlsbad,
and last but not least…"One More Time!"

I love you guys and miss you bunches!

Rush of
PLEASURE

CHAPTER ONE

The hotter the pleasure...
the sweeter the burn.

Destiny is what you are supposed to do in life.
Fate is what kicks you in the ass to make you do it.
—Henry Miller

Sacred, Louisiana

THE END OF the world was a strange motivator,
providing the kind of impetus that could make
a man do things he'd sworn he would never be
caught doing. Like coming back to places he'd
vowed he'd never return to… Or seeking out
people and memories he knew were best left to
the past. The problem, of course, was that the
past had ways of sneaking up on a guy.

In cases like this, it could even make you feel
as if you were making the biggest mistake of
your life.

As Noah Winston walked inside Broussard's,
the rickety bayou bar where he'd worked as a

teenager, that's exactly how he felt. Like a man walking the plank, heading toward his doom. And in Noah's case, that doom came in the form of a woman. A woman who just so happened to be from one of the craziest families the state of Louisiana had ever known, and who, incidentally, also happened to be a too-powerful, too-stubborn, pain-in-the-ass caste of witch.

His best chance of surviving this visit in one piece was to get the information he needed, and then get the hell out of Dodge before that particular hellion ever set eyes on him. The faster, the better. If he were lucky, she'd never even know he'd been there.

Despite that comforting thought, a clammy, uneasy feeling crept over his skin as he made his way into the dim interior of the bar, the door sliding shut behind him. A bead of sweat snaked slowly down his spine while chills spread over his arms, the whirring blades of the ceiling fan swaying precariously over his head doing little to battle the oppressive heat. At one o'clock in the afternoon, the business was deserted but for the two beer drinkers playing pool near the back wall and the towering brute lurking behind the till, polishing shot glasses that looked absurdly small in his beefy hands. The bartender eyed him with a look of bored indifference, until he caught sight of his pale blue eyes. Noah took a

quick sniff, his heightened sense of smell alert-
ing him to the fact that the guy was no more
"normal" than he was. A grizzly-shifter, if he
was reading the scent right.

Noah might have been more or less human,
but that "less" part of the equation was becoming more evident with each day that went by.
With every passing hour, his senses were becoming sharper, allowing him to interpret the world
around him in a way that was more monster
than man. His human self, it seemed, had become another casualty of the war that he and his
friends were currently waging against an ancient
evil named the Casus. Fortunately, Noah and his
buddies, a group of shape-shifters and vampires
called the Watchmen, had finally managed to
defeat the majority of the monsters nearly two
months ago back in May. But the Casus leader,
Anthony Calder, had mysteriously disappeared
at the height of the battle, before Noah could kill
him. They didn't know where Calder was, but
Noah had a good idea of *who* he was with. He
also knew the bastard wasn't going to stop until
he got what he wanted, and Noah was willing to
die to keep him from getting it.

But that was going to be a battle for another
day. For the moment, he was after the solution
to a different problem. One that was less personal, but no less important. And one he knew

he could help with, if he managed to stay a step ahead of Calder.

As if aggravated by the thought of that particular Casus, his arm ached with a renewed wave of pain, the scar left from Calder's fangs throbbing with a dull pulse. Though the injuries he'd sustained on the day Calder had been snatched from his grasp were nearly healed, Noah still didn't feel...right. Too many changes were taking place inside him, his system in a constant state of flux that often left him jittery and tense. Or maybe that was just his current bitter outlook on life. Either way, he was a guy who others went out of their way to avoid these days. One who no longer even tried to hide the raw, constant burn of worry weighing heavily in his gut.

Heading toward the bar, Noah kept his gaze locked on the giant behind the till. The guy set down another shot glass, slapped the dish towel over his shoulder, then braced his beefy hands against the scarred but gleaming wooden counter. Thick, graying brows drew together in a deep scowl over his suspicious gaze. "You thirsty, Casus? We don't welcome your kind here, but you can take something to go."

"I'm not a Casus." Noah fought to keep his tone easy, knowing it wasn't going to do him any good if he started shit with the shape-shifter.

"And I don't want any trouble. I just need some information."

"Not Casus?" The guy snorted. "You looked at your eyes in a mirror lately, son?"

Noah ignored the question. Thanks to his maternal bloodline, he had the same ice-blue eyes as the Casus, but he wasn't one of them. Not yet, at any rate. "I'm looking for Jessie Broussard," he said, making an effort to sound patient. "Do you know where I can find her?"

The scowl deepened. "What's yer business with Jessie?"

"I need her help."

"S'that right?" the guy drawled.

"I'm willing to pay for the information." He reached into his back pocket, pulled out a wad of folded bills and slapped them on the counter. The scent of the money filled the air, sharp in his nose, but the shifter didn't so much as blink.

Leaning closer, the guy eyed Noah with a dark, steady stare. "Do I look like the sort to be bribed?"

"You don't want the money, fine." His voice was tight, his irritation rising like the heat spilling in off the murky waters of the bayou that lurked just beyond the bar's entrance. "But I'm not leaving until I've spoken with Jessie. It's a matter of life and death."

"For who? You?"

Noah clenched his jaw as he pocketed the money. "Let's just say that I'm here on behalf of the Watchmen."

A gritty laugh rumbled from the giant's chest. "Those crazy-ass shifters? Hell, what makes ya think I care what they're up to?"

"Because a helluva lot of people are going to die if you don't."

The seconds stretched out, marked only by the whirring of the ceiling fan and the distant sounds of the pool game, while he stared the older man down.

Finally, the shifter muttered, "You can find her out back. Last cabin on the left."

"Thanks."

"Hell, don't thank me yet." Laugh lines crinkled at the corners of the bartender's eyes as he smiled. "Knowing Jessie, she's liable to shoot ya before you get yer first word out."

"Tell me something I don't know," he grated under his breath, turning and heading for the door. It was common knowledge that the Winstons and Broussards had never gotten along. The human residents in Sacred believed the decades-old disagreement had been spawned by a particular piece of land that bordered both their properties. But those locals who were a part of the ancient clans—nonhuman races who lived hidden among the humans—knew the truth.

That truth being that *Chastain* witches generally disliked any species that fed on blood, such as the Deschanel, or vampires. And the only species they hated more than the vamps were the Casus.

The Broussards didn't care that Noah's family was human. Nor did they care that the only reason the Winstons had Casus blood running through their veins was because one of his ancestors had been unfortunate enough to be raped by one of the monsters a millennia ago. They distrusted the Winstons' ice-blue eyes, and they feared the day when the Casus would escape their immortal prison called Meridian and return to this world, using families like Noah's as their human hosts. It wasn't a fair prejudice, but was one that had been bred into Jessie's grandparents, her parents and into Jessie herself.

About the time that Noah turned sixteen, the local sheriff had had enough of their constant bickering and proclaimed it was time the two families learned to get along. Jessie was ordered to give Noah a part-time job at the bar, which she'd inherited from her father, and her nephew Harris had been ordered to help out at Noah's grandfather's garage on the weekends. Though it took a few months, and a couple of brawls, he and Harris had surprised everyone by breaking the legacy of distrust and becoming friends. The hostilities between the families had cooled for a time—but Jessie had still scared the crap out of him.

Heading around the side of the building, toward the cabins that had been built in the woods behind the bar more than a hundred years ago, Noah figured the once ramshackle cabins must have been renovated before Jessie moved into one of them. The lady might have been one egg short of a dozen, even for a *Chastain* witch, but he remembered Jessie as a silver-haired woman who enjoyed things exceptionally neat and clean.

Wondering just how loudly she was going to screech when she set eyes on him today, Noah set off down the winding path that wove through the lush woods. He told himself he wasn't afraid of Jessie Broussard, but an uneasy feeling still burned in his gut like bad whiskey. His instincts urged him to turn and get the hell out of there, but he couldn't do it. Desperate times called for desperate measures, and he'd already wasted too much damn time as it was. He'd known for months now that this visit needed to happen, and yet, he'd put it off. Dragged his feet like an old woman. Yeah, he'd sent letters, but he hadn't really expected the Broussards to respond to them. And he'd known that trying to email or call would be pointless. The Broussards had always trusted modern contraptions about as much as they'd trust a cranky cottonmouth. Twelve years might have passed since he was last in Sacred, but there were some things that just never changed.

So, yeah, he'd known this visit was unavoidable. But he'd stalled, because he hadn't wanted to spend what might be his last days scraping off emotional scabs that had never quite managed to heal. Crap like that sucked. Left you raw. Bleeding. And he already had enough problems to deal with.

Following the path farther into the woods, Noah lifted his face as a cool breeze fluttered its way through the trees and he pulled in a slow breath that had him instantly jerking to attention.

There was something there. Something rich and sweet beneath the verdant scents of the forest. Something primal and female that called to those increasingly visceral parts of him. But despite the instinctive hardening of his body and the almost primitive impulse to hunt and take, he knew he had to maintain control. Damn it, he *knew* that scent. Knew precisely who owned it.

Willow.

With his heartbeat pounding in his ears and a low curse on his lips, Noah scanned his surroundings, knowing beyond a doubt that Willow Broussard was there in the forest with him. That mouthwatering scent was his first clue. The delicate little hand suddenly whipping around his shoulder, pressing a sharp blade against his throat was his second.

With her other hand fisting the collar of his T-shirt, wrenching his head back, she spoke quietly in his ear. "What the hell are you doing here, Winston?"

He choked back a frustrated growl and forced his body to remain still, unwilling to fight her for his freedom. She sounded irritated, but she wasn't going to kill him in cold blood.

At least, he didn't think she would. They hadn't parted on the best of terms twelve years ago. No way to know how she felt about him now—but he figured it would be wise to play it safe. Especially for a guy with luck as crappy as his had always been.

"I asked you a question, Noah." The soft weight of her body pressed closer against his back, making it damn hard for him to concentrate. He could feel the sexy shape of her breasts, the tightness of her nipples, and knew damn well that she wasn't wearing a bra. Sweat broke out across his forehead that had nothing to do with heat and everything to do with the woman breathing into his ear. "What are you doing here?" she repeated.

It was a mistake to pull in another deep breath through his nose, his temperature spiking when her scent flooded his senses, his brain derailed by the feverish surge of lust ripping dangerously through his system. Determined to stay in control, he managed to rasp, "I need...to talk to your aunt. To Jessie."

Her low, husky laugh was one of the sexiest damn things he'd ever heard, and he wondered how sick it was that he had a hard-on for a woman who was holding a knife to his throat.

"You've *got* to be kidding," she drawled.

"I'm not. I swear. You know I wouldn't be here if it wasn't important."

Silence, punctuated only by their sharp breathing and the rustling trees, and then she muttered a quiet, colorful curse and lowered the knife. She was taking a step back as he turned to face her. He tried to give himself time to prepare, but there was no way to hide the fact he was floored. Damn near knocked on his ass by the sight of her, just like he'd been the first time he noticed her transformation from a scrawny, troublesome tomboy into a beautiful girl. It'd been a sweet shock to his system, as well as painful as hell, since Noah had known he couldn't have her. His unlikely friendship with her older brother, Harris, had been part of the problem. Harris would have kicked his ass if he'd known

Noah had a serious case of lust for his younger sister, and he hadn't wanted to lose that friendship. Then there'd been Jessie, who would have skinned him alive if he'd so much as looked at Willow with a whisper of interest.

It hadn't been easy, but Noah had somehow managed to fight the rising attraction...until that hot summer night when he'd come across her fighting off Johnny Stubb in the front seat of the bastard's Corvette. Raw, possessive fury had taken hold of him, and his resistance had shattered, along with Stubb's nose when it met with his fist.

But she was no longer that reed-thin little urchin who'd tried so hard to hold her own with the boys. The features that had once been a little too bold for her age were now stunning within her heart-shaped face, the long braids replaced by sexy, light blond curls that brushed her shoulders. She hadn't gained much in height, but her five-sixish frame was leanly muscled and beautifully curved in all the right places. She looked earthy and gorgeous, completely at home there in the primeval surroundings of the forest.

She didn't blush under his heated appraisal, her rosy mouth tilted at a wry angle as she looked him right in the eye. Slowly, she said, "I never thought I'd see the day that Noah Winston came slinking back home."

"It's…good to see you," he murmured, giving her a wary nod as he shoved his hands in his pockets, figuring it was the safest place for them. He watched as she slipped the knife into the sheath strapped to her tanned, bare thigh, her cutoff shorts and skimpy halter top revealing far too much flesh for his peace of mind. He was a little shocked to see her wearing the weapon so openly, but knew he shouldn't be. Any woman who was related to Jessie Broussard was bound to be hell on wheels, and Willow was obviously no exception. Her parents had been killed in a boating accident when she was only five, and it was Jessie who had raised Willow and her siblings. Raised them and loved them like her own.

Clearing his throat, he added, "It's been a long time."

She dragged her gaze over him, then slid him a taunting smirk. "You look like hell."

And you look good enough to eat. Or lick. Or nibble on, he thought, keeping the provocative, no doubt dangerous, words to himself. Instead, he said, "You look…pissed."

She arched one slim pale brow. "I'm sure that doesn't come as a shock. Most girls never stop hating the first guy who trampled their heart. We have long memories."

"I didn't do a damn thing to your heart," he said tightly. Her body, yes. He'd kissed it and touched it and had been on the verge of taking things too damn far before they'd been interrupted. Just thinking about it made his insides burn. He'd been about two seconds away from burying himself between her sweet little thighs when Harris had shown up. Then his mother... followed by Jessie. Before he knew it, a goddamn crowd of relatives had surrounded them.

"You know what?" she murmured, her voice growing softer. A chilling light flickered wildly in her big brown eyes, the unique color reminding him of gold-dusted cinnamon. "You're right. You didn't do a damn thing, Noah. You just cut out and ran."

He scraped his palm across his scratchy jaw, silently reminding himself to stay calm. He couldn't let her rile him, which was exactly what she was trying to do. "We haven't seen each other in years, Will. Can't we at least be civil?"

"You can be whatever you want," she drawled.

"I didn't come here to fight with you."

With a sharp sigh, she crossed her arms under her breasts and cocked her hip. "Exactly why *are* you here?"

"I already told you. I need to talk to your aunt. Ask her some questions."

"And would this have anything to do with your little quest to save the world?"

Surprise had his eyes going wide. He knew

she'd become some kind of hotshot private investigator for the ancient clans who still walked the earth. But he hadn't imagined she would ever waste her time keeping tabs on him. "You've been spying on me?"

She shrugged, and Noah couldn't help but notice how the motion pushed her breasts against the thin cotton of her shirt. "I'm not deaf," she replied, the lazy, liquid cadence of her speech striking him as incredibly seductive. He'd spent so much time on the West Coast, he'd forgotten just how sultry a true Southern accent could sound on a woman. Like something hot and sugary that would melt on your tongue. "I've heard the talk spreading among the clans. You're a part of the Watchmen now. Or whatever the separatists have decided to call themselves."

Separatists? He almost laughed, imagining what Kellan, one of his werewolf buddies, would say to that. Idiot would probably love it.

"Look, it's important that I talk to Jessie." Before she could tell him her aunt wouldn't want to hear anything he had to say, Noah played his ace. "It's about your family."

HER FAMILY? Though she tried to play it cool, Willow knew he'd seen the truth in her eyes. That initial blast of wariness and fear that had caught her by surprise. He couldn't mean... No, that would be impossible. She didn't know with any certainty that he was talking about Sienna. Hell, there were Broussards scattered all over the world, each one as crazy as the other. Any one of them could have stumbled into trouble. Noah was just sticking his nose in where it didn't belong.

Taking a deep breath, she ran her hands over her arms, wishing she were wearing more clothes. A woman needed full emotional battle armor when faced with a man like Noah Winston. Carefully, she said, "I don't see how that could be possible. You don't know a damn thing about my family, Noah."

A warning flashed in his shadowed gaze, making her stomach bottom out. "I know something you're going to want to hear. Trust me."

"As if. I'm not in the habit of trusting the Casus," she murmured, deliberately baiting him. She knew damn well that he hadn't been taken over by one of the monsters. Yet. He was still Noah. But for how long? Without sustenance, the Casus had become shades while trapped within their metaphysical prison. From what she understood, they were forced to take human hosts when they returned to this world—but not just any humans. They needed ones who had a trace of Casus blood in their ancestry, and the Winstons fit the bill. Hell, they were practically the headliners.

"Stop the bullshit," he growled, finally losing his temper as he took a step toward her. "You know me."

Shaking her head, she said, "Wrong. I knew you, as in past tense. I don't have a clue about who you are now."

"I'm still me. Nothing's changed."

Like hell it hasn't, she thought. But she kept the resentful words to herself. She didn't want him thinking she was still bitter over his desertion. A girl had her pride, and a *Chastain* witch had more than most.

And even though it appeared as if he'd just walked through the fires of hell, he still looked damn good. Gone were the boyish looks that had made all the girls in Sacred pant after him when he'd been nineteen. He'd matured over the years, and he wore that rugged maturity well. He was attractive in a dark, sinister kind of way, his long body wrapped entirely in black—black jeans, black boots, black shirt. His thick black hair was spiky from the wind, his mouth almost cruel, but sensual. And then there were those ice-blue eyes that should have looked cold, but burned like smoldering flames instead.

"What happened to your arm?" she asked, changing the subject as she eyed the wicked-looking scar that was still healing on his forearm. She didn't want to think about how hot he looked, or how badly she wanted to strip off that black T-shirt and see for herself if he was even half as muscled as he appeared to be. He was all sleek, predatory strength, ripped and hard and mouthwateringly gorgeous.

"I got bit," he finally forced out in response to her question, the memory of the event clearly not a good one. Not that she had expected it to be.

"By what?"

"A bastard."

"You kill him?" she asked, lifting her brows.

"No." For such a simple reply, it held a wealth of emotion. Fury. Regret. Maybe even a touch of desperation.

"Weren't fast enough?" she murmured, clucking her tongue. She was being a total bitch, but she couldn't help it. It was as if the sight of him had cracked the cool, calm, nothing-can-hurt-me attitude she'd been hiding behind for years. With every second that went by, a little more of that fragile veneer was crumbling, leaving her feeling small and tense. She hated it. Hated that he could reduce her to this, when she was normally so good at shielding herself and keeping men in their place.

Shaking his head, he said, "Someone decided to save him before I got the chance."

Dread spilled through her system. "Your bad guy had a guardian angel?"

"It seems that way." Tiny lines fanned out from the corners of his eyes as he held her stare. "Wanna know her name?"

"It was a she?" The words were so soft the wind nearly carried them away, the panic in her veins burning like acid.

He nodded, and Willow could tell from the look in his ice-blue eyes that he didn't like what he was about to do. "It was a she," he said quietly. "A woman that I know."

She crossed her arms tighter and ground her jaw. "I have a feeling you know a lot of women, Noah. So why should I care?"

"Because this one," he told her, his deep voice rough with regret, "just so happened to be your sister."

CHAPTER TWO

"YOU'RE WRONG! There's not a chance in hell that Sienna would help those monsters! Not. A. Chance."

The angry words Willow had blasted at him were still ringing in Noah's ears as the two of them neared Jessie's cabin. Not that he blamed her. He could understand how difficult it was for her to hear that kind of news, much less believe it. Noah had seen Sienna collaborating with the Casus on two different occasions, with his own eyes, and it was still hard to accept. It was likely impossible for Willow to reconcile the image of her lovely older sister with a woman who would align herself with someone like Anthony Calder.

What could have prompted Sienna to make such a dangerous alliance? He remembered her as a sweet, beautiful young woman who had always been kind to him. His friends, however, knew her only as the witch fouling up their plans—which was why he hadn't risked giving this job to one of them instead.

He and Willow had wasted a good ten minutes arguing before she finally demanded that he give his bullshit version of events to Jessie herself. He'd seen the surprise in her big eyes when he hadn't balked at the idea of facing her aunt with his claim, but had simply agreed. Surprise, and a shadow of fear at the realization that he just *might* be telling the truth.

As they climbed the wooden steps to Jessie's cabin, she said, "I guess you've got more balls than I thought you did, to come back here this way. Jessie despises you."

"It's either balls…or stupidity."

She was carefully avoiding his gaze, but he could see the corner of her mouth twitch with a tight smile. "In your case, probably both."

Though he'd expected to be sweating bullets by the time he got to this point, standing at Jessie Broussard's door, Noah was surprised to find that he was more concerned about the woman standing beside him than the one he would soon be facing. All he had to do was look at her, and he felt that same uncomfortable, edgy sense of *need* that had always spiked through him whenever she was around. A bad place to find himself in, seeing as how nothing could come of it. For one, she probably hated him as much as her aunt did. And it wasn't like he could stick around to change her mind. Once he had the information he wanted from Jessie, he'd be gone. And the odds of him coming back were... Well, they definitely weren't good.

The maudlin thought made him frown, and he searched his mind for a diversion. "I thought you would have moved away by now. Didn't expect you to still be around."

She snickered. "You mean you were hoping not to run into me."

"That's not what I said."

"But it's what you were thinking," she offered in a slow drawl, finally lifting her hand to knock on the door that was painted a bright, sunny yellow. "And I'm not still around."

"You're here, aren't you?"

"Only for a visit between cases." She turned her head a little and shot him a look from beneath her thick, golden lashes. "Guess you're just unlucky. I'm only in town to spend a few days with Jessie. The 'no technology' lifestyle she's so desperately clinging to makes it difficult to stay in touch."

"Where do you live?" he asked, surprised that she apparently no longer adhered to Jessie's "no technology" lifestyle. He would have thought she'd be too stubborn to change. "Are you still in Louisiana?"

She rolled her eyes. "Like I'd tell you."

Before he could respond to her smart-ass answer, the door opened and Noah found himself caught in Jessie Broussard's dark, "witchy" stare. That was how all the local kids had described Jessie when he was growing up. Witchy eyes, witchy hair, witchy attitude. She was considered the scariest female in the state, and while Noah figured she could help him, he couldn't help thinking the woman was probably going to make him pay for that help in blood.

Her face was remarkably unlined for her age, her nose still covered with a sprinkling of freckles. She wore a flowing green sundress, and what looked like...well, she was wearing what looked like a rabbit. On her head. A dead one, but a rabbit all the same. Or at least the animal's skin, complete with head and eyes made of dark glass, the rabbit's long ears hanging down the sides of her temples like some kind of macabre hair accessory. Any hopes that this particular *Chastain* witch would have mellowed with age had obviously been futile. She was clearly as crazy now as she always had been.

With an odd light burning in her midnight eyes, she took her time looking between him and Willow. "Noah David Winston," she finally murmured, settling that disturbing gaze directly on his face. "To what do I owe this surprising... pleasure?"

Willow spoke in a rush, her voice strained.

"Play nice, Jessie. He has information about Sienna."

One slim white brow arched with surprise, the pale color in sharp contrast to the darkness of her eyes and the rabbit's fur. "Does he now?"

Noah nodded his head respectfully. "It's true, ma'am."

"Hmm. Then I guess you should come in out of the heat," she said, turning and heading into the shadowy recesses of the cabin.

Noah allowed Willow to go first, then followed her inside.

"Have a seat," Jessie told him while she settled her slim frame into a wicker-back rocking chair. With a push of her bare foot, she set the rocker in motion, the steady creak of the wood seeming strangely ominous in the sunlit sitting room, where soft beams of gold poured in through the numerous windows.

Despite the unhampered wash of sunlight, the house was wonderfully cool, thanks to what must have been a kick-ass air conditioner. Noah took a seat on the edge of a small sofa, his elbows braced on his spread knees as he leaned forward and laced his fingers together. Jessie just kept staring at him, waiting for him to begin, so he finally cleared his throat and got on with it. "For about a year now, I've been working with the Watchmen."

Willow immediately interrupted him. "You keep calling them that, but rumor has it they're not the Watchmen anymore."

Shooting her a quick look, he said, "I guess they're not." Until recently, the purpose of the Watchmen had been to act as the eyes and ears for the Consortium, the group of leaders who governed over the remaining ancient clans. Disgusted by the Consortium's refusal to take action against the Casus, many of the Watchmen units located around the world had finally decided they'd had enough. "The Watchmen I'm working with have broken with the Consortium," he added, "along with a lot of the other units. But they still haven't decided on a name for their new organization."

"And what does any of this have to do with Sienna?" Jessie asked, the slight tremor in her voice the only sign that she was worried about what he had to say.

Clearing his throat again, Noah got back to telling his story. "Every time we've killed one of the Casus and sent them to hell, a portal has opened into that section of the pit that holds the souls of the condemned clansmen and women. These condemned souls are called the Death-Walkers, and each time the portal has opened for a Casus soul, one has escaped. Last month, we finally found Meridian, the Casus prison, and destroyed nearly all of the bastards, but that victory has led to another problem."

Jessie nodded with understanding. "When so many of the Casuses' souls were sent into hell at once, it allowed the Death-Walkers to escape from the pit in greater numbers. How many are we talking about?" she asked over Willow's quiet cursing.

"We don't know," Noah replied. "Likely thousands. Enough to be causing more trouble than we can handle." Holding Jessie's dark-eyed stare, he said, "They're attacking small towns and villages, infecting some humans, feeding on the others. At the rate they're going, containment is nearly impossible and the loss of life catastrophic. It needs to come to an end."

"Do you know how to kill them?" Willow asked.

"Not yet." Noah caught Willow's gaze as he reached into his back pocket and pulled out several folded sheets of paper. "But these are copies of a section in a journal we found a few months ago. We call it the 'death journal,' because it's filled with instructions on how to kill a variety of clan species, some we've never even heard of." Looking back at Jessie, he said, "We think this section contains instructions on how to kill the Death-Walkers."

"Then what's the problem?" Willow asked, no

doubt eager to get on to the part about her sister. "Are the instructions difficult?"

"We don't know. We can read the heading for the section, but not what's written beneath it." He offered the folded sheets to Jessie. "Take a look for yourself."

Opening the folded sheets of paper, Jessie studied the passage. She spoke after a moment, but kept her gaze focused on the strange symbols that Noah and his friends had been unable to decipher. "It's in a demonic dialect. A very rare one that I've seldom seen used."

He choked back a sharp curse. "We were afraid it might be something like that."

Jessie's gaze lifted from the papers, trapping Noah in its grip. "So you'd like my help deciphering this." It wasn't a question. She knew exactly what he'd come there for.

Noah gave a sharp nod. "We've had specialists from all over the world look at the passage, but no one's been able to help us. I'm hoping you'll be able to make something of it."

Her gaze didn't waver. "I think that might be possible."

"Great. So that's settled." Willow's voice was sharp with impatience. "Now tell us what you know about Sienna."

Scraping his palm over his jaw, Noah said, "When we were in Meridian, we got to Anthony

Calder, the guy who's been leading the Casus, and almost killed him. But then Sienna somehow popped into the middle of the battle. She came in through some kind of portal and grabbed him. They both disappeared, along with a few other Casus shades, and then the portal vanished."

"There has to be some kind of reasonable explanation." Surging to her feet, Willow began pacing from one side of the room to the other, her beautiful face pale with strain. "Maybe she means to kill him."

"I don't think that's the case, because that wasn't the first time we'd seen her." Both women locked their troubled gazes on Noah, waiting for him to explain. "In February, I saw Sienna in the Wasteland. She was working with a particularly nasty Casus named Gregory DeKreznick. Gregory killed a good friend of mine named Jamison. The guy was only twenty-six, and Gregory gutted him."

"That isn't possible," Willow whispered, shaking her head. "She wouldn't work with someone like that. Not Sienna."

"Tragedy changes people," Jessie murmured in a thin voice, looking as if she'd aged fifteen years in five minutes. The chair was no longer rocking, her body held perfectly still. "It can make them...desperate."

Noah went on saying, "According to Gregory,

he and Sienna had an arrangement. Some kind of deal that they'd worked out, but I couldn't get her to tell me what it was. He claimed that she'd sought him out because she needed something from him. When it was clear he'd been defeated, she said that she'd have to find someone else to help her. That's all I know."

"What did she do?" Willow asked, her golden eyes glistening with tears. "How did she help him, I mean?"

"She used some kind of spell to freeze us in place, until my buddy Kellan, who's a shape-shifter, broke her hold and managed to go after Gregory. Then Sienna disappeared. I didn't see her again until she popped into the middle of the battlefield in Meridian and grabbed Calder. We're assuming she's made a similar deal with him."

"Oh, God." She took a deep breath, looking as if she was trying to collect herself before she was ill. "When you talked to her, did she admit to being Sienna?"

He shook his head, and her face flushed with triumph.

"Then it wasn't her! It could be an imposter. Someone trying to trick you."

"I understand how badly you want to believe that, Will. But at the moment, there's no way to know for sure."

"I'll get proof," she vowed, her expression one of fierce determination.

Protective instincts rose up with surprising speed, catching him off guard. The last thing he needed was Willow running around trying to hunt down Calder. The headstrong woman would end up getting her ass killed. "Damn it, Will. This isn't some deadbeat dad or petty criminal you'd be trying to track down. You have no idea what you'd be going up against."

Her lip curled with a sneer. "This is my sister, Noah. I'm getting her back from that bastard, even if I have to go into hell to do it."

"You're going to have to find her first," he shot back, realizing she was just as stubborn now as she'd always been. "And that's nearly impossible."

"Just because you haven't been able to find her doesn't mean I won't!"

"He's right," Jessie interrupted, her quiet voice barely audible over the rushed sound of their angry breaths. "If this is our Si with those monsters, it would take some old, dark magic to make her this powerful. Shielding me from finding her. Locking warriors in place with her mind. It's not something that comes from the light." Jessie blew out a ragged breath, and adjusted the bizarre rabbit on her head. "If she doesn't want you to find her, then you won't."

Willow spun toward her aunt. "Are you telling me she's gone Vader?"

"Vader?" Noah muttered.

She waved her hand in the air toward him. "You know. To the dark side."

Jessie's voice was soft, but firm. "Pain has a way of breaking even the strongest of hearts, Will. Instead of judging her, remember how much you love her."

"What do you mean about pain?" Noah asked. "I've been searching the internet for months, but there's been nothing reported in the news. What happened to her?"

Instead of answering his question, Jessie locked her gaze with his and asked one of her own. "Why have you waited so long to bring us this news?"

Okay. This was where he needed to be careful. "Ever since I first saw Sienna, I've been trying to get information about her. I've searched newspaper articles and online sources, but haven't been able to find anything."

"That's because we would never mix our family business with the police." Jessie sounded horrified by the very idea.

Noah started to speak, but Willow cut him off. "It's been five months, Jessie. He obviously wasn't planning on *ever* telling us. We're his last resort."

"It's true that we've exhausted all the Watch-men's sources and no one has been able to help us with the journal," he grated, hating the way Willow was looking at him. "But I wouldn't have kept the information about Sienna from you."

Her smile was sharp. "Right."

"Damn it, I mailed letters to the bar," he growled, moving to his feet.

"What letters?" she demanded, glaring up at him. But there was a flicker in her eyes that made him think she didn't want to believe the worst of him.

"There were several," he muttered, scraping a hand through his hair. "They said that I had information about Sienna. I'm assuming no one ever bothered to open them."

Willow looked at her aunt. "Did you get his letters?" When Jessie didn't answer, she crossed her arms over her chest and demanded, "What happened to them?"

Jessie, who'd been studying the papers in her hand again, looked up and shrugged. "I probably tossed them on the weekly bonfire."

Willow closed her eyes, apparently counting to ten. When she opened them again, she looked at Jessie and said, "If you refuse to use modern forms of communication, then you need to take the time to open your mail."

"But I didn't want to read anything from Noah."

"I get that," she snapped. "But we could have known about Sienna months ago."

Jessie's eyes looked owlish as she blinked. "How was I to know that?"

"You would have known if you'd opened the bloody letters!"

"You expect me to open every piece of mail that comes to the bar?" Jessie shuddered, as if the idea were revolting. "Do you have any idea how many people send me letters?"

Willow's nostrils flared. "You know, Jessie, if you don't like reading mail, then get a bloody telephone. Or at least have one put in at the bar."

Jessie sniffed, then turned her attention back to Noah. "There's something else I want to know. Why didn't you send one of your friends? There was no reason for you to come here yourself. One of the others could have done it just as easily."

Shoving his hands in his pockets, he gave her the truth. "They don't know...what Sienna used to be like. After the things she's done, I didn't want to take the chance that I would be putting any of you in danger."

"You haven't told them about her family? About us?" she asked with surprise.

He shook his head. "They're aware that I

know her, because I called her by name. But I've refused to tell them anything else about her."

Willow gave a short, bitter laugh, as if the idea of him doing something honorable was funny, but Jessie simply smiled. "So you came yourself to protect Si and her family? I appreciate that. And I find that admirable, even if you are a Winston. But what about your own skin?"

CHAPTER THREE

His own skin?

"What about it?" Noah hedged, wondering where this was headed.

"Your family is one of the strongest Casus bloodlines," Jessie murmured. "During the thousand years that the Casus were trapped within Meridian, they turned to shades, requiring a human host when they managed to escape and return to this world." Jessie was clearly demonstrating just how much she knew about the Casus and their history. "If the big guy is free with his right-hand men," she added, arching her brows, "aren't you worried?"

His laugh was harsh. "It would be stupid not to be."

"Very true," she agreed. "Why do you suppose none of your family has been taken as hosts before now?"

Noah rolled a shoulder. "Who knows? Rumor has it they were saving us for last. But I don't know what will happen now. The few shades that got away with Calder, if they still need hosts, will probably come after us. But we haven't seen any sign of them yet."

Thanks to the Watchmen, he had sources all over the world keeping an eye out, but so far there'd been no sightings of Calder or the Casus shades that had escaped with him—and while he wasn't eager for a confrontation, Noah hated not knowing what the holdup was. He'd thought the bastard and those who'd followed him through that portal would strike hard and fast after the battle in Meridian, but weeks had gone by and there'd been nothing. No sign of them. No attacks. But his gut told him not to lower his guard until the monsters had been found and killed.

As if Jessie had been reading his mind, she said, "Well, whatever this Calder and his men are up to, I don't think you and your family are off the hook. As far as the Casus leader sees it, you're living on borrowed time. I've heard Calder wants you, specifically."

Noah's eyes narrowed. "And where did you hear that?"

The corner of Jessie's mouth curved with a wry smile. "I listen to voices, Noah."

Christ, any minute he expected her to spout some line like *I see dead people.* And why the hell hadn't these voices told her about Sienna? If he were Jessie, he'd be having a chat about what they considered pertinent information.

Willow walked over and nudged him in the shoulder. "What does she mean about Calder wanting you?"

He ground his jaw and ignored her, refusing to answer.

"What about your brothers?" Jessie asked. "Where are Jackson and Bryce?"

"I've had them placed in protective custody. One of the Watchmen units has taken care of it."

The older woman laughed, making the rabbit on her head jiggle. "I bet that went down well. When this is over, they'll likely be on my doorstep, eager to purchase a spell for some payback against you."

He winced, thinking she just might have it right. His brothers were probably cursing him to hell and back at the moment, but he hadn't had any choice. Now that Calder was free, he needed to make sure they were as safe as possible.

"Actually," Jessie said, "I'm surprised you didn't come here on behalf of your family."

Noah frowned. "What do you mean?"

"For my help with the Casus."

She'd caught him off guard with that one, and he was sure that it showed. "If I thought you could help us," he said, his voice low, "I'd have come here a long time ago. But I don't see how you could do anything." Which wasn't exactly true. Jessie's talent with spells was legendary, as was her knowledge of the occult. He just hadn't thought she'd be willing to raise a finger to help a Winston—or that she'd actually offer to help out with Calder.

The smile she was giving him said she knew exactly what he'd thought...and she was enjoying proving him wrong. With a soft spill of laughter on her lips, Jessie moved to her feet and headed across the room toward a tall, weathered chest of drawers, the bells at her ankles tinkling as she walked. If not for the rabbit skin on her head, she would have been a beautiful woman, and Noah found himself wondering if the strange getup with the rabbit was her way of scaring off interested males. There'd been rumors when he was younger that she'd lost the love of her life in a tragic accident when she was only twenty-one, and the surge of sympathy he felt took him by surprise. He couldn't help but wonder what Jessie had been like before her heart had been broken.

When she turned back around, she was holding something small in her right hand, the papers he'd handed her still clutched in the left. As she headed toward him, she asked, "Why aren't you wearing the Dark Marker that you've brought with you to Sacred? The one you left in the truck you parked back at the bar."

His eyes went wide again, but he didn't ask how she knew about the Marker. If you were around Jessie long enough, you came to accept that there were just some things you couldn't hide from her. The powerful cross he'd left in the truck was obviously one of those things.

The Dark Markers were ancient crosses that acted as talismans against the Casus. They were also the only known weapons that could destroy a Casus's soul and send it to hell. Noah and his friends had spent the past year collecting the twelve Markers needed to break into Meridian and destroy the Casus shades. After the battle, they'd taken the crosses back to England with them, to the ancient manor house where they were currently living.

Answering Jessie's question, he said, "I brought the weapon to kill Calder, in case I run into him. But its powers aren't going to protect me from him, if he tries to make me his host. So I didn't see the point in wearing it."

"Well, it's foolish to take chances. You should make full use of its protection. Now lean down here so that I can reach you." He shot a worried glance toward Will, who seemed to be enjoying his discomfort, then did as Jessie said and leaned forward a little. She lifted a small leather pouch dangling from a black cord and slipped it over his head. "If you're smart," she told him, "you'll keep that on. It's a special charm of mine that should prevent Calder from getting inside you."

Holy shit. Noah wondered if he looked as floored as he felt. "Can you give me some to send to my brothers?"

"Of course."

He swallowed, and somehow managed to force out an awkward "Thank you."

"You're welcome," she murmured, patting his shoulder in a gesture that was almost...comforting. "Now, if you'll excuse me for a moment, I'm going to step back into my office. I need to have some time alone with these papers you've brought me."

Noah watched her glide from the room and shook his head, wondering if he'd slipped into some kind of alternate dimension. Rubbing his thumb over the strange pouch now hanging around his neck, he lifted it to his nose and sniffed. He could pick up traces of sandalwood and something...richer. Something strangely exotic. God only knew what it was, but at least it smelled good.

"I must be out of my mind," he whispered under his breath, cutting his gaze toward Will. "Am I crazy for thinking this thing might work?"

"You should listen to her, Noah. Jessie's an amazing woman."

His laugh was soft and rough. "It just seems kinda strange, putting faith in a woman who's wearing a rabbit on her head."

Willow clucked her tongue. "Are you really that judgmental? Because you know what they say about people who live in glass houses..."

He brushed that off with a grunt and turned toward her, locking her in his hooded stare. For one dangerous moment, he had to fight the driving impulse to reach out and pull her close, locking her against his body, as well. But somehow he fought it down. "What's going on with Sienna?" he asked quietly. "You can talk to me, Will. I want to help."

"I...can't. It's too much." Something tragic and aching flashed in her eyes, twisting his insides, as if the pain were his own. It was strange, how badly he wanted her to trust in him enough to share her secrets. There was no basis for the feeling. No logic, either.

"Have you had any contact with her?"

She shook her head. "I've been searching for her ever since she disappeared. That was late last year. But there's been nothing. I'm starting to think she just doesn't want to be found." Her lower lip trembled with emotion, but she took a deep breath and hardened her expression. "After what you've told us, I guess I was right."

He wanted to ask more, but knew she wouldn't give him the answers he wanted. Not yet. The creak of floorboards announced Jessie's return, and she came back into the room with a somewhat stunned look on her face, her odd gaze settling on Willow for a charged moment, before moving to Noah. She still held the papers in her hand, but they now looked singed around the edges.

"Have you ever asked yourself why that particular passage is written in a language that's different from the rest of the journal?" The question was obviously rhetorical, since she didn't wait for a response. "It's because it's a spell."

"A spell?" That wasn't what he'd expected. "A spell for what?"

"For a weapon."

Okay. That was more like it. "And it will kill the Death-Walkers?"

She raised her brows. "From what I can tell, this spell will kill anything."

Whoa. He definitely hadn't expected that. "What do you mean by anything?" he rasped, his eyes narrowed on her smiling face.

"Mortal. Immortal. From heaven and hell and everything in between."

Noah's pulse roared in his ears, his heart

hammering so hard he was sure the two women would hear it. Yeah, he had the Marker he could use against Calder, but that meant getting close to the bastard. And getting close meant giving the Casus the chance to get inside him. If there was another way to kill him, he wanted it. Badly.

"Can you write the spell down for me?" he asked, his voice sharp with excitement. "Is it one that can be used by anyone? Or do you need to be a witch?"

Jessie held up one slender hand in a sign for him to slow down. "There's something I need to tell you, and it's going to be a bit…well, surprising."

Dread punched into his stomach with the force of a kick, knocking the air from his lungs. "What is it?"

"I was able to translate the main catalyst for the spell."

"And?"

She slid a quick look toward her niece, then said, "You're going to need a virgin's blood."

"Come again?" he rasped, while Willow started to choke and cough.

"A virgin's blood," Jessie repeated, resuming her place in the rocker. "And not just any virgin's. It must be from an adult warrior. Not human, but of the clans."

"Jesus Christ." He took a deep breath and

scrubbed his hand over his eyes. "This has to be some kind of sick joke."

"Come on, Noah." Willow's voice sounded odd, like a strange cross between horror and amusement. "You didn't actually think it would be something easy, did you?"

He scowled as he looked at her. "Easy, no. But a little sanity wouldn't hurt. I mean, call me a pessimist, but I don't think a nonhuman, adult, warrior virgin is going to be all that easy to find these days. Whoever came up with it must have had some screwed-up mind!"

She shrugged, still looking as if she was struggling with her own reaction to the bizarre news. "The spell is obviously old magic, and virgins were considered sacred."

Sacred. Right. Not to mention extremely rare in the twenty-first century.

God, he was tired of this war.

Blowing out a rough breath, he said, "What exactly is the spell, Jessie?" He had a bad moment where he imagined himself lurking over a boiling cauldron, reenacting the scene with the witches from *Macbeth,* but Jessie just frowned.

"I'm sorry, Noah, but I'm afraid that's where my expertise ends."

"What do you mean?"

"The passage is incredibly difficult, and I

could only grasp bits and pieces. You're going to need a demon to fully translate it."

"A demon?" Willow gave a low whistle. "Must be one helluva spell."

"This just keeps getting better and better," he growled. "Where the hell am I going to find a demon?"

"Hell would be a good place to start," Jessie offered helpfully, as if she'd just suggested he run down to the corner store and grab a gallon of milk.

Noah pinched the bridge of his nose and struggled for patience. "I know this might come as a shock to you, Jessie, but I don't travel into hell all that often."

"Hmm." She pursed her lips, lost in thought, then clapped her hands together. "You could try finding an earthbound demon."

An earthbound demon? Christ. Noah had heard of them. They were demons who had either escaped from hell and were now on the run, or who had been forced out for one reason or another. The hell dynamic was so complicated, he'd never gotten a good understanding of it when his mother had tried to explain the hierarchy to him. He'd never thought he'd need to…until now.

With a tired sigh, he said, "I don't suppose you happen to know an earthbound demon who could help me out? Or even where I could find one?"

"No," Jessie replied, her dark eyes almost glowing in the sunlit shadows of the room. "But…I think Willow can help with that."

OH. MY. GOD.

Lifting her hand, Willow pressed it to the center of her chest and glared at the woman who'd raised her. She felt as if she'd been dealt a physical blow, the bitter burn of betrayal ripping painfully through her insides. She couldn't believe it. Had Jessie lost her friggin' mind?

"Will?" Noah's voice was soft. Cautious.

Keeping her hard gaze on her aunt, she said, "Forget it."

Noah looked between her and Jessie, who was just sitting there with a serene smile on her face, pretending she hadn't just thrown Willow into the fire. "Would someone please tell me what's going on?" he demanded.

"Willow has a friend," Jessie explained. "His name is Damon."

Noah grunted, the supremely masculine sound almost making her smile. "And this Damon is a demon?"

"Maybe," Willow muttered, ready to strangle her aunt. Bracing herself for the coming argument, she shifted her gaze to Noah. "But I need to be searching for Sienna. I don't have time to get involved in your problems, no matter how serious they are."

"The Death-Walkers aren't *my* problem, Will. They're everyone's problem." He paused for a second, his dark brows pulling together...and there was a strange light in his eyes that told her she wasn't going to like what he said next. "If you want to find your sister, then sticking with me is probably the best chance you'll get."

"How do you figure?" she asked, thinking he looked as surprised by what he'd just said as she was. If she hadn't been so angry, the situation might have actually been funny.

He recovered quickly, vibrating that hot male energy at her while he pulled back his shoulders, as if getting what he wanted was a foregone conclusion. "Think about it, Will. What Jessie said is true. Calder wants my body."

She shot him a cheeky grin. "He got the hots for you, Noah?"

"You know what I mean," he growled, an endearing flush of color burning along his cheekbones.

Yeah, she knew. But it was easy to see why Noah would be considered prime host material. What male, no matter how much of a monster he was, wouldn't want to wear that sexy skin? Women probably threw themselves at him on a daily basis, begging for the chance to touch and taste all that rugged, mouthwatering perfection.

She was truly playing her role as the awful bitch to a *T,* but it couldn't be helped. After all, it was easier to be angry than hurt, and God, did it hurt. Just looking at him was a kind of physical torment. Just being near him. Breathing him in.

Noah had been the first boy who had ever made her feel like a sexy, desirable female. Who had blown her mind with pleasure that was so intense, it'd felt like she was dying…but in a good way. And no one had ever quite managed it since. It was like the bastard had marked her, every other man she'd known paling in comparison.

Still, considering the cards she'd been dealt, it was, in a way, good that things had turned out the way they did. Thanks to a certain pain-in-the-ass prophecy, nothing could have come of her crush on Noah Winston. But that didn't mean that the way he'd ended things hadn't stung. Having a guy tell you it was a mistake to touch you was never a good thing. As far as set downs went, it sucked the big one.

And yet, despite all of that, she knew she couldn't refuse to help him. At least, not completely. Her goddamn guilty conscience wouldn't let her, no matter how badly she wanted to.

"Fine. I'll track down Damon for you," she grumbled, pulling her phone out of her back pocket, so that she could enter Noah's number. She knew Jessie was going to have a lot to say to her, but that didn't mean she wanted Noah Winston around to hear it. Better to clear out to her own cabin, and come back to see Jessie later, before she left. "You got a cell number where I can reach you?"

His dark brows drew together in a straight line over those sharp blue eyes. "Reach me?"

She tried not to sound huffy. "Finding Damon isn't going to be easy. He's trying to avoid his ex, who has it out for him big-time, which means he's gone silent. No phones. No pagers. I've got to hit the road to look for him. It might take a few days, but once I've found him, I'll call you."

He worked his jaw, something grim and angry darkening his expression. "That's not how this is going to work."

Willow lifted one brow in a slow arch and cocked her hip. "Did I miss something? I thought you wanted my help."

"I do. But you're not going after the demon on your own."

"You want that spell translated?" she snapped, pointing her finger at the papers in Jessie's hand. "Or not?"

"Yeah, I want it. But we get it together." He

crossed his arms over his chest, his eyes narrowed to hot, glittering slits. "The Death-Walkers aren't idiots. If they catch wind of what you're doing, they'll come after you like a force from hell. Literally. I intend to be there to make sure you don't get hurt. And I want to hear the translation straight from the demon's lips."

"No," she breathed out, shaking her head. *Hell, no.*

"If you want your answers about Sienna, this is the only way."

"I'll get my own answers," she snarled. "You've got to be out of your friggin' skull if you think I'm just going to tag along with you for the ride!"

"The bastard who has her wants me, Will. That means you need me."

"Maybe, but you need me, too," she shot back, her temper getting the better of her. She never had been able to suffer arrogant men. And Noah Winston was as cocky and arrogant as they came. "You need me a lot. Remember? Damon might be the only shot you have at getting those pages translated!"

"That's right. So we work together."

Her stomach damn near bottomed out. What the hell had just happened? Closing her eyes, she stumbled back a few steps, until she came up against a wall. "Jesus, Noah. That's a bad, bad idea," she whispered, deciding she was going to have to add *tricky* to his list of character faults.

"I'm no happier about it than you are," he said in a low voice, "but I don't see that we have a lot of choice here. Unless you're willing to tell me where I can find this demon of yours on my own?"

Huh. At least he knew better than to gloat. But she was still pissed as she opened her eyes to glare at him. "I can't tell you something I don't know. And he'd kill you before agreeing to help you."

He gave a sarcastic snort. "Sounds like a great guy."

Her smile was meaner for the fact she knew she was going to have to give in. The bastard was going to win, she was going to be stuck working with him, and God only knew what other horrors awaited.

CHAPTER FOUR

INSANITY MUST BE contagious. Considering the circumstances, that's certainly what it felt like. Noah was trapped in his truck with Willow, surrounded by that mouthwatering scent, and the goddamn road seemed to stretch on forever, punishing him for the sexual thoughts that kept slinking their way into his brain.

Ever since his family had taken off in the dead of night twelve years ago and driven from Sacred to San Francisco, Noah had hated road trips. They made him irritable and tense. He'd been on more than he could count since joining the Watchmen, but he couldn't recall ever feeling this restless while cruising down the open highway. He couldn't even keep his damn eyes on the road, constantly stealing sideways glances at the woman sitting beside him.

She'd changed her clothes before they'd headed out, trading the halter top and shorts for a T-shirt and jeans. He'd hoped the change might be easier on his system, but no such luck. The outfit might have covered more skin, but the way it clung to her curves was just as sinful.

He should have known it was going to be like this. That he'd lose his friggin' mind the instant he set eyes on her again. If he'd had any brains at all, he'd have holed himself up in some cheap hotel room with an even cheaper woman for a few days and screwed his brains out before setting foot in Sacred. Then he wouldn't have had any left to fry. As it was, all he could hear was the slow sizzle of his thought processes as they smoldered and burned, surprised he didn't have smoke coming out his ears.

Scrubbing a hand down his face while the other had a death grip on the steering wheel, he made a desperate attempt at conversation. "You gonna tell me why your aunt was wearing that rabbit on her head?"

Maybe she needed the distraction as much as he did, because instead of telling him to shut up, she gave a throaty laugh, the rich sound doing something funny to his insides. "You should have seen the look on your face when she opened the door wearing Rufus."

"Rufus?"

"He was her pet, until he keeled over from old age. That was a few years ago."

"Okay." He ran his tongue over his teeth, trying to wrap his mind around what she'd said. "So then Jessie wears him out of affection? To keep him...close to her?"

She rolled her head over the back of the seat to look at him, the side part in her hair giving her an Old Hollywood look, with those glossy curls falling over the side of her face. It was sexy as hell, making a man want to stroke those soft locks back, so that he could touch his mouth to the smooth curve of her cheek. The tender corner of her eye. The feminine arch of her brow. On any other woman, he'd have thought it was a practiced pose. Something meant to entice and allure. But there was nothing superficial or calculating about Willow. She was just naturally sexy, without even trying. And it was hell on his system.

"She doesn't wear Rufus to keep him close," she murmured with a crooked smile. "She uses him to project her loony persona."

"Why does she want people to think she's crazy?"

She rolled her head back toward the window, staring out into the starless night. "A woman can have all kinds of reasons for projecting a persona," she murmured. "In Jessie's case, I think she likes the protection her reputation affords her. With fear comes a certain amount of respect. But I also think it helps to keep away those who might have a romantic interest in her." Another husky laugh rolled off her lips, the throaty sound making his muscles twitch. "And Rufus certainly does a good job of that."

So he'd been right, after all. Maybe ol' Jessie wasn't nearly as batty as she appeared to be.

Keeping one hand on the wheel, Noah reached up and touched the charm she'd given him, wondering if there was a chance in hell it would actually work. After all, if anyone could pull off that kind of spell, it would be Jessie. The woman had an understanding of the occult that was unlike anything he'd ever seen. And then there were her *Chastain* powers, which were truly impressive.

The *Chastain* were at the high end of the power spectrum for witches—but unlike most of the other castes, they could mold their abilities into one of three specific specialties. There were the spell-makers, the warriors and the healers. Jessie, obviously, had devoted her life to the first, Willow to the second and Sienna to the third. As far as he knew, a *Chastain*'s ability to gain power was essentially limitless, depending on their lineage and how strongly they chose to train. In Willow's case, considering her leanly muscled physique and the way she'd handled that blade that she carried, it was clear that she'd trained *hard*. But she hadn't crossed over into the "dark side" of the occult, the way her sister had, which meant she'd be at a disadvantage if the two ever faced off together.

Noah hoped it never came to that, but then, he'd learned the hard way that just hoping for something wasn't always enough.

"So now that you've blackmailed me into this working arrangement," she said, "I have some questions for you." She stretched as she spoke, rolling her shoulders back until her breasts strained against the confines of her T-shirt. From the corner of his eye, Noah stared at the delicate shape of her nipples, wondering just how much of a bastard he must have been in a past life to deserve this kind of torture.

Apparently a really, really big one.

Kneading the muscles at the back of her neck, she asked, "What are you guys doing about them?"

He blinked, trying to remember what they were talking about—but his mind had been blanked by lust. "Them?"

"The Death-Walkers."

"Uh, not much," he rumbled, quickly forcing his attention back on the road, where it wasn't likely to get him into trouble. "At the moment, they're pretty much handing our asses to us. We're in deep pick-up-the-pieces mode, rather than prevention. We have no idea where they're going to strike next, or when. Or even how many of them escaped when we fried the Casus in Meridian."

"Have there been any problems with the media?"

"A few." It was costing the Consortium a fortune to "buy" the silence they needed from witnesses in order to ensure the secrecy of the clans. Not to mention some questionable intimidation tactics that made him and the guys in his unit uncomfortable as hell. They understood the necessity, but that didn't mean they had to be happy about it.

"And what about the Collective?" she asked. He wasn't surprised Willow knew about the Collective Army. She was a part of the clans, after all, which meant she knew to be on guard from the fanatical organization of human mercenaries who devoted themselves to purging the world of all nonhuman species.

"The Collective are pretty busy at the moment trying to save face."

"That's hardly surprising," she drawled. "They screwed up, big-time."

They had definitely done that. In an ironic twist, the Collective had partnered up with the Casus after being offered a deal they had hoped would lead to the death of the clans. Instead, their greed had left the Army looking like idiots.

"The Collective generals might covet blood,

instead of money or power, but it all ends the same," he said. "In misery and death."

He could feel the press of her stare as she looked at him. "And what do you covet, Noah?"

Apparently you, he almost muttered. But he managed to choke down that colossal blunder.

"I mean, what is it you're trying to do?" she asked, without waiting for his answer. "Buy yourself some good luck? You should be trying to find Calder. Not worrying about how to stop the Death-Walkers."

"I honestly don't know." He worked his jaw, uncomfortable with the topic. Hell, he didn't waste time psychoanalyzing his actions. He just went with his gut and tried to keep his head on straight, which meant keeping busy. He didn't like sitting around and thinking everything to death. Shit like that drove him mad.

"What about you?" he asked, wishing he hadn't smoked his last cigarette. He'd never been much of a nicotine addict, but the past few months had been a bitch. And it wasn't like there weren't worse vices he could be indulging in.

"What about me?"

Noah slid her a speaking glance, then returned his attention to the road. "From the bits and pieces I've heard over the years, you've earned quite a reputation as a badass investigator. One who isn't afraid to mete out some rough punishments every now and then. Kind of like a judge, jury and executioner all rolled into one."

"Well, it does pay to be a little bit bad," she said with a smile in her voice. "And I never hurt anyone who's innocent."

"And what about those who are guilty?"

"That," she murmured with almost feral satisfaction, "is a different matter altogether."

"Is that why you decided to focus on warrior training? So that you could mete out justice?"

"Oh, you know," she said airily. "It was either that or go into Jessie's line of work and end up wearing a rabbit on my head."

"You got a thing against ol' Rufus?" he teased, sliding her a lopsided smile.

"Naw, I just didn't like the idea of anything squishing my hair."

A burst of laughter rumbled up from his chest, and he was surprised by how good it felt, the husky vibration feeling almost new. Jesus, had it really been that long since he'd laughed?

"And really," she continued, "I couldn't see myself doing anything other than what I do. It just…works for me. I enjoy the travel. The freedom. And it probably sounds corny as hell, but I enjoy helping people."

"What kind of cases do you normally take?"

"There's a lot of jerk-offs bailing on their families, leaving the wife and kids behind and shacking up with clueless chicks half their age. The whole deadbeat-dad thing, just like you said. But I also work a lot of missing-persons cases, which can just about kill me if we're talking about a child. Those are the…" Her voice trailed off, and he watched from the corner of his eye as she rested her temple against the darkened passenger's window. "Those are the hardest, but they're also the ones that bring the greatest reward, if I'm able to make a difference. Most of my clients have nowhere else to turn, since it's difficult to involve the police when your child isn't human."

Something weird turned over in his chest, and he rubbed at the spot with the heel of his palm. "I wish there were more people like you in the world, Will. It would be a helluva lot better place if there was."

She gave a soft, self-deprecating laugh, then turned back toward him. "It's strange to hear you talk."

He slid her a curious look, wondering if he had a speech impediment he didn't know about. "Why's that?"

"You just don't sound as Southern as you used to."

With a grin, he said, "It's easy to lose an accent in California. No one in my family sounds all that Southern anymore, except for my mother."

"What are your brothers up to?"

"Jackson's been running my bar for me back in San Francisco."

"Winston's, right?"

"That's right." He waited to see if she would expand on that, wondering what else she knew about the life he'd left behind in California, but she kept silent. "Anyway, he's a good kid. Mom was pissed that he dropped out of college, but he couldn't take it. He damn near already knew everything they were trying to teach him, so it bored the heck out of him. He's taking it easy for now, content at the bar, trying to figure out what he wants to do with the rest of his life."

If he has one.

The intrusive thought made him flinch, and he shook his head, surprised when she reached over and put her hand on his arm. "It's okay, Noah." Her voice was soft with understanding. "He'll make it through."

"Thanks," he grunted, enjoying the touch of her hand. And missing it when she pulled away, settling her hands in her lap. Giving himself a mental shake, he got back on topic. "And Bryce is a family man now."

"No way."

"I swear to God. He married a woman who's

part panther, and she keeps his crazy ass in line. They have a little girl named Zara, who's the cutest damn thing you've ever seen."

"I can't believe you're an uncle."

He smiled. "I'm not just *an* uncle. I'm her favorite."

With a quiet laugh, she said, "I bet she misses you."

"Yeah, I miss her, too. I haven't seen her since we moved the unit's headquarters to England."

"It seems so odd that you live there."

"Why?"

"I don't know. I guess I just never pictured you as the English-manor type."

Dryly, he said, "I try not to drag too much mud through the place."

"I wasn't saying you're not classy enough, Noah. Just that you're too…" She seemed to be searching for the right word, but couldn't find it. "Never mind. But it wasn't an insult. I didn't know you were so… Well, you're pretty touchy, you know that?"

"And you're pretty bitchy," he drawled, liking it when she gave another soft laugh.

They finally caught sight of the motel Will had said would be a good stopping point, and he pulled into the lot. At this time of night, the place was nearly full with travelers and truckers, but the clerk knew Will and managed to scrounge

up a room for them. It was clear from the look
in her eyes that she wasn't thrilled about having to share a room, but she didn't openly com-
plain. Instead, she simply tossed her bag on the
king-size bed and told him she was grabbing a
shower.

As he sat on the foot of the bed, listening to
the rattle and hum of the pipes, Noah considered
the situation he and Will now found themselves
in. They'd never really been friends. They'd been
more like thorns in each other's sides when they
were younger, always bickering and snapping.
Constantly rubbing each other the wrong way.

And then everything had come to a head on
that last night he'd been in Sacred, and all that
prickly energy that'd always been between the
two of them had transformed into something
mind-blowing. Into something that'd shocked
the hell out of them both.

Now, twelve years later, they still weren't
friends. Were more strangers than anything else,
and yet, it didn't feel like he'd just spent hours
with a stranger. In some ways, the span of years
since he'd last seen her seemed nonexistent—
but at the same time, everything had changed.
What had happened between them that last time
they'd been together had irrevocably altered the
cadence of their relationship. Like a match to
flame, all that restless, uncomfortable energy

had spectacularly combusted, flaring into something violent and raw and explosive, creating a feeling that was… Well, it was…

Damn it, he didn't know how to explain what it was. Noah only knew it was something he'd never felt before. That he'd never come close to feeling since. And it was still vibrating in the air between them, impossible to ignore.

He just didn't know what to do about it.

"But I knew this was going to be a mistake," he muttered under his breath, shoving his hands back through his hair so hard that his scalp stung. He rested his head back on his shoulders, staring at the motel's water-stained ceiling, and told himself that he needed to start focusing on the mission.

He also needed to check in with the others back in England.

Taking a seat in the cheap wooden chair that matched the room's even cheaper desk, Noah booted up his laptop and then clicked on the icon that would initiate a secure video connection via satellite. He knew exactly why Kellan had uploaded the software onto his system, insisting that he use it while he was in the States. His friends back in England wanted to be able to see him—to check his expression and read the look in his eyes—so that they could be sure he was still Noah…and not some meat-puppet being controlled by Calder. Not that he blamed them. If he was in their shoes, he'd have done the same thing.

As he waited for someone to connect on the other end, Noah admitted to himself that while he missed his friends, he was glad for the time away from them. As happy as he was for the guys, their luck in the love department had started wearing him thin. All the laughter and smiles and satisfied looks of pleasure. They weren't naive. They knew there was still work to be done. Knew the fate of the world was resting in the balance. And they were prepared to deal with it. But it didn't stop them all from wallowing in romantic bliss. It was enough to make a single guy sick to his stomach.

"It's about damn time you checked in." Kierland Scott's deep voice suddenly cut into his thoughts, and Noah jerked his gaze back to the laptop. The werewolf was buttoning up a white shirt, his green eyes sharp with concern. He sat behind one of the desks they'd set up in the new high-tech room they all referred to as command central and stared up at the video monitor mounted on the wall. "We've been worried."

"Yeah, I'm sorry about that," he rumbled. "It's, uh, been an eventful day."

"I'll just bet it has," Kellan groused, coming into the room and pulling up a chair beside his brother. He was shirtless, his auburn hair mussed from sleep, and Noah realized he'd probably pulled them both from their beds. He hadn't thought about how early it was there. "And?" Kellan demanded, while he scratched the auburn stubble darkening his jaw. "Did you find what you were looking for? Is the mystery over? Can you finally tell us what all the fucking secrecy was about?"

Kellan really hadn't taken well to Noah's insistence that he make the trip to Louisiana alone, but then neither had any of the others.

"I've gotten a good start," he said, keeping an ear out for the sound of the shower turning off, "but before we get into it, I need to quickly explain a few things. First of all, I know the witch. The one who was working with Gregory, who took Calder out of Meridian."

Kellan rolled his eyes. "We figured as much, considering you called her Sienna," he offered dryly, scratching his chest.

"Yeah, well, what you didn't know is that I grew up with her." While his friends listened, Noah quickly explained his connection to the Broussard family, telling them about the feud and his friendship with Harris. He left out the part where everything had gone to shit between him and Willow, simply explaining that tensions between the two families had prompted the Winstons to relocate.

He also admitted why he hadn't filled them in on any of this before, and then he told them what had happened when he'd shown the spell to Jessie. When he was done, he sprawled back in the uncomfortable chair and waited for them to rip into him.

It didn't take long. He didn't need to hear the guttural curses to know how pissed they were with him. Their expressions said it all. What he hadn't expected was the hurt he could see in their eyes.

"We protect our own, Noah." Though Kierland kept his voice soft, it resonated with anger. "You should have known that."

"Yeah, I know," he muttered, scrubbing his hand down his face. "And I'm sorry. I was a dick not to trust you. I just haven't been thinking straight lately."

"You're also a dumbass," Kellan added, and Noah barked out a gruff laugh.

"Yeah, that, too."

Getting back to the issue of the journal, Kierland said, "You told us the aunt was able to decipher the catalyst for the spell, but you didn't tell us what it is."

Leaning forward in the chair, Noah braced his elbows on his knees. "I know this is gonna sound crazy, so I'm just gonna say it. We need an adult virgin. One with a warrior's blood. And she can't be human."

Kellan gave a low whistle and shook his head. "Well, hell, that leaves me out."

"Now there's something we didn't know," drawled a deep voice with a slight Scandinavian accent, and Gideon Granger walked into view, the vampire's arms crossed over his chest as he lounged against the wall behind the desk. The Deschanel vampire and his brother, Ashe, had been working with the Watchmen for months now, and Gideon was staying at the house in England more often than not these days.

"I don't like this," Kierland rasped. "It doesn't feel right."

Gideon gave a low laugh. "I tried to warn you, Kier, that you might not like what has to be done in order for you and your friends to survive."

"This isn't about our own asses," Kellan growled.

Kierland shifted in his chair, cutting a dark, suspicious glare at Gideon. "Did you know it was going to be a virgin's blood that was needed?"

The vampire shook his head. "Not specifically. But I was afraid there might be something like that involved. Considering we're dealing with dark magic, it seemed...fitting."

"Well, I've got a lead on a demon who should

be able to help us decipher the rest of the spell," Noah said. "I'm hoping to track him down in the next day or two."

"In the meantime," Kierland told him, "we'll research virgin rituals. See what we can dig up."

"Ask Saige," Noah suggested. "She knows all about this kind of crap." Saige Buchanan was an anthropologist who was engaged to one of the Watchmen in their unit, and her knowledge about clan history was extensive.

"Will do," Kellan assured him. And then, quick as a snake, he said, "You planning on telling us who's in the shower before you head off?"

Noah made his expression blank. He'd deliberately left out the fact he was traveling with Will, wanting to avoid the inevitable questions. "I don't know what you're talking about," he lied, refusing to give in gracefully.

Gideon snorted as he glanced from one Scott brother to the other. "Does he think we're deaf?"

Kellan looked into the camera and smiled like an idiot. "I can hear it all, big boy. Even the race of your pulse. You got a new lady friend with you?"

"I doubt he'd call me a friend," Willow murmured, her voice coming from just behind Noah's left shoulder, and he damn near jumped out of his skin. He'd been so focused on the conversation with his friends, he hadn't heard her slip out of the bathroom. "I'm sure Noah would just tell you I'm a pain in the ass."

Gideon gave her a slow, appreciative smile. "If they all look like you, sweetheart, I think I'll have to get one for myself."

Noah scowled. "Keep a leash on the vamp, Kier. Or better yet, a muzzle."

Gideon's brows arched with amusement. "You're awfully touchy, Winston."

"Oh, you guys have no idea," Willow said with a laugh, the fresh, mouthwatering scent of her skin damn near making him drool. A wave of possessiveness swelled up inside him, strange and unsettling, and he had to choke back a snarl as he turned to look at her.

And that was his second mistake.

He'd seen a lot of beautiful women in his time, their naked bodies displayed in erotic poses that would have tempted a saint—but none of them had ever made him feel the way he did when he saw Willow standing there in nothing but a tattered white towel, her hair falling in a tumble of curls over the right side of her face, her red mouth curved in a wicked smile. Christ, she was gorgeous. Droplets of water still clung to the feminine slopes of her shoulders, her skin dewy and soft from the heat. He wanted to put his tongue to her and lick those drops right off her skin. Wanted to slide his tongue into places that were even wetter…and pinker.

Knowing damn well that he was about two seconds away from completely losing it, he growled, "For God's sake, Will. Put on some clothes."

"If you insist." She started to drop the towel, but his hand shot out and snagged her wrist.

"Don't even think about it."

Turning back to the computer, he glared at every one of the grinning jackasses staring back at him and then disconnected the connection. The instant the screen went blank, he moved to his feet, towering over Will as he tightened his hold on her wrist, but she didn't back down. Instead, she stared up at him as she licked her bottom lip with a provocative sweep of her tongue… taunting him. Screwing with his mind.

Was this some kind of game to her? Did she just enjoy flirting…or was she trying to push him? And if so, where the hell did she want him to go?

Needing to find the answer, Noah released his hold on her wrist and stepped back, crossing his arms over his chest as he leaned against the desk. "If you're so eager to get naked in front me," he rasped, running his heavy-lidded gaze down the front of her body, before looking her right in the eye, "then do it."

CHAPTER FIVE

NOAH'S HEART POUNDED, his pulse a thrashing, violent roaring in his ears, while he waited to see what Willow would do. The seconds ticked by like a countdown inside his head, jarring and loud.

And then it ended.

"I'm sorry," she whispered, a surprising flush of color creeping up her throat, her lashes lowering to shield whatever he might have seen in her eyes. She pressed both hands to the knot at the top of the towel, squeezing so tightly her knuckles turned white. "I don't know why I did that. It was a…mistake."

"That's what I thought you'd say." Using a harsh laugh to cover the sharp blast of disappointment that swept through him, Noah turned and sat back down at the desk. He kept his back to her while she went about getting ready for bed, and tried his damnedest not to think about sex. Or that lush body that she'd almost bared for him. Or how right it felt to have her with him.

How much he liked her smiles and her laughter, even when they were edged with sarcasm.

And since when did he obsess over a woman's smiles? That sure as hell wasn't normal.

Damn it, why hadn't he gotten laid when he'd had the chance?

Meaningless, harmless, easy sex wouldn't have solved all his problems, but it would have taken the edge off this gnawing, frustrating need. Or at least he liked to think it would have. But Noah was beginning to have his doubts. This hunger tearing through his system was so raw, he probably could have screwed his way through twenty casual encounters, and still been in the same world of hurt. Because sex with Will would be…well, anything but casual.

And if he had to bet on it, he'd wager it would be unlike anything he'd ever had before. He didn't doubt that for a second.

That was the problem right there. Nothing about burying himself inside Willow Broussard would be meaningless. Or harmless. Or easy. It would likely blow his mind, and he was already on shaky enough ground as it was. Did she have any idea how dangerous it was to play games with him, tempting him to lose control?

Trying hard to get his mind on something else, Noah took off his boots and socks while he waited for her to slip into bed. As he removed the knife and sheath he kept on his calf, he heard the rustle of covers as she slid between the sheets and turned off the lamp on her bedside table. There was still a faint glow of light spilling around the cracked bathroom door, and a frown pulled at the corners of his mouth. Had she left the light on so he wouldn't be stumbling around in the dark? If she'd asked, he could have told her he didn't need it. Thanks to the bite on his arm, his night vision was improving rapidly. He could damn near see as good in the dark now as he could in the light.

At any other time in his life, Noah would have probably been excited by the change in his sight, knowing it would make him better in a fight. But he couldn't ignore the wary voice in his head that kept reminding him the changes in his body were only linking him closer to the monsters.

Choking back a bitter curse, he grabbed the gun tucked into the back of his jeans and set it on his bedside table. Then he pulled his shirt over his head, tossing it on the back of the chair, and shucked off his jeans. He'd just grabbed the top of the covers, getting ready to pull them down so that he could slip beneath, when Willow lifted her head, shooting him a surprised look over her shoulder, the smooth skin bare but for the slim strap of a tank top.

"What do you think you're doing?" she gasped.

Stretching out in the bed, Noah put his hands behind his head. As he stared up at the ceiling, he tried not to think about how insubstantial that tank top was and answered what he considered a fairly ridiculous question. "What do you think I'm doing, Will? I'm going to bed."

He wasn't crazy about sleeping in the same bed with her, since it was going to be damn hard to relax with her body so close to his—but it's not like there were a lot of alternatives and he was dead on his feet.

He jumped when she twisted around and poked him in the arm with her finger. "Damn it!" he yelped, rubbing his arm as he shot her a scowl. "What was that for?"

"You are not sleeping in this bed," she informed him, the haughty tone of her voice setting his teeth on edge. "You can sleep on the sofa."

"Like hell," he grumbled, wondering what her problem was. It's not like he was going to attack her, no matter how badly he might like to. And there were acres of empty space between them. "That sofa's three feet too short for me. And I bet it feels like plywood."

Her eyes narrowed. "Tough."

"What is it with you? You were ready to bare

your ass to my friends a little while ago, but now you're too shy to sleep in the same bed with me?"

"Not too shy," she shot back with a grim smile. "Just unwilling."

His temper started to slip away from him, and he forced his response through gritted teeth. "I'm not going to touch you, so just chill."

She studied his face in the soft darkness, no doubt noticing how worn out he looked, and finally relented. "Fine. Whatever. Just stay on your side of the mattress."

He grunted, wondering if he should be insulted that she'd apparently just decided he was too tired to be a threat. "The same goes for you," he ground out with a disgruntled thread of amusement, certain it was the first time he'd ever warned a woman to stay *away* from him in bed.

She muttered something colorful in response as she gave him her back, and despite his shitty mood, Noah found himself grinning. He lay there for a long time in the quiet darkness, listening as her breathing eventually evened out with the calmness of sleep. He must have eventually dozed off, because sometime in the night he drifted slowly back to awareness. He knew, in an instant, that he was dreaming. And he didn't want to wake up. Not yet. Unlike the gruesome nightmares that had plagued him for months, this one was too damn good to miss.

He was standing in the middle of a forest... and he was with Will. A bloodred moon hung low over the trees, scarred by the jagged edges of dark cloud that stretched across the sky. The air was warm, sweet with the scent of Willow's skin, the night silent but for the whispering of the wind and their sawing breaths.

They were both dressed in jeans and T-shirts, but her nipples were pressed tight against the thin cotton, and Noah felt himself reaching out for her, covering the soft weight of her breast with his hand. She gasped, her head falling back, and with a low growl on his lips, he took her mouth in a desperate, searching kiss, as if he was trying to find the answer to something important. Something...vital.

Noah didn't know how long they stayed in that tight, clutching embrace, arms wrapped around each other, the tenor of the kiss bordering on violence. He thrust his tongue against hers with a greed that left him shaken, then nipped at her bottom lip, unable to get enough of the sleek, petal-soft textures...the warm, honeylike taste. It was a rich, drugging sweetness that made his blood go thick, his cock pulsing with a raw, insistent ache. He ran his hands down her back until he gripped her ass, then yanked her close, her body soft and pliant against his hardness, melting into him.

God, he needed this. Even if it was only a dream. He needed all of her. Needed her on his tongue, on his skin. Needed to spread her open and drive his body inside hers until she'd taken every demanding inch of him. Until he could feel the hammering of her heartbeat thrumming around the heavy length of his cock as he stretched her open, her arms and legs locked tight around his body, holding him close. Binding him to her.

His hands gripped tighter as he lifted her up, grinding her against his erection with an animal-like sound of pleasure. He moved forward a few steps, trapping her against the gnarled trunk of a towering oak tree. Curving one hand around the back of her neck, tangling his fingers in her soft curls, he slid the other down the back of her thigh. As he lifted her leg higher on his hip, the position allowed him to rub more fully against the warm cushion of her sex. She moaned in response, whispering his name, and the soft sound of longing pierced right through him, like a bullet. It struck with a violent force that ripped him from the lush, delicious depths of the dream, jerking him back to a shocking awareness.

With his chest heaving, Noah opened his eyes and took in the startling reality of his surroundings. The cheap motel room, instead of the forest. A scarred headboard instead of the gnarled, towering tree. But Willow was still in his arms. Still moaning and writhing against him, her legs hugging his hips, his knees braced in the bedding. She moved like she wanted to crawl under his skin, driving him out of his mind.

Driven by blinding urgency, his hand shook as he grasped the hem of her tank top and shoved it up, his mouth closing hotly over a sweet, pink nipple. She cried out at the intimate contact, the throaty sound making him wild. He used his tongue to stroke and lick, nipping with his teeth, before sucking on her with a hunger that just kept rising. He could *not* get enough. Not of her taste or her skin or those provocative little sounds she kept making. The way she arched against his mouth, seeking more…or the breath-taking quiver of desire shivering through her limbs. The way she wound her fingers in his hair, tugging him closer.

God…I need her. Want her.

Just her. Her. Her…

In that moment, all of Noah's concerns were forgotten. He was an animal, primal and male, at the mercy of his baser hungers. He grunted with feral satisfaction as he lifted her body higher, trapping her against the headboard with the burning heat of his body, his muscles coiled hard and tight. Her dazed eyes went wide as he gave a raw, guttural growl, just before he covered her mouth with his, his blood roaring in his ears as visceral craving bore down on him, obliterating reason and logic. Smashing it with a violence that should have shaken him…but he was too far out there, existing in pure sensation.

She didn't fight him, but her mouth had been shocked into stillness beneath his—passive, simply taking, accepting—and he wanted her hunger. Wanted the bite of her nails and her mind-blowing passion.

He wanted her wild for him.

"Goddamn it, kiss me back," he snarled, holding the side of her face in his hand. She moaned, tilting her head, fitting her mouth more closely to his. "Please," he gasped against her silky lips, his voice cracking as he begged her…pleading. "Kiss me back, Will." And then he felt the soft, sweet stroke of her tongue, and his body shuddered violently in response to that delicate, seeking touch. Within seconds, the kiss became something explicitly carnal, devastating in its power. Noah kissed her like he wanted to consume her. Like he never wanted to stop. And he didn't. He wanted it to last forever. Wanted to keep drinking in that warm, heady flavor, loving the way she tasted on his tongue. Loving that for once in his godforsaken life, reality was so much better than the dream.

With another feral, rumbling growl, he broke the kiss, pressing his mouth to the sharp point of her jaw as he sucked in lungfuls of her mouth-watering scent, his chest heaving. Heat shot up his spine, roaring through him as he reached for the waistband of her pajama bottoms, wrenching them down as far as he could get them with her legs wrapped around his waist. His body shuddered as he pressed his hand between her thighs, stroked through the plump, slippery folds that were drenched with heat, then thrust a long finger inside her. She cried out again, panting against the side of his face, her nails biting into his shoulders, while her inner muscles spasmed, clasping him tighter, fighting to hold him inside her. He made a thick sound as he pressed deeper, loving the way she clung to him, so tender and hot, and he pulled his head back so that he could watch her eyes. Watch the pleasure climb, shocking her, the moment so intimate it made his chest hurt. He'd done this with too many women to count, and yet, in that moment, he couldn't remember a goddamn one of them.

Not. A. Single. One.

All he could see was Will.

It was mesmerizing, watching the emotion flash through her dark eyes as he stroked inside her, penetrating the plush sheath, pushing deep, then slipping his finger back out and swirling the callused tip wetly over her clit. She trembled, her mouth open for a soundless word that looked like *More,* and he locked his jaw as he pushed back in, giving her two fingers this time. Her sex was tight and wet and scalding around his fingers, burning him alive, and he braced her with the press of his body so that he could free his other hand to shove down his boxers.

She cried out again, his name spilled huskily from her kiss-swollen lips, and the next thing Noah knew, long, lethal fangs were bursting into his mouth, heavy and throbbing and hot—just like the ones he had in his nightmares. But he was too far gone to care. He pressed himself against her, stroking the heavy head of his cock through her slick, swollen folds, his breath leaving his chest in ragged bursts as he buried his face in the crook of her shoulder. Her skin was deliciously smooth against his scratchy cheek, her scent an intoxicating lure. Unable to resist, he put his mouth against the tender column of her throat, the hunger demanding that he possess and mark her in the most primal, savage way that a male could mark his mate.

Just as the blunt tip of him nudged her entrance, he scraped his fangs across her sumptuous flesh, on the verge of taking his first bite, when she gripped two handfuls of his hair and wrenched his head back.

"Whoa," she said breathlessly. "Noah, wait!"

"I won't hurt you," he groaned, lowering his head and flicking his tongue against her throat, loving the way her wet sex felt against the bulging head of his shaft. "I—"

"Noah! Listen to me. I said *no!*"

He pulled back a little, confused. He could sense her withdrawal, but couldn't understand exactly what she wanted. Her words were fuzzy in his ears, their meaning not getting through to his brain, like she was shouting at him through soundproof glass while he struggled to read her lips. He shook his head, trying to concentrate, while the import of those words fought to break their way through the deafening fog of hunger and lust.

"Goddamn it, Noah!" She shoved hard against his shoulders, then slapped him with so much force that his head whipped to the side. "Move back!"

The words busted through that time, like a douse of cold water in his face. He brought his face back around and looked into her eyes…and reality came back in a slow, sickening slide.

Shit, he thought dully, shaking his head again, while the details of the situation came into sharper focus. Her warm body crushed against his chest. The thick, granite-hard length of his cock pressing against her inner thigh. The kiss-swollen shape of her mouth beneath eyes that were burning with hot, vibrant emotion. Christ, he could *not* be doing this. What the hell was wrong with him?

"Damn it!" He curved his hands into shaking fists, lifted his arms and slammed his fists against the wall, making her jump. A muscle in his jaw pulsed with fury as he narrowed his eyes at her. "This isn't going to happen," he snarled. "I am *not* going to bang you against the wall in some cheap motel room. Not for our first time!"

"Hey!" Indignation filled her expression. "It wasn't like I asked for this. *You're* the one who grabbed *me*. And I'm the one who told you to stop!"

"You think I don't know that?" he shouted, hitting the wall again. "I know I fucked up and I'm sorry!" He felt the heavy, uncomfortable fangs start to recede, and almost sagged with relief. His fists unclenched, his hands flattening against the wall as he closed his eyes. "I didn't mean to scare you," he added in a halting rasp, the burning in his gums a stark reminder of what had almost happened. "I…I thought you were… with me." His eyes opened, and he locked his gaze with hers. "I thought you wanted me."

CHAPTER SIX

WILLOW SWIPED HER tongue across her lower lip, fully aware that Noah was waiting for her to tell him he'd been right, that she *had* wanted him. When he realized she wasn't going to say anything, his expression tightened and he pulled away from her, a blast of cold hitting her as she lost the feverish heat of his body.

He kept his face averted as he jerked up his boxers—too fast for her to get a good look at him—and moved to the other side of the bed, where he sat with his long legs braced over the side, elbows on his knees, head in his hands. His back was strong and beautifully muscled, his skin misted with a light sheen of sweat. She licked her bottom lip again, tasting him on her mouth, and he tasted like wicked things. Like sin and sex. Like something that she could get addicted to, if she didn't play it smart.

Problem was, she'd been wanting to be un-smart all friggin' night. When he'd challenged her about the striptease, she'd been so tempted to call his bluff. To just drop the towel and see if he would make good on the carnal, provocative threat that had burned in those piercing ice-blue eyes. Noah Winston at nineteen had been the most gorgeous thing she'd ever seen. But at thirty-one he was to die for. Dark, devastating and enticingly dangerous. He all but oozed sex appeal, one crooked slant of that sensual mouth and she was ready to beg. It was only through sheer force of will that she'd managed to resist the urge.

She'd actually been proud of herself, thinking she was stronger than she'd thought where he was concerned, until he'd shut down his computer and started taking his clothes off. She'd been watching him in the mirror over the dresser, and her eyes had all but bugged out of her skull when he'd pulled off his shirt. No doubt about it, the man was built. To perfection. His shoulders were hard and broad, his muscles ripped beneath golden skin that looked silky and warm. There was a particularly nasty scar running along his rib cage that she wanted to ask about, as well as other souvenirs from his time with the Watchmen. She'd had no idea just how good that hard-worn look would suit him.

She wanted him so badly she could taste it, and if she were any other woman she probably would have said to hell with pride and taken what he was offering. But she couldn't. Damn it, there were reasons she couldn't have sex with him. Circumstances that were beyond her control. That she could do nothing to change at this point. It sucked, but this was the hand that fate had dealt her, and no matter how much she hated it, Willow knew she couldn't change it.

But that didn't mean she wasn't tempted. And by a man with a wicked set of fangs, no less. Go figure. She didn't hold the prejudice against those breeds that liked to drop fang now and then, the way most of the *Chastain* did. But then, it'd never been something that had turned her on, either.

Not that she was admitting any of it to him. There was too much baggage between them. Too many feelings that were tenuous and raw. Too much unknown. Too much...everything.

She was, however, eager for an answer about what had just happened. Quickly sorting out her pajama bottoms and tank top, she dropped down into a sitting position, pulling her knees to her chest. "Is there something you want to tell me, Noah? Because the last I knew, you were human. As in *sans* fangs."

"I'll tell you...what's happening. I promise." His breathing was still ragged, his shoulders glistening with sweat. "Just not now, Will. Please."

She accepted that…for the moment, but only because she wasn't entirely certain she wanted to know the answer.

Still, she wasn't afraid.

And it wasn't like she was without resources. Her blade was close by, sitting on the bedside table. Or, if she'd wanted, she could have blasted him with a shot of electricity, thanks to her powers. But she hadn't wanted to hurt him. And in spite of everything, she didn't believe he would ever harm her.

But if that was true, then why was her heart hammering like a freight train, her breath still tight in her lungs? Was it Noah she didn't trust… or her own weak-kneed, gimme-your-body-now reaction to him?

Believing he would never harm her physically was one thing—but there were all kinds of hurt. Endless ways to cause pain. Her body might be safe…but her heart was a different matter altogether.

"Fine. I'll accept that for now," she said, studying the back of his neck, appreciating how beautiful it was in the soft spill of light still glowing around the bathroom door. Masculine, strong. She loved the shape of his hairline and his ears. Loved the strong cords of muscle and sinew that connected his neck to those powerful shoulders. Yum.

"I'm sorry, Will." His rough voice pulled at her, making her want to reach out to him. "If it makes you feel any better, I feel like shit about… what just happened."

"I don't know what you're so upset about. I wanted you to stop, and you did. You didn't hurt me, and I'm hardly going to be traumatized by…a few kisses. I'm not a child, Noah." And it's not like she hadn't been kissing him back, rubbing all over him. When she thought of just *how* eager she'd been, heat climbed into her face, and she had to fight the urge to cover her burning cheeks with her hands.

He exhaled a shaky breath. "Yeah. I, uh, definitely know that you're not a child."

"And it's not like this should be new for you. I happen to know that you never had any trouble banging girls in cheap motel rooms before."

His head whipped to the side in a flash, his eyes hooded as he caught her gaze over his shoulder. "How the hell do you know that?"

Her lashes lowered as she shrugged. "I know lots of things about you."

"You've spied on me with women?" he rasped, his eyes widening with shock.

She snorted softly. "Don't flatter yourself. But I had ears when we were younger. And I was sneaky. I used to listen in when you and Harris were talking. I know all about the girls you slept with."

Willow watched him digest that bit of news, an eloquent curse on his sensual lips. Then she said, "I'm still waiting for an explanation."

He drew his brows together. "About what?"

"About why you seem to find the idea of banging me in a cheap motel room so distasteful."

She thought he'd decided not to answer that question, as well, when he shifted position and propped his back against the headboard, one leg bent at the knee, the other still hanging over the side of the bed. "Because you deserve better."

The stark, poignant response reverberated through her like a tender caress, and she felt herself slipping into a fiercely emotional place she couldn't afford to go to. "Why touch me at all, Noah?"

"I couldn't touch you before," he said in a low voice, staring down at his palm as he opened and closed his fingers. "But most of the reasons why I couldn't are no longer relevant." He blew out a deep, careful breath of air. "We're gonna have to talk about that."

Couldn't touch her? She'd been there—she knew damn well that he'd *touched* her that night. In intimate, wonderful places that had made her scream.

In her innocence, she'd been embarrassed by

the force of her reaction to the delicious things he'd done to her body. She'd been unable to contain her husky cries of excitement, his deep voice rough with hunger as he'd whispered in her ear. She'd been shocked by the explicit images he'd painted in her mind, while those talented fingers had pushed her deeper into that blinding, shaking madness.

But they'd been discovered before they could go any further. Before he could put his mouth on her. Before he could bury himself deep inside her, like he'd promised her he would. And there wasn't a day that went by that she didn't regret that loss.

"Noah," she said softly, hugging her knees closer to her chest. "You *did* touch me."

"Not nearly as much as I wanted to." His fingers curled into a powerful fist, and he gave his head a hard shake, his jaw so tight it looked painful. "You were too innocent for the things I wanted from you that night. Your brother was right to warn me off."

"You could have just practiced a little self-control." God knows she'd been practicing it for years.

He gave a gruff laugh, relaxing his hand. "Maybe, if you were just some pretty girl I'd wanted to score with. But it was more than that."

It was? "More...how?" she asked, unsure of where this was going.

He shoved his hand back through his hair, leaving it spiked out in every direction, making it look as if he'd just come from a hot, sweaty sex-fest. She couldn't help but notice that he wore that just-got-laid look exceptionally well.

"Haven't you ever wondered why I cut and bailed?" he asked, suddenly turning his head and locking his gaze with hers. "Why I didn't tell our families to mind their own damn business that night and just stayed in Sacred?"

"No," she lied. "I didn't see any reason to waste my time trying to figure you out." Which was another big, fat, whopping lie. "Jackasses don't need a reason to act like jackasses, Noah."

He made a harsh sound in the back of his throat. "I was crazy about you, Will. I had been for a long time. Long before that night ever happened."

Oh...God. Hiding her reaction to those devastating words was one of the most difficult things she had ever done. But she forced herself to do it.

"Wow, that's really rich," she managed to drawl, using everything she had to keep her voice from trembling with shock. "Tell me something, Noah. Do you think I'm stupid? Or do I just have an I Love Bullshit sign plastered to my forehead?"

Well, hell. That'd come out even better than she'd hoped. She'd blown her own mind with that stellar response. She deserved a freaking Academy Award!

"I'm serious," he said, the quiet words striking against her composure like a hammer. Just those two simple words, and it was *Bye bye, Oscar*.

She covered her trembling mouth with her hand and blinked. "That's impossible. You couldn't stand me. We fought like cats and dogs."

"Haven't you ever asked yourself why that was?" His eyes held hers in the shadowy darkness, his gaze deep and searching, as if he was trying to see inside her mind.

"Lots of people fight," she said shakily. "It doesn't mean they're lusting for each other. Or anything else."

"It did for us."

"Don't be arrogant," she snapped, hating that she felt so out of control. "You don't know how I felt."

He arched one dark brow with a cocky arrogance that made her want to slap him again, as if he was remembering how she'd melted the second he touched her.

"I don't understand what you want from me, Noah. Why are you telling me these things?"

"I don't know," he admitted with a strained laugh. He pushed his hands back through his hair again, locking his fingers behind his neck as he hung his head forward. His voice was gruff when he spoke. "Maybe I just don't like you being angry with me about leaving. Maybe it's some kind of deathbed confessional to ease my conscience in case the worst ends up happening."

Her stomach rolled. "God, don't say that. It's not funny."

He lifted his head and looked at her. "I just... I need you to believe me about this, Will. I wasn't just screwing around with you that night. I'd been falling in love with you for a long time. I just didn't know how to handle it."

She took a shaky breath, beyond shocked that he'd just said that. And nearly destroyed by how badly she wanted to believe it. By how tragic it would be if it were true, because it would mean she'd lost so much more than she'd ever realized.

She swallowed the lump of emotion in her throat, and tried to keep her voice from quivering as she said, "Even if what you're saying is true, which I still don't believe, you sure as hell fell out of love pretty fast."

He flinched, his expression pulling tight again. "I didn't want to hurt you."

"But you did." There was no sense denying

it. She'd had no pride that night, begging him to stay.

"I didn't see that I had much choice." He looked away, staring across the shadowy room. "Not after that scene with our families."

"You know, even if what you're saying is true, I...could deal with what you did to me. I think I could even forgive you for it. What I can't forgive is what you did to my brother."

His head whipped back to the side. "To Harris? I didn't do a damn thing to him."

"That's not true." Willow forced herself to hold his stare. "You cut out on him, too. Left him behind."

His nostrils flared as he ground his jaw. "Trust me, Will. After what he found us doing, he wanted me gone."

"He wanted to protect his little sister. That doesn't mean he wanted to lose his best friend. His *only* friend."

His deep voice was tinged with disbelief. "You're serious, aren't you?"

"I knew when you and Harris became friends that it wouldn't work out. That you would end up hurting him. And I was right. You did."

"Damn it, that's not fair," he grated. "I couldn't stay. Not with you there."

"We could have made the situation work," she

argued, but there was no heat in the words. "We could have just avoided each other."

"Not good enough!" he barked, slapping his hand against his bedside table so hard that the cheap lamp crashed to the floor, the sudden explosion of temper revealing just how on edge he really was. "I wanted you too bad to hold back. The only answer was to get the hell away from you!"

With a disbelieving smirk, Willow slowly shook her head. "Honestly, Noah. You make me sound like some kind of femme fatale."

"YOU MIGHT AS well have been," Noah muttered. Sparks had always flown between him and Will. She'd made him feel restless and edgy. Made his skin feel too tight for his body. And that strange, unsettling attraction hadn't eased with time. He'd barely gotten a taste of her, but over the years it'd been Willow who invaded his dreams at night, even when he was lying beside another woman.

"Come on. I was a sixteen-year-old tomboy." Her tone said she thought he was being ridiculous. "I'd only just made my way out of an A cup."

"It didn't, *doesn't,* matter what size your breasts are. They were beautiful." Unable to help himself, he lowered his gaze to her chest. "They still are. But I was scared."

"Of what?"

"My feelings." He lifted his gaze, locking it with hers. "Maybe of what you would come to think of me. I can't change what's inside me, Will."

She licked her lips, a kind of dazed look in her big brown eyes. "No one's perfect, Noah. But I thought you were damn close. I didn't care about your bloodline. I never have."

He took a swift breath, and just sat there... staring at her...wanting so badly to believe her. Tension vibrated in the air like an electrical force, sizzling against his skin. "I did what I thought was right."

"You mean what you thought was *easy*."

His body trembled with a renewed wave of anger. "Like hell. Leaving you was the hardest thing I've ever had to do. I need you to understand that."

"I don't know why. Excuses never make a difference. What's done is done. You went off to start a new life. And I've got mine." She paused to sort out the sheets, then slid back beneath them, her hair spread out over her pillow. "We've also got a long day tomorrow, so you should try to get some sleep."

He grunted, but didn't argue, watching from

the corner of his eye as she pulled the covers up to her chin, her gaze focused on the ceiling. "Just out of curiosity," she murmured, "are you seeing anyone at the moment?"

"No. Hell, I can't even remember the last time I went out with a woman."

"Hmm."

"Well?"

"Well, what?" she asked, the thread of light from the bathroom playing softly over the delicate shape of her profile. God, she was gorgeous. It didn't seem fair, the way he wanted her even more now than he had before.

Remembering what he wanted to ask her, he said, "Are you involved with anyone?"

"Good night, Noah." She rolled over, giving him her back. "And just so you know, come at me again like that, and you're going to wish you hadn't."

He gave a weary sigh. "At the risk of repeating myself, you've turned into a real bitch, Will. But you probably hear that a lot."

"Actually, my friends all love me." The quiet words vibrated with emotion. "Past boyfriends and lovers all think I'm a great gal. I'm trustworthy. Would die for those I care about. Always keep my promises. It's only the rest of the world's population who find me difficult to deal with."

I want to be your friend. He bit back the words, knowing damn well she would just throw them back in his face. And he didn't want to hear any more about those past boyfriends and lovers.

"And just so you know," she added, "I wouldn't have had sex with you twelve years ago, even if you had stuck around."

"Talk about pretty lies. You were so hot, you'd have let me lay you down in your front yard and cover you in Jessie's flower bed. You would have—" He cut himself off, surprised by the force of his reaction. Why was he even bothering to challenge her? It was pointless, since he'd been the one to destroy what they could have had.

"I didn't say I wouldn't have wanted to," she whispered. "But…we don't always get what we want."

There was something behind the words that pulled at him, making him want to dig deeper, but he knew better than to push. She was already pissed. So he rolled onto his side instead, and closed his eyes. But all he could see was Will and the way she'd looked when he'd been touching her…seconds away from taking her.

He pushed his fingers into his eyes, wanting to block out the images, but it was impossible. She'd been burned into his brain. Her taste, her scent. The feel of her. He'd always known it would be like that between them. That he hadn't imagined how good it felt to have her against him all those years ago. And he needed more. So much more than what he'd gotten.

He was wrecked. Destroyed by the thought that he might have just missed his only chance to get his mouth on her. Not knowing how she tasted on his tongue wasn't something he could live with. Neither was not knowing what kind of cry she'd give when she came against his mouth in a sweet, mouthwatering rush of pleasure. Or how she'd look when she was coming apart on his cock, taking it from him hard and deep.

He had to know those things. *Had to*. They were as vital as the need for air in his lungs. Something he could *not* do without.

And after that…he didn't know—and he was too bloody confused to figure it out tonight. Considering what was coming after him, there might not even be an after.

Noah was still churning the whole complicated mess around in his mind when his cell phone started ringing on the nightstand, the shrill sound jerking him out of his troubled thoughts. His gut cramped with unease as he reached for the phone, knowing he was about to get some bad news. "What's wrong?" he grunted, swinging his legs over the side of the bed.

It was Kierland's voice that crackled over the connection. "There's been another attack."

"Shit. Where was it?"

"Wisconsin. Raine could only pick up on a few flashes of information, but it was enough for us to pinpoint the location."

Raine Spenser was engaged to Seth Mc-Connell, the only other human, besides Noah, in their unit. A former Collective soldier turned good guy, Seth had become a close friend, and so had Raine.

Thanks to her psychic abilities, Raine had been doing her best to help the unit keep an eye on their enemies as much as she could, but she was having a hard time getting a clear read on the Death-Walkers. Their thoughts were too chaotic and warped. According to Raine, it was like trying to see a clear picture on a TV with crappy reception, everything distorted and out of focus. Like a bad acid trip.

She'd also tried to read Calder for him, but found that the signal was being intentionally blocked. Noah had no doubt that it was Sienna doing the blocking.

"Is it bad?" he asked. A stupid question. The attacks were always bad. But he couldn't stop himself from asking.

"The Death-Walkers took out an entire town. The local Watchmen unit will be on the scene in the next five minutes. Ashe and Gideon are flying over to help them out." Ashe Granger was Gideon's brother, the two vampires more than qualified to deal with the situation.

Noah told Kierland to keep him posted, then set the phone on the table. He rubbed a hand over his eyes, wishing like hell that this thing was over.

Behind him, Willow sat up. "What happened?"

"Another attack. The Death-Walkers took out a small town up in Wisconsin."

"Ohmigod."

"It's gonna take an act of God to contain this." Moving to his feet, he grabbed his jeans and started to pull them on. "You okay sleeping in the truck?"

"I can sleep anywhere."

"Then let's hit the road," he muttered, knowing damn well that he was too wound up to get any rest. "The sooner we find this demon, the better."

CHAPTER SEVEN

SOMETIMES, BEING DEAD was better.

Sienna Broussard Jones knew it was a strange idea, but was afraid it might be true. Whenever anyone had asked Jessie about the man she'd lost when she was a young woman, Sienna had heard her say the part that hurt the most was living on, when you shouldn't be alive. That it was the continued empty existence when those you loved were already gone that could grind you down. Change you. Turn you into something that you weren't.

Jessie must have been right, because look at what had become of her eldest niece. Sienna was in a hell of her own creation, and one that was becoming more macabre with each day that passed by.

She was currently standing in the middle of a field in southern Mississippi, the night winds snarling through her hair, whipping it painfully against her face. A face she doubted her loved ones would even recognize, her once pleasant features now ravaged by the memories of what she'd lost…and the horrible things that she'd done.

The field lay silent and empty, but for her and the four figures huddled in its center, standing over a man's body. Overhead, the full moon watched on like an avid spectator, too shocked to turn away from the gruesome display of savagery taking place down below.

It was 3:00 a.m. The witching hour. When things best left to the dark often came out to play.

On the ground lay a Casus male who was living within the body of a human host, his arms and legs spread wide, his hands and feet nailed to the ground with heavy iron spikes. He'd been cruelly tortured, chunks of flesh missing from his torso and limbs, and she shuddered in shame at the broken, mewling sounds of agony that spilled from his throat.

Beside her, Anthony Calder gave a low, demonic laugh and shook his head. "Listen to that whimpering. I should have known that even in death you'd be weak, Richard."

"You have no right to do this," the Casus cried, straining against the spikes that held him in place. "I've been loyal to you! I've followed all your commands!"

"Really?" Calder's brows lifted with challenge. "Did you or did you not fail to capture

Jackson Winston before the Watchmen hid him away?"

The Casus coughed, choking on a mouthful of blood, his gaze wild with pain. "I couldn't get there in time. That's not my fault!"

A cold, serpentlike smile lifted the edge of Calder's mouth. "Oh? So I'm supposed to be lenient because you're incompetent?"

"You can't do this!" Richard roared, struggling to lift his head from the blood-soaked ground. "You need all the Casus soldiers you can find. After what happened in Meridian, our numbers are too low to lose another."

"I'd rather have a strong few than legions of weaklings," Calder murmured. "And I can, I assure you, do anything that I want. Just ask our lovely little witch here."

He smiled as he said the words, the curve of his lips pulling awkwardly at the decomposing flesh of his face. He blamed Sienna for the gruesome condition of his body, because of the way she'd ripped him from Meridian. Of course, he'd have likely been killed in the battle, had she not kidnapped him, but that argument had done little to change his mind. As she had quickly learned, there was no reasoning with a monster. And Calder was one of the most evil, despicable beings she'd ever encountered. Which was why she needed him.

But first, she needed him strong.

Sienna wasn't sure why Calder and the three shades who had followed him through the portal had been so traumatized by the incident. Perhaps it had been the portal itself. She was hardly an expert where the metaphysical doorways were concerned, her ability to make them a skill she'd only recently acquired, as her understanding of the workings of dark magic grew stronger. For that reason, Calder refused to allow her to "pull" him through another one.

However, the portal might not have been the problem at all. Another possibility was the fact that Calder and his men had begun regenerating while still trapped inside Meridian, gaining substance from those Watchmen they had killed, then fed on, during the battle.

Whatever the cause, the result was a problem she'd been forced to deal with. Though Calder had tried to simply continue the regeneration of his true form, the process had failed. It was as if his shade no longer knew how to exist in this realm. He and the others had been forced to take the bodies of the closest human hosts they could find, but they had yet to succeed in retaining one for long. No matter what kind of fortification spells Sienna tried, the host's flesh began to decay from the moment they slipped inside.

Using her powers, she had been helping the

four of them to move from one body to the next, and they were steadily regaining their strength. But it was a slow process, and Calder was anxious to get on with his plans.

"Considering you came back a failure," he said to Richard, "I'd say it proves that you're not only incompetent, but stupid, as well. And we can't have any weak links in this war. However…you *will* have the opportunity to redeem yourself."

"What?" Richard gasped. "What the hell are you talking about? How?"

The wind tore across the field as Calder explained. "Now that the gate to Meridian has been broken, our shades can no longer return there. But neither can I send you to hell without one of the Markers. So, when this body you're in dies, your shade will simply be forced to find another host."

"So then this is just for fun?" Richard demanded, still struggling to break free. "You twisted son of a bitch!"

Calder's eyes narrowed. "This is to teach you a lesson so that you don't make the same mistake twice. Weakness will not be tolerated."

Suddenly, the man's gaze cut to hers, and Sienna flinched at the blast of hatred pouring from his pale blue eyes. "You honestly think he's going to keep his end of the bargain you made with him?"

"He'll keep it," she whispered, her voice steady, devoid of emotion. "Or I'll kill him."

"You'll never get the chance," he growled.

"That's enough!" Calder barked, cutting him off. Then he nodded to the others, giving them permission to begin their feeding.

As the Casus began ripping Richard to pieces, Sienna turned her face away, unable to stomach the gruesome sight.

She'd made a deal with the devil, and she'd burn for it, eventually. But there were some things in life worth burning for, and she'd once had one of them. And now she wanted it back. Even if it was just for a day. For an hour.

After she'd lost her last accomplice, the Casus named Gregory DeKreznick, she could have given up and gone home. But when she'd tried, she…couldn't. She wanted her baby back too badly. Wanted her husband. Her family. If she had to go to heaven and hell to get them, she was willing. So she'd gone after the leader. Gone after Calder, himself.

Now, all she had to do was ensure Calder continued to regain his strength, until he was strong enough to take the body he wanted. And what he wanted was Noah Winston. He wanted the man who had dared to come after him. Wanted to break him down, then take him over.

Only then would the bastard go into hell for her and bring back what *she* wanted.

"Poor Sienna." Calder's icy hand touched her chin, lifting her face until she was looking him in the eye. Despite the ice-blue color, his gaze reminded her of a shark's. Soulless and cold. "You look positively green, my dear."

"You'll have to forgive me for not rejoicing in such a vulgar act."

"A few more killings, and I'll be strong enough. It's time for you to collect the Winstons for me." He slid a disappointed glance at the ground, where his men were still feeding. "I can't trust the others to make this happen on their own. They need your help."

"I understand."

His gaze locked with hers once more. "Fail me, and I promise you'll never see that man of yours again."

"I will *not* fail." Her voice was hollow, the complete opposite of the fast, happy notes that had always made her husband smile. He'd been big and gruff and so in love with her she hadn't known what to do with all the happiness. Maybe that was the problem. Maybe she'd had so much it had upset the balance in nature, and so she'd lost everything to even the score. She didn't know the why or the reasons. All she knew was that she wanted her family back.

And she was willing to do whatever it took to get them.

CHAPTER EIGHT

A DAY AGO, if anyone had told Noah that his best day in nearly a year would be spent on a road trip with Willow Broussard, he would have told them to unload their money on a shrink. Especially after the way the night had gone. And yet, despite everything that had happened and his worry about what was to come, it was true.

Not even Kellan's endless text messages demanding to know more about his "mystery woman" had been able to irritate him. He'd simply ignored the texts, which had made him smile, since he knew it would drive the good-hearted idiot out of his skull.

And oddly enough, he wasn't even obsessing over the fang episode, which kind of surprised him. Noah didn't know what it meant, the fact that he'd suddenly spouted a set of fangs when he'd been on the verge of driving inside her—and he wasn't sure he wanted to. Whatever the reason, it wasn't likely to be good, but he decided he could worry about it later.

Which had left him free to focus on Will.

They'd taken turns driving, which had allowed them to both grab some sleep earlier on. It was nearing twilight now, and though they'd searched four bars that day, they hadn't had any luck finding the demon. About an hour ago, they'd crossed the state line into Tennessee and were now heading to the fifth bar on Will's list of possible places she might track the demon down. Considering the situation, Noah figured he should have been edgier than ever, but instead, he found himself feeling almost...mellow. Yeah, the sexual need was always there, growing more urgent each hour that went by— but he'd also experienced a strange kind of pleasure in just spending time with her. In eating burgers and fries and talking about movies and places they'd been. In trying to figure out how her mind worked, and what was important in her life. What she hated, and what she loved.

As if by some silent agreement, they seemed to be avoiding those topics that were bound to make them argue. He hadn't asked her about Harris, and she hadn't brought up what had happened between them the night before. That is until she turned toward him and said, "Are you going to tell me about that bite on your arm?"

Noah glanced at the scars Calder's fangs had

left in his skin, the wounds finally beginning to lose that raw, angry color. "What about it?"

Carefully, she said, "It's hardly my field of specialty, but after last night, I'm thinking Calder's bite might have come with some...side effects."

He cut her a sharp look, but she had her face turned away from him, staring out the windshield. After a moment, she asked, "Exactly what changes are you experiencing?"

"Sharper senses. Faster reflexes. Shit like that. And I'm not complaining. In a way, I like it. It's making me a better fighter. But..."

"But what?"

He rubbed his fingers along his jaw, which definitely needed a shave. "It's just that I've been having some fairly gruesome dreams lately." Ones that involved lots of violence...and blood, like something from a horror flick. But he kept those disturbing details to himself, and simply said, "They had started before the bite— but they've gotten a lot worse since it happened. That part I could do without."

"Hmm." She took a deep breath, then slowly let it out, as if she was preparing herself for something difficult. "Do you, um, want to tell me about them? About the nightmares?"

"Not particularly," he muttered.

"Okay." Noah could feel the power of her gaze

as it settled against the side of his face. "But do you think that's healthy?"

His voice was getting rougher. "You got something you want to say, Will?"

"Only that I think you shouldn't be so hard on yourself," she told him. "The dreams are probably nothing more than a natural reaction to stress. And as for the changes...well, I don't think you should worry that you're turning into a monster."

He grunted in response, more than a little irritated that she could read him so easily. And hell, if it turned out he *was* turning into something monstrous, he knew what to do. The minute he thought he was a threat to her safety, he'd put himself down. End of story. He could eat a bullet if it was needed. Hardly the most palatable solution, but it was the best he had. And it meant he could have a little more time with Will.

Noah was trying to work out how he might be able to talk her into sticking around a little longer, once they'd found this demon friend of hers, when she asked him a question he'd been dreading. But one he knew she'd ask eventually.

"When you saw Sienna," she murmured, "what did she look like?"

Noah locked his jaw, wanting to tell her anything but the truth. An honest answer was only going to cause her more pain. So he didn't give her one. "She just looked like Si. A little older than I remembered her, but still beautiful."

Taking another deep breath, she lifted her chin. "I know you don't want to tell me the truth, Noah. But I need to know."

He arched his brows. "And just how do you know that wasn't the truth?" he drawled. "You read minds now?"

"No, but I'm good at reading your expressions." She gave a wry, breathless laugh as she leaned her head back against the seat. "When we were younger, I used to study you for hours on end when you were working at the bar, or just hanging out with Harris. You never knew I was there, but I was watching you. Learning you. So I know when you're lying."

Noah exhaled in an audible rush, caught off guard by how easily those intimate words slipped under his skin. How powerfully they affected him. "It's not something you want to hear," he grated, his voice suddenly raw with frustration. "Damn it, Will. I don't want to hurt you."

"I've been hurt before, and I've survived." There was no heat or anger in the words. They were a simple statement of fact. But they still made him feel like shit. "And it'll hurt more if I don't know what to expect. The odds are high that we'll be seeing her, and I...I don't want to be caught unprepared."

He cursed something foul under his breath, knowing he was going to give her what she wanted. That he didn't have any choice.

Before he could think better of it, Noah reached out and caught hold of her hand, gripping it in his. "When I saw her, I knew it was Sienna, but...she's changed. A lot. She's much thinner now, almost...gaunt. She looks kind of like she's just...wasting away."

She trembled, her hand cold in his, but she didn't try to pull away. Instead, she tightened her grip, holding on to him while she stared through the windshield at the endless stretch of highway. "Did she look like she'd been... hurt?"

"Not from what I could see." He stroked his thumb against her palm, too aware of her to miss the way she shivered in reaction, even though she tried to hide it. "But she won't be easy for you to look at," he added, frowning as she pulled her hand from his and crossed her arms over her chest. She huddled in on herself, as if she were cold, so he reached down and turned off the air conditioner.

She didn't say anything more, looking as if she were miles away, completely lost in her thoughts. Noah waited until she finally began to relax again, some of the tension easing from her frame as she lowered her arms and leaned back against the seat, before saying, "So, about this demon."

WILLOW BIT BACK a brief smile. She'd been wondering how much longer Noah was going to be able to hold out before he asked her about Damon. She was actually surprised he'd lasted as long as he had.

Rolling her head toward him, she watched the way the ethereal shades of twilight played over the rugged, masculine angles of his face. It didn't seem fair for one man to be so delicious. "What about him?" she asked, flicking her gaze over him. It was impossible not to notice how the soft denim of his jeans hugged his muscular thighs…as well as the impressive bulge behind the fraying fly.

"Why's he hiding out in bars?"

The sound of his voice made her give a little jump, and she quickly jerked her gaze back to his face, before she got caught ogling his package.

"Aren't there other places that would be less… conspicuous?" he added.

The bubble of laughter in her throat was a welcome relief after the choking tightness she'd felt only moments before. "I could tell you, but I think it'll be more fun for you to figure that one out for yourself."

He grunted, clearly not caring for her answer. "Then tell me why he's in hiding."

"I already told you when we were at Jessie's that it's because of his ex. His ex-wife, to be precise."

He slid her a quick glance, before turning his attention back to the road. "An acrimonious divorce?"

A wry smile touched her mouth. "You could say that. She did something not only illegal, but downright evil, and Damon turned her in for it. It was the right thing to do, but she escaped the demon prison she'd been put in, and now she wants revenge."

"She serious about it?"

Willow nodded. "Enough that she plans to carve off pieces of his body, one by one."

He gave a low whistle under his breath. "I'd say that's pretty serious. No wonder he's on the run."

"Luckily for Damon, he does the whole running thing like a pro," she offered with another quiet laugh. For all his faults, Damon was just one of those males it was impossible not to love, so long as you weren't *in love* with him.

"You seem to know him pretty well," he said,

his voice sounding a bit grittier than before. "You date him?"

The knuckles on the hand he gripped the steering wheel with turned white, and Willow almost believed he was actually jealous. He certainly sounded it. And with that muscle suddenly pulsing in his clenched jaw, he definitely looked it.

So what exactly was she meant to do with *that?*

He'd told her, last night, that the reasons he'd had for not sticking around twelve years ago no longer stood. Which meant…what? That he planned on touching her again? And if that was the case, then what the hell was he after now? An affair? A one-night stand? Not that it mattered. She couldn't give him either of those things, even if she wanted to.

And yeah, she definitely wanted. Which just pissed her off, since there wasn't a damn thing she could do about it.

With a frown pulling at the edges of her mouth, she shifted into a more comfortable position. Or tried to. But it was damn hard to get comfortable when your insides were getting twisted like a pretzel.

Instead of answering his question, she asked two of her own. "Why all the questions about

Damon? Are you really that interested in my love life?"

"Just curious." His shrug was casual, but she could still see that telltale tension in the set of his jaw. "From the sound of it, you've been… busy."

"And what about you, Noah? How many wrecked hearts have you left behind over the years?"

The shadows were deepening around them as the lavender of twilight faded into evening blue, and his eyes burned in the soft glow of the truck's instrument panel. "Sex doesn't equal love."

"Meaning what?" she asked with a stunned laugh.

He jerked his shoulder again. "Just that the women I get involved with don't expect anything more."

"What a crock," she said, shaking her head. She rolled down her window, enjoying the feel of the summer-scented air as it blew against her face. It was rich and warm, like a living thing, offering a kind of primal comfort from the chill creeping through her system. Keeping her face turned away from him, she quietly added, "They may not own up to it, Noah, but all women are looking for love. Some just hide it better than others."

He didn't say anything in response, and she was almost starting to drift off, lulled by that sweet, warm breeze, when his deep voice broke the silence. "You didn't answer my question about the demon."

"No, I never dated Damon," she admitted with a tired sigh, deciding to give him the truth. "He's a great friend, but he would have been more than I could handle as a lover."

He made a guttural sound that was anything but happy. "What does that mean?"

"It means I can only juggle so many things in my life at one time, and Damon would have taken up a lot of…space." Maybe not the complete truth, but close enough. And all he was getting.

"Ever thought of settling on just one guy?" he rasped.

He clearly thought that by "things" she meant "men," and she didn't bother to correct him. "I might, if I ever met one who was worth it."

"Christ," he said with a low laugh, the husky sound quick and rough. "That's harsh, Will."

"I'm just being honest." She turned to look at him, for no other reason than he was just really good to look at. "It would take a helluva man to make me settle down."

He chewed that over for a while, his eyes glittering in the darkness, but she wasn't concerned.

Despite the menacing air of danger and violence that flowed around him these days, he was still the Noah she'd grown up with. He was no monster, no matter how worried he might be about those changes he was going through.

And he was definitely worrying.

She could see the soul-deep exhaustion he was trying so hard to hide, the bruise-colored shadows under his eyes a testament to the fact that he wasn't sleeping well. But they didn't detract from his looks. He was beautiful in a dark, fallen-angel kind of way, the shadows under his eyes only making the unusual blue seem brighter beneath the ebony strands of hair that kept falling over his brow.

They'd eaten up a good chunk of highway before he said, "So how did you meet him?"

"Who?"

He braced his elbow on his door, stroking his hand over his jaw again. "This Damon guy."

"Oh." She rubbed her arms, chilled by the memory. "It's a long story," she hedged.

"We've got the time," he murmured.

"Okay, if you really want to know, we met on a case I was working. An eight-year-old little girl had gone missing. Her father was human, but her mother was a demon who had gone to school with Damon's sister. The mother hired me to find the little girl, and Damon's sister asked him to help. We didn't have many leads, but the parents were suspicious of a neighbor who hadn't been seen since the girl went missing."

He cursed something foul, the low words thick with dread.

With a hard swallow, Willow cleared the husky note from her throat and continued her story. "We found her before she was killed, but not before that monster had managed to terrify the living hell out of her. Damon was beside himself. I've never seen anyone so enraged. He literally tore the man apart with his bare hands. Then, while I drove, he cradled the little girl in his arms all the way back to her mother."

"What happened to her? Is she okay?"

A soft smile touched her lips at the worry in his voice. "She's growing into a beautiful young lady. And Damon has stayed in close contact. She adores him. He's like her favorite uncle. He's promised to look out for her, to be there if she ever needs him, and he'll keep his promise. He would die before letting anything happen to her."

"Huh. A demon with a soft spot. Who knew?"

Irritated by his tone, she narrowed her eyes at him. "Damon's a good guy, Noah. And he's a friend. I won't have you being ugly about him."

"He's a demon, Will. How great can the guy be?"

She ran her tongue over her teeth, and aimed

low. "At least he was never too afraid to admit that he wanted me."

His hands clenched on the wheel so hard she thought it might break. "It was never a case of not wanting you," he forced through his gritted teeth. "I couldn't have you."

"Oh, please. Spare me the drivel. So you have Casus blood in your veins. Who gives a damn? I sure as hell never have."

His laugh was sudden and harsh. "You didn't even know until that night. I saw the surprise on your face when Jessie told you the truth about the feud between our families. When she told you about the Winston bloodline."

Ah. She'd always wondered if he'd noticed her reaction to that little revelation.

"So I was surprised," she muttered, crossing her arms. "So what? Did you bother to stick around to ask me how I felt about it?"

"No, I didn't." He popped his jaw, his voice flinty as he said, "Your family made it clear that wasn't an option."

NOT TO MENTION his own family, Noah thought. Hell, even his mother had been against them. She'd told him how disappointed his father would have been if he'd still been alive. She'd said a *Chastain* witch could never be trusted to be there when you needed her. Told him that

Willow would turn on him. That she'd come to hate him. And he'd believed her.

Had he been a fool? Or had it been the smartest decision of his life? He no longer knew, and it was pissing him off.

He didn't doubt that he could make Willow Broussard want him physically. But would that be all there was to it? Would he become just another lover that she reminisced about, while he went through life hungering for something he could no longer have?

"Get ready to pull over," she said, ripping him from the darkness of his thoughts. "That's the place."

Noah pulled into the dirt parking lot and reversed into a space at the back of the rambling wooden structure, the neon sign that sat on its sloping roof flashing nearly blinding bursts of color against the truck's windshield. As he cut the engine, he sent a dubious look toward the building. "What makes you think he's here?"

"I don't know where he is," she replied, reaching for the handle to her door. "But we're going to hit every clan hangout that I know of until we find him."

They made their way across the lot, entering through a side door, and Noah fought back a grimace. Christ, the place was even worse than he'd suspected. Music blared from the corner where a live band was playing some kind of death rock, the dance floor set up in front of the stage packed with a rough-looking crowd that spilled over into every corner of the room. As they headed past the bar, a gruff voice sounded from off to his left. "Well, well, well. If it isn't one of those Casus assholes." A beefy hand grabbed hold of his shoulder and jerked him around. "What makes you think you can waltz in here without getting your ass kicked?"

Noah stared the paunch-faced shape-shifter right in the eye. "I'm not a Casus."

"Sure you aren't," the guy sneered, sending a laughing look at his buddies. "You hear that, guys? Blue Eyes here doesn't think he's a Casus."

"I'm only going to say this once." Noah moved in closer, going nose to nose with the male. He was pretty sure the shifter was a Lycan, but it was hard to get a clear read on his scent under all the booze. "If you don't want it broken, get your hand off my shoulder."

The shifter snickered. "Make me, Casus."

"If that's how you want to play it." Noah's smile was slow and sharp. "But don't say I didn't warn you."

Before the werewolf could so much as blink at him, Noah wrapped his fingers around the asshole's wrist and stepped back, yanking him off his bar stool. The shifter threw a heavy left hook that Noah easily dodged, using the man's momentum to spin him around, then twisting his right arm up behind his back. The shifter tried to catch him in the face with the back of his head, so Noah wrenched the jerk's arm up higher against his back, and the guy gave a high-pitched, gurgled cry. "Are we done here?" he rasped. "Because I don't appreciate you pulling this shit in front of my...lady friend."

"Okay," the guy wheezed. "We're done."

"That's what I thought," he said in a low voice, releasing his hold on the idiot and taking a step back.

As he watched the shifter rubbing his sore arm, Noah ran a hand over his mouth, more than a little surprised by how easily he'd taken down the werewolf. Yeah, he was used to fighting things that weren't human, and he was damn good at it. That wasn't ego talking—it was fact. But this had been...different. He'd acted on pure instinct, and he'd been faster. Stronger.

And a helluva lot angrier than he usually was.

Side effects? Obviously. He was just damn glad the fangs hadn't made another appearance.

Turning around, Noah expected to find Willow waiting right behind him. But she wasn't there.

With a graveled curse, he immediately scanned

the crowd. Raw, burning fury scalded his veins when he spotted her. While he'd been dealing with the Lycan, the little idiot had taken on the bastard's friends by herself!

From the looks of it, she'd already downed two of the guys, and was currently exchanging words with a third. They were standing at the edge of the crowded dance floor, the band still making enough racket that Noah couldn't hear what she was saying to the man. Whatever it was, he looked angry about it, his lip curled in a sneer. The guy took a swing at her, which she blocked as she spun, bringing her leg around in a kick that struck him across the backs of his thighs.

For a moment, all Noah could do was stare. Then he stalked forward and yanked her off the jackass, leaving him to the two bouncers who were finally making their way over. He couldn't have cared less about the jerk. All he cared about was Will.

And judging by how pissed he was, he cared a helluva lot more than he should. It was stupid and insane and was no doubt going to land his ass in a world of hurt. But there didn't seem to be a goddamn thing Noah could do to stop it.

CHAPTER NINE

GRABBING HOLD OF her by the arms, Noah lifted Willow off the ground and shoved her against the nearest wall. "Have you lost your fucking mind?" he shouted, his voice shaking with fury. "Tell me, Will. What the hell did you think you were doing?"

She blinked back at him. "That's a stupid question, Noah."

The calmness of her voice, when his composure had just been shredded with fear, made him want to shake her.

"I was helping you," she added.

"Helping me?" Oh, yeah, he really wanted to shake some sense into her. The logical part of his brain knew she'd had the male under control; it was the rest of him that was scared shitless. "You could have been hurt," he snarled, the rough words biting and sharp. "Do not *ever* do anything that reckless again. Do you understand me?"

"I understand that you're being an idiot.

What's the big friggin' deal? Was I just supposed to stand aside and let them gang up on you?"

He leaned forward, putting his face close to hers. So close that he could feel the soft panting of her breath against his chin. "If something goes wrong, I don't want you getting dragged down after me." He fought for a measure of control, but couldn't find any, and his voice lowered, the quiet words thick with emotion. "I couldn't handle it if anything happened to you."

She stared back at him, those cinnamon-colored eyes turning warm with understanding, and he felt like she could see right through him. Right down to the fear that was seething so painfully in his gut. Softly, she said, "I'm sorry I scared you."

He locked his jaw and looked away, his body stiff with tension as he lowered her to the ground and stepped back. Taking a deep breath, he scraped his hands through his hair and tried to calm down.

"Oh, God," she groaned, her gaze focused a little to his left, back toward the bar. "This is all we need."

Following her line of sight, he simply said, "Shit."

"Damn it, Hank, you know the rules!" the bartender roared, pointing a shotgun at the man Noah had been fighting. The one who was currently turning into a massive werewolf, his hands already sporting a deadly set of claws.

"No shifting inside the premises!" the bartender added. "You cut this shit out, or I *will* shoot you!"

Hank glared at the bartender, staring down the barrel of the gun, then chuffed as he jerked his shoulder and began returning to his human form. The bartender, however, didn't look in any hurry to lower his weapon.

"Come on," Willow muttered, putting her blade away before she reached out and grabbed hold of Noah's hand. "Let's look for Damon and then get the hell out of here. The sooner, the better."

He allowed her to pull him along behind her, taking an uneasy pleasure in the simple act of having her delicate hand in his again. It was embarrassing, how hard he had to work to keep from crushing her in his grip, wanting to cling to her so tightly she couldn't pull away. He was unbearably off balance, too many violent emotions crashing around inside him, his thick skull feeling like it might crack from the pressure.

Jesus. Barely twenty-four hours together and he was already losing it.

They made their way through the front room without any further incidents, most of the other

customers giving them a wide berth as news of
what had happened with Hank and his buddies
spread through the bar. When they finally made
it through to the back room, Willow stood on her
tiptoes and looked over the crowd, squeezing his
fingers when she glanced into the far corner.
"He's here! That's Damon over there!"

Because of his height, Noah had a clear shot of
the man she was pointing to. But he still couldn't
believe what he was seeing. "Oh, come on," he
groaned. "A blond-haired, blue-eyed demon?"

He glanced at Willow just in time to catch her
impish grin. "He's adorable, isn't he?"

"Yeah, he's friggin' precious," he muttered,
surprised by the strange burn of jealousy ripping through his gut. Jealousy was *not* an emotion he'd ever had to deal with before. Nor was
it one he particularly cared for, and he had a bad
feeling about this. One that got worse as Willow
tugged him along behind her, obviously eager to
reach the demon's table.

Then Damon turned his head to the side, tilting a beer bottle up to his mouth, giving Noah
a clear view of the demon's hair, as well as the
side of his neck, and he damn near stumbled over
his own two feet.

I don't bloody believe it.

There was a dark blue streak in the demon's
blond, shoulder-length hair and a knotted sym-

bol at the side of his throat. The symbol was the same color blue as the streak in his hair, and Noah knew they were the markings of his demon subspecies. He also knew that this particular species was one of the most notorious.

"You've gotta be kidding me," he growled, grinding to a halt, his hold on Willow's hand forcing her to stop, as well. "He's a goddamn sex-eater!"

She shot him a bright-eyed look over her shoulder and laughed. "Listen to yourself. You'd think you'd never seen a guy who fed off sex before."

"I haven't," he bit out, understanding now why the demon was hiding out in bars. A guy had to have his nourishment, after all. And with all the scantily clad women in the place, the demon had an endless variety to choose from.

Willow arched one of those pale, sweeping brows as she studied his grim expression. "I didn't take you for such a prude, Noah."

"I'm not a prude," he forced through his gritted teeth. He just hated, *hated,* the thought of Willow hanging out with a good-looking demon who, if the rumors about his breed were to be believed, was able to stay hard for hours on end, enjoying multiple orgasms off one erection. Not to mention what they could supposedly do to a woman *with* that erection.

He was thinking it might be good if he went and locked Willow in the truck, leaving him to talk to the demon on his own, when the guy caught sight of her. Pleasure instantly transformed the demon's fierce expression.

"Low!" he called out, coming around the back of the table so fast he nearly knocked it over. "Get your ass over here, woman!"

"Low?" Noah muttered, fighting the urge to toss her over his shoulder and run like hell.

"That's what he calls me," she explained, her voice all breathless and happy. "You know...Willow."

She pulled away from him, leaving him to make his own way as she rushed forward and threw herself into the demon's brawny arms. The sight of them together, hugging and laughing, hit Noah like a kick in the gut. The demon had to be nearly six-five, with the muscle to match, his smile one of genuine affection as he spun Willow around in a fast circle that sent her golden curls flying.

Her laughter filled the air, and Noah couldn't help but compare this particular reunion with the one he and Willow had shared the day before. Damn. Instead of pulling her knife on the demon, she had her arms wrapped tight around his neck, holding on as if she never meant to let go—and with a longing that nearly floored him, Noah suddenly found himself wishing that things could have been different between him and this woman. That he could have stayed in Sacred and lived a life that included Willow.

It was a screwed up kind of torture, but he couldn't help thinking how incredible it would be to come home and be greeted like this, with her laughter and her beautiful smile, and those strong arms wrapped tight around him, holding him close.

Noah was still lost in his unsettling thoughts when the demon finally set Will back on her cherry-red Doc's, wrapped a possessive arm around her shoulders and looked right at him. With an accent that sounded oddly Southern, considering the demon had likely been born in hell, he asked, "Who's your new friend, Low?"

Willow quickly made the introductions, and the demon's eyes shot wide with surprise. "So you're the jackass from her past," Damon Mac-Caven murmured, looking him up and down. "Well, hell. I've always wondered what you'd be like."

"Willow told you about me?" Noah didn't know whether to be pleased by the fact that she'd talked about him...or worried about what she'd said.

Arching one blond eyebrow, the demon pulled her closer to his side, crushing her against his body. Then he gave Noah a smart-ass smile. "She told me enough to know that you're an idiot."

Shit. So much for being pleased.

"She also said you were human." Damon leaned forward and sniffed, his dark blue eyes burning with a hot, soft glow. "But you sure as hell don't smell human."

"I'm surprised you were able to figure that out on your own," Noah drawled, his temper getting the better of him as he crossed his arms over his chest. "I'd always heard demons weren't too bright."

A slow grin curled the guy's mouth. "That's just 'cause we're so pretty. People are usually amazed that we can have such great looks *and* brains."

Willow cleared her throat, cutting an uncertain look toward Noah, no doubt sensing his mood. Then she stared up at the man holding on to her and shook her head, looking as if she was fighting back another smile. "I see your ego is still enormous, Damon. Can you at least try to behave yourself?"

"I'm sorry," he murmured, without sounding the least bit contrite. "I haven't seen you in forever, Low. And you know how crazy that makes me." Then the bastard lowered his head and kissed her, right on the delicate edge of her jaw, and Noah started thinking that this just might be the night he finally discovered if demons were really as hard to kill as he'd always heard. If not for the fact that he needed Damon to decipher that damn spell, he just might have given it a try.

"I'm curious, Will." Noah sounded like his throat had been scraped with sandpaper. "Is he like this with all women? Or just the ones who've turned him down?"

She winced, but the demon only laughed as he deliberately ran his hand over her hip, then glanced at Noah. "You never know, Winston." His voice was a deep, sensual rumble. "Maybe tonight'll be my lucky night."

Noah took a step closer, getting right in the demon's face. "Try it, and I can promise you're not going to be nearly so pretty come morning."

"Way I've heard it," Damon rasped, his blue eyes narrow and dark, "you're not the kind who sticks around till morning."

"You don't know a goddamn thing," Noah snarled, his hands curling into fists.

Damon sneered, his own temper suddenly raging from his eyes. "I know you had better have a damn good reason for coming back into her life!"

"Stop it!" Willow suddenly cut in, sounding tense. As well as distracted. "I get that this is obviously a blast for the two of you, but is it possible we could save the drama for later?" She was looking away from them, staring through the window that was located just off to her side. "If not, I'll just go outside and deal with the monsters lurking in the woods behind the parking lot on my own, while you two keep playing barbarian."

Noah gritted his teeth, wondering how much worse this night could get.

"Monsters? What the hell are you talking about?" the demon grumbled.

She pointed toward the window. "Take a look for yourself."

"It's the Casus," Noah muttered, spotting the same eerie, malevolent glow of ice-blue eyes that had caught Willow's attention through the glass. He walked over to the window for a better look, and could see the bastards standing just inside the line of trees that bordered the back lot, near where he'd parked his truck, probably waiting to ambush them when they left the bar.

"You sure it's the Casus?" Damon asked, coming to stand by his side.

"I'm sure," Noah replied. He knew that icy color by heart, considering he saw it every time he looked in a mirror.

While they were watching, an SUV drove through the rear lot, its headlights illuminating two of the Casus. The monsters were still in their human forms, their impatience etched into the eager lines of their expressions.

Damon whistled under his breath. "Is it just me, or do those guys look like they're waiting for something?"

Willow gave a strained laugh. "Oh, they're waiting for something all right."

With raised brows, the demon looked at Noah, then at Will. "Well, is somebody gonna tell me what it is?"

"Me," Noah grunted, his muscles coiling as he felt the sharp rise of a lethal, primal fury surging through his veins. One that was anything but human. "They're waiting for me."

"I'm assuming there's a good reason for that." The demon's voice was wry, as was the look on his face as he studied Noah through his golden lashes. "Let me guess. Your charming personality has made you irresistible to them?"

Noah slanted the demon a narrow look. "Let it go, MacCaven."

Damon's chest shook with a gruff bark of laughter, and he slid a grin toward Willow. "I'm actually starting to like this guy, Low. Maybe you should keep him around."

"I'm afraid he's not mine to keep," she said tightly. "We're working together, and we tracked you down for a reason. An important one, but it's going to have to wait until we deal with what's out there."

Noah turned his attention from the window and pinned her with a glare. "*We're* not dealing with anything, Will. Your little ass is going to stay inside and out of danger. I'll handle this on my own."

"That's a great idea," she said breathlessly, feigning an exhilarated expression, "except for two things."

"Yeah? What?"

"One, you're being an idiot." She shot him sweet smile. "And two, I don't take orders from anyone. Least of all you."

Looking at Damon, he growled, "Keep her here."

Damon shook his head and grinned back at him. "No can do, buddy. I gave up trying to control Low a long time ago. The witch does as she pleases."

"Some help you are," he muttered, turning and making his way out of the crowded room. Unfortunately, they followed along right behind him, but at least there was no sign of Hank and his friends as he headed through the front room. Nor was there any sign of the band, who must have been taking a break, the place blessedly devoid of music. When he reached the side entrance, a group of purple-haired pixies poured into the bar and blocked the doorway while Willow and the demon caught up to him. Damon crossed his arms and leaned his shoulder against the wall, and Willow placed her hand on Noah's arm.

"Please, just think about this before you go rushing out there." Her voice was rough with concern. "If Sienna is with them, then—"

"Sienna?" Damon grated, cutting her off. "As in your sister? *That* Sienna?"

"Yeah, and it's a long story." She took a deep breath and shoved a handful of curls behind her ear. "But she isn't exactly playing for our side anymore."

It was clear from the demon's expression that he felt bad for her. "Shit, Low. That sucks."

"Tell me about it." Looking back at Noah, she said, "Sienna might freeze you in place, just like she did before, and you won't be able to do a damn thing to keep Calder off of you. But *I* can."

"What do you mean?" he asked.

She licked her lips, then quickly explained. "I might have followed the warrior's path, but do you really think Jessie ever let any of us do anything the easy way? She made sure I studied a little of all three specialties, so I'm pretty good with spells. I should be able to counteract whatever Si tries to use on you."

Damon moved away from the wall and cracked his knuckles. "And I'll get a kick out of pounding some Casus ass. Never have liked the stories I've heard about those jerk-offs."

"This isn't your fight," Noah said to the demon, wondering why the guy was even offering to help.

Damon shrugged, the casual gesture stretching the confines of his white T-shirt. "Low seems to like you," he said in an easy rumble, "which means I can't kill you. So I might as well help keep you alive." He rolled his head over his shoulders, then released a set of vicious-looking talons from the tips of his fingers. "Now, what do these guys want with you?"

Willow quickly explained about Noah's bloodline and how Calder intended to use him as a host. She also told him about the Dark Marker that Noah had, explaining that it was the only weapon that could send the Casus to hell. The demon took it all in stride, still ready to stand by them, and Noah shook his head, thinking it was a shame he hadn't met Damon MacCaven under different circumstances. He might have actually liked the sex-eater, if not for the situation with Will. But, as things stood, he had no choice but to hate the guy.

"So then this Calder needs a host to survive outside his prison, right? But what's so special about Winston here? I mean, he's pretty enough. But there's got to be more to it than that."

Before he could respond, Willow said, "Noah sided with the enemy and dared to fight against the Casus. He stood up to these bastards. Refused to sit around and wait for them to screw up his life. That's why Calder wants him." She turned her warm gaze on Noah, and a grin crossed her mouth. "Noah's strong, and Calder wants that strength."

What the...? Noah swallowed the lump of shock in his throat, stunned by her words. By the pride and admiration in her soft voice. But he knew he didn't have time for the sentimental reaction, so he shook it off and reached for the door.

"One more question." Damon put his arm out to block the doorway, and locked his gaze with Noah's. "What happens if we kill one of those host bodies without a Marker?"

The demon's question made him realize there were still a few things he needed to explain. Clearing his throat, he said, "Before we broke into Meridian and destroyed the gate, the shades would be sucked back into the prison whenever we killed a host body without using a Marker. But we've had some new intel from a Watchmen unit in Australia who killed a Casus a few weeks ago."

"And?" Will asked.

"The bastard they killed didn't go to Meridian. He just hopped into another body. They know that's what happened because the second host was a friend of one of the Watchmen."

Willow's eyes darkened with worry. "So if Calder's out there, walking around in some other body, and we kill him without a Dark Marker, then he *could* try to jump right into you. Do I have that right?"

Noah shrugged. "For all we know, he might be able to do it without waiting for the host body to die."

Her surprise was obvious. "Has that happened before?"

He shook his head. "Not that I know of. But with Sienna in the mix, I think it's best if we don't rely too much on history. She's powerful enough to change the rules."

Willow looked pale at the thought of going up against her sister, but she wasn't backing down. "Make sure you protect the charm Jessie gave you," she told him. "Don't let them rip it off you."

Noah nodded, pressing his hand against his shirt, where he could feel both the Marker he'd brought with him and the leather pouch. He'd already mailed the other two charms Jessie had given him to his brothers. He hoped like hell that the charms worked, but in the event that they didn't, he needed to tell Willow what to do.

Reaching inside the neckline of his shirt, he grabbed the Marker and pulled it over his head. Then he held it up for her to see. "If at any point you suspect me, you get this away from me and you use it."

"What are you saying?" she asked with a frown.

"Calder could be out there, and we don't know for sure that Jessie's charm will work." His voice was getting harder. "If you think he's inside me, don't even think twice. Just do what needs to be done."

Her eyes went wide as she realized what he was saying. "What the hell, Noah? You want me to kill you?"

"Do. Not. Hesitate." He forced the words through his clenched teeth, and prayed she would listen. "I mean it, Will. If you hesitate, you could die."

Her nostrils flared as she flicked her gaze over the cross. "Noah, even if I wanted to, I don't know how to use that thing as a weapon."

"You just hold it flat against your palm. That puts the cross into weapon mode. Your arm will turn into something that's called an Arm of Fire, and you use it to punch right through the back of the Casus's neck."

She kept her gaze on the cross as she exhaled a deep breath of air. Then she swallowed, and lifted her gaze back to his. "I'm *not* going to kill you."

Frustration roared through him, the cold suck of fear in his gut freezing him to the bone. "Damn it, Will. I need to know that you'll be safe."

"You don't need to worry about me," she said, lifting her hands in front of her. "I can protect myself."

"Will...?" Hardly able to believe his eyes, Noah blinked at the sight of the small balls of fire flickering in her palms.

"Cool, huh?"

"I've never heard of a *Chastain* witch being able to manipulate fire."

Her smile was cocky. "I bet you've never heard of a lot of things I've learned to do in the past twelve years," she told him, the flames disappearing as she closed her hands.

He hated that she was right. Knowing that nothing good was going to come out of his mouth at that moment, he turned and walked out the door. And they followed right behind him.

As they walked across the parking lot, Damon fell into stride on his left, Willow on his right. There was a grass-covered border of land that stretched from the back of the lot to the edge of the woods, and they stopped when they reached it, standing near Noah's truck. Across that strip of grass, the trees swayed, but there was no sign of the Casus. Not even the chilling, ice-blue glow of their eyes.

Damon cupped his hands around his mouth and shouted, "Come out, come out, wherever you are!"

Noah counted the beats of his heart, reaching ten before three Casus males stepped out of the woods, stopping at the opposite edge of the grass, their bodies still in human form. But there was no sign of Sienna.

"Where is she?" Willow rasped. "I don't feel any kind of spell on the air."

"Maybe she didn't come with them," Damon replied.

"Which one of you is Calder?" Noah demanded, while back in the bar the band started up again.

"He's otherwise occupied," the one in the middle replied. "So he sent us to collect you."

Noah ignored the wave of relief that spiked through him, and gave the monsters a snide smile. "I guess he was just too chickenshit to do the job himself."

The Casus ignored the taunt, spreading out as they released their claws and fangs. They stepped onto the edge of the grass, and the light from the sign shone on their faces.

"Whoa," Damon muttered under his breath. "Is it just me, or do these guys look a little... dead?"

CHAPTER TEN

WILLOW UNDERSTOOD EXACTLY what Damon meant. The Casus looked waxen, their skin sagging on their bones, as if their host bodies were already decomposing while they were still walking around inside them. "I don't think the hosts are agreeing with them," she murmured.

"They must be the shades who came through with Calder," Noah scraped out, palming the hilt of the knife he'd taken from his calf sheath in one hand, still clasping the Marker with the other. She'd seen him put his gun in his bag earlier that day, and knew the weapon was still locked in the truck. "None of the other host bodies have ever looked like that," he added.

Reaching for her own knife, she said, "Maybe Calder's having the same trouble."

"If he is, that might explain why he was reluctant to come on his own," Damon murmured.

"They're getting ready to attack, so be ready." Noah's voice vibrated with rage, and she had no doubt he was going to be deadly in the fight.

"Try to take them down without killing them if you can. Then I can fry them with the Marker before they move to another host."

Willow was about to ask how easy a host body was to kill, when a familiar voice came from off to their right, farther down the grassy patch of land. "You know, for someone who claims he isn't a Casus, you keep some interesting company, boy."

Oh, shit. She'd wondered why she hadn't seen Hank and his pals on the way out of the bar, and this was obviously why. They'd been waiting to confront Noah in the parking lot, where the bartender and his shotgun couldn't interfere.

"This has nothing to do with you," Noah growled, cutting a quick look toward the group. They must have added a few more —shapeshifters to their numbers, because there looked to be six of them now, including Hank. "If you're smart, you'll all turn around and get the hell out of here."

"That's some good advice, Winston. But I don't think those shifters look all that clever," Damon drawled, and in the next instant, they attacked. All of them. The Casus and the shapeshifters, and it was a goddamn bloody mess. Willow felt like she'd landed in the middle of a freaking war zone, but instead of guns and rockets, this was a battle being fought with claws and steel.

"Don't let them kill him!" one of the Casus shouted to his comrades, obviously worried about the shape-shifters going after Noah. "We're meant to take him back alive!"

The battle was fast and violent, and Willow cut and slashed as opponents came at her one after another, careful not to make any of the injuries fatal. The shape-shifters were assholes, but she didn't want to be responsible for their deaths. And she knew Noah wanted the Casus killed with the cross he'd slipped back inside his pocket. But despite the Casuses' strength, their flesh tore easily beneath her blade, the rotten stench of their blood making her want to gag. And she wasn't the only one having a problem.

As Damon grabbed the arm of the man he was fighting, the Casus's arm tore away from its body with a wet, sticky pop, and the demon looked like he might hurl. "Jesus," he groaned, tossing the arm over his shoulder with a visible shudder of disgust. "Anyone else feel like we're trapped in some bad zombie flick? This is just *wrong.*"

The Casus snarled as he lunged, swiping his remaining hand at Damon's face, and the demon had to lurch back to avoid the monster's claws, tripping over the groaning body of one of the

felled shifters. Willow started forward to help
him, ready to take on the one-armed Casus before he could reach Damon, but another Casus
grabbed her from behind and pinned her arms
behind her back, his low laugh rumbling in her
ear. The one-armed Casus gave an evil smile as
he started toward her, his intention clear, and
she screamed, knowing Damon would never get
there in time to stop him.

And then everything seemed to happen in
slow motion. From the corner of her eye, she saw
the look on Noah's face as he whipped his head
around at the sound of her scream. There was
fury and fear, as well as the understanding that
he couldn't reach her in time to use his Marker
on the approaching Casus. Instead, he started
running as he threw the Marker to Damon, who
caught it in one hand, while using his other hand
to toss an unconscious shape-shifter out of his
way.

"Put the cross against your palm!" Noah
shouted. "Fry him!"

Just before the monster sliced through Willow's throat, Noah dove between them, blocking
the blow and tearing what looked like a wicked
set of claws across the Casus's chest. The guy
reeled back, clutching his chest with his remaining arm, then dropped to his knees on the
ground.

"Hurry!" Noah grunted, already back on his feet and delivering a crunching punch to the nose of the Casus who held her. "Fry him before he dies!" he shouted at Damon, his fist flying over Willow's head as he punched the Casus again.

This time, the guy went down, and took Willow with him.

She landed on top of the Casus, and Noah wrenched her out of the monster's hold, tossing her aside so that he could finish him off. Sitting up, she watched, stunned, as Damon moved behind the one-armed Casus, his own arm glowing with molten, vibrant flames. The demon followed Noah's earlier instructions, burying his burning arm in the back of the monster's neck and Willow looked away just as a deafening explosion tore through the night, signaling the Casus's death.

When she returned her gaze to Damon, he was sprawled on his ass with a stunned look on his handsome face, his blond-and-blue hair covered with falling ash as it floated on the wind. Looking around, she saw that the shape-shifters had gathered their wounded and finally run, obviously deciding this was a situation they didn't want any part of. She envied them that choice, since she knew she was stuck there to the end.

Noah was still fighting the other Casus who had managed to get back on his feet, and the last one was standing by the trees, his face bloodied from his battle with the shifters. She figured there was something clever she should be doing, but she was in shock, stunned by what Noah had done. By the way that he'd risked his life to save hers. And she was still reeling from that bombshell, when she got slammed with another.

"Witch!" the Casus shouted into the woods. "Get your ass out here!"

As a gaunt figure walked out of the trees, Willow couldn't believe her eyes. Despite Noah's warnings, bile rose in the back of her throat as she got a good look at the wasted, almost skeletal woman who barely resembled her beloved sister. A sister who was helping those trying to hurt Noah.

"Sienna?" she croaked, her eyes burning with the hot sting of tears. "How could you?"

Her sister winced, her voice almost painfully hollow as she spoke. "I'm sorry, Willow. I didn't know you were going to be here."

"And that makes it okay?" she shouted, surging to her feet. "These assholes are trying to kidnap Noah! And you're helping them!"

"I know…I know you'll never be able to understand, but I don't have any choice."

"Like hell you don't," she argued, while Noah moved to her side, the Casus he'd been fighting scrambling away to take shelter behind her sister. "These are killers, Si. Is that what you've become? A murderer?"

"You don't understand," Sienna repeated, her pale, tangled hair moving over her shoulders as she shook her head. "You can't possibly understand."

Tears clogged Willow's throat, but she managed to ask, "What would Mike think of this? Do you think he'd want to know that this is what you've become?"

Sienna flinched so hard, it looked like she'd been slapped. "I'm sorry, Willow." The husky words were little more than a whisper. "But I made a deal and I have to keep my end of it. I have to let them take Noah."

She stepped in front of Noah, shielding him with her body, and made her voice hard. "I'm sorry, too, Si. But I can't let you do that."

Sienna's frail body shook harder, the look on her thin face one of tormented agony. "Damn it, Willow. I don't want to fight you." But even as she said the words, she lifted her hands, preparing to unleash some kind of spell.

Willow's heart broke.

"I don't want to fight you, either," she choked out, the words hoarse with pain. "But I'm not letting you have him." Then she took a deep breath, dropped her knife and lifted her palms.

Noah couldn't believe what he was seeing. Damon had moved in close to Will's other side, and now a towering wall of fire surrounded the three of them, offering them protection, the violent flames licking the skies like the flick of a dragon's tongue.

"How long can you keep this up?" he asked, hating the strain etched into her beautiful face.

Sweat misted her skin as she panted, "Not long enough."

"We need a plan," he growled, looking at the demon.

"What exactly is this thing made of?" Damon asked, bouncing the Marker on the palm of his hand.

"I don't know," Noah snapped, wondering why the demon even cared. "I think it's some kind of material that can only be found in hell, but I have no idea what the name is."

Damon grinned. "That's all I needed to know."

"Why? What are you going to do?"

The demon's sly grin spread into a smile. "Trust me. This'll be more fun if you just watch."

Knowing Willow was in pain, he snarled, "Whatever the hell it is, do it now!"

Damon rubbed his thumb over the dark metal of the ornate, Maltese-shaped cross, and then looked at Will. "When I say the word, honey, you drop the flames. Okay?"

She nodded, and Damon closed his eyes, his brow creased with concentration as he muttered to himself in a strange, guttural dialect. The cross began to glow, burning a deep, dark red, and then the demon opened his eyes and growled, "Now!"

Will dropped her hands, extinguishing the wall of fire, and Damon shoved his arms forward, the glowing cross still trapped within his fingers. A thunderous blast of wind flew from the demon's outstretched arms, slamming into Sienna and the two remaining Casus, flinging them back toward the trees. And then they simply vanished, and Damon lowered his arms.

"What did you do?" Willow rasped, appearing equal parts pleased and terrified, no doubt worried about her sister.

"I just sent them on a little trip." Damon leaned against the side of Noah's truck, none too steady on his feet. "They won't be far," he explained, running a shaky hand back through his blue-blond hair, and Noah noticed that the blue streak, as well as the symbol on the side of the demon's neck, looked paler than before. "Maybe a county or two over."

"Oh," she breathed out, the relief in her eyes easy to read.

As his claws retreated into his fingertips, Noah put a comforting hand on Will's shoulder and offered the demon a gruff thank-you for his help.

"I see you've got a backseat in this thing," Damon rumbled, patting the truck. "You guys mind giving me a lift? I don't know about you two, but I'm more than ready to get out of here."

"Didn't you drive here?" Willow asked, picking up her knife and cleaning the blade on her jeans, which were already covered in blood. Thankfully, it didn't look as if any of it was hers.

The demon gave a tired sigh. "No, and before you ask why, it's a long story."

She shook her head and almost managed a grin. "They always are with you."

As Noah and Will climbed into the front of the truck, Damon sprawled himself in the middle of the backseat. "While we drive, maybe the two of you could explain what it is you need me to do. But first—" he groaned, sounding as if he was in pain "—we need to find me some food. You guys got here before I could eat tonight, and pulling shit like that spell always zaps me. I'm down to nothing."

"We'll find you a drive-through," Noah told him, turning his key in the ignition and cranking the engine.

Damon laughed. "How the hell am I supposed

to do my thing in a drive-through? I'm flexible, but...damn, Winston. I don't think any man should be *that* limber."

Noah looked over his shoulder. "What the hell are you talking about?"

Willow placed her hand on his arm, and he turned his head, studying her face in the crazy neon glow flooding through the windshield. She was so damn beautiful, it stole his breath. His chest felt hot, soft, like something was melting in there, and he knew that couldn't be good.

With a smile twitching at the corner of her mouth, she said, "I don't think Damon means *that* kind of food, Noah."

His eyes went wide. "You mean...?"

"Yep. He needs to find a woman. One who's willing and able, and, knowing Damon, stacked like a brick house."

"Well, shit." Noah was pretty damn sure they weren't going to run across a drive-through for *that*. Then he thought about the strange interchange they'd just shared, and he started to laugh.

They were battered and bloody, had nearly lost their lives, and he'd discovered that in addition to fangs, he'd also managed to release some pretty deadly claws that they still hadn't talked about. He should have been worrying about what it meant, or driving Will's crazy little ass back home, where she'd be safe. But he wasn't doing any of those things. Instead, he was going to make sure they got the demon somewhere he could get laid.

If he'd called his friends back in England and tried to explain the situation to them, they wouldn't have believed him. Hell, he hardly believed it himself.

"Okay, then," he finally said in a strange, kind-of-strangled voice as he adjusted the air conditioner and put the truck in gear.

As the open road stretched out before them, Noah realized that in a world where nothing was making a lot of sense to him, there was one fact that he could be certain of, without any shadow of a doubt.

He might have managed to hold on to his body for another day, but he'd finally lost his mind.

CHAPTER ELEVEN

DAMON'S IDEA OF dinner turned out to be a night-club located across the street from the hotel where they'd managed to get the last two available rooms. Since Noah refused to stop before he'd put some distance between them and the bar, Damon had been forced to wait for his meal. The demon had used the time to explain how the Marker was made of powerful "hellstone." He'd used it to channel his energy into a spell that transported Sienna and the Casus to a different location. Then Willow had told Damon about the Death-Walkers, the journal and why they needed him.

Damon had agreed to take a look at the spell, but only after he'd done something about his hunger pains. They'd parted ways in the lobby, and Willow now found herself in the same situation she'd been in the night before.

Alone. In a hotel room. With Noah.

As she sat on the edge of the bed, she looked over the beige, almost painfully drab room,

thinking it was a step up from the motel they'd
stayed at last night. She didn't know how much
time they'd spend there. Probably only enough to
get cleaned up, considering they were all a mess,
and maybe grab a few hours' sleep. She knew
she needed the rest, but as she looked over her
shoulder, settling her gaze on Noah, all thoughts
of sleeping fled her mind.

He was standing on the other side of the bed,
setting his knife on the bedside table, along with
the gun he'd taken from his bag. He checked the
clip on the handgun, then pulled off his ruined
shirt, leaving him in a pair of low-slung jeans.
Willow tried not to stare, but it was impossible.
Like trying to tell someone not to look at the
Grand Canyon when they were standing right on
its edge. His body was that stunning. All hard
and muscular and mouthwatering.

Last night he'd said they were going to have
to talk about his physical reaction to her. She
suddenly wondered if that was a conversation
they could just act out instead. Because she had
some really important things…to say.

She knew she'd never be able to trust Noah
Winston with her heart. She just didn't have that
kind of faith inside her anymore. But she trusted
him with her body. The man had already proven
he was willing to risk his life to save hers. As
long as she stayed in control and set the limits,

she wanted to touch him…and to be touched. Damn it, she wanted as much of him as she could get. And she knew, without any doubt, that if she didn't do everything she could to get her fill of him now, she was going to regret it for the rest of her life.

But a shower was mandatory, since she smelled of Casus blood, so she grabbed her bag and headed for the bathroom. She didn't take long, and Noah went in right after her, leaving her to prowl the room in her sweats and tank top, too restless to lie down.

She was standing at the window, staring through the blinds at the silver moon, when the bathroom door opened, and she listened as Noah took a seat on the couch. Resting her shoulder against the window frame, she said, "I didn't want to believe you. About Sienna."

She'd been trying not to think about her sister all night, but flashes of memory kept stabbing into her brain like a knife. When Sienna had walked out of those woods, she'd looked like something from a horror movie. Long, ragged white dress splotched with blood. Snarled, waist-length hair that was nearly white. And those cold, almost lifeless eyes.

"I've been trying not to think about her," she added, "but I can't stop."

When he spoke, his voice was low and deep,

brushing across her skin like a physical touch. "I want to be able to help, Will. But I need to understand why she's doing this."

Her throat constricted. "Who knows?"

"Come on, Will." His voice was soft, but she could hear the bite of impatience he'd tried to hide. "I've been searching for information about Si for months, but haven't been able to find anything. Nothing in the media or from the authorities."

"There wouldn't be," she murmured, closing her eyes as she leaned her head against the window frame. "You know what my family's like. We keep things private. Jessie wasn't joking when she said we never go to the police."

"Will, please trust me."

She opened her eyes and stared out at the dark, endless landscape of the night. Trees swayed in the wind like dancing figures in an ancient ritual, and she kept her gaze focused on those swaying limbs as she said, "It happened last spring. Do you remember Mike Jones?"

"The guy who played high school football with Bryce, then went on to play at Ole Miss?"

"That's him. He came back home after he'd been injured his junior year, and he fell in love with Si. They got married, and later had a little girl named Angie." She took a shaky breath, wrapped her arms around herself and went on.

"Angie was killed last spring while over at a friend's house. The friend's family was attacked by a couple of rogue vampires who had flirted with the little girl's mother earlier that day. They hadn't liked the way she'd blown them off, so they followed her home and waited until nightfall. No one in the house was left alive."

He cursed under his breath, and she could hear him move to his feet. He paced from one side of the room to the other.

She cleared her throat, then went on. "Despite being human, Mike managed to track down the vampires who were responsible and he got his revenge after a long, bloody battle. But he didn't survive his injuries, and Sienna lost him, too."

"Christ," he grunted. "Poor Si."

"It was awful," she murmured. "Everything she loved was taken from her so quickly. She went from having everything in the world, to having nothing at all."

"I remember Sienna studying healing when we were kids. Was there nothing she could do to bring them back from the dead?"

She shook her head as she turned to face him, her arms still wrapped tight around her body, as though they might be able to hold her together. "We're taught the Life-Spell from an early age, but few have ever used it successfully. I've only heard of three cases in history where a *Chastain* was actually able to bring someone back from the other side, and it was done within minutes of them dying. By the time she'd found Mike's body, it was too late. And it was the same with Angie."

"What do you think she wants with Calder?" he asked, his hard muscles coiled with anger. He was still moving in that restless, powerful stride, like a tiger pacing its cage. Predatory and primal. And stunningly gorgeous.

Realizing the mouthwatering sight of him had sidetracked her, she cleared her throat and answered his question. "Mike's parents had never liked Sienna. They believed the rumors they'd heard about our family. I think they were even afraid of Angie, who was already showing signs of incredible power."

He stopped in his tracks, his handsome face etched with shock. "They were afraid of their own granddaughter? Jesus, they sound like idiots," he growled, and she loved him for thinking that.

Letting her head fall back on her shoulders, Willow stared at the ceiling, but she didn't really see it. All she kept seeing was her sister's gaunt, skeletal face. That soulless look of pain that had been in her eyes. "Anyway, Mike's parents were awful when they learned what had happened. They told Si that their son was burning in hell because he'd taken lives in anger, and they accused her of forcing him to make the kills. Said she'd controlled him with witchcraft and that she was to blame for his death…and his punishment."

She sniffed, and there was a tremor in her words as she continued. "Sienna was never the same after that. I stayed home to help Jessie take care of her, and we tried everything we could think of to reach her. But she just kept drifting further away. Then I woke up one morning and she was gone. I hadn't seen or heard from her since." She lowered her head and found him staring right at her, his blue eyes burning with emotion.

"Until tonight," she whispered.

"I'm sorry, Will." He was no longer pacing. Just standing there, watching her, the searing heat of his gaze rushing against her like a hot wind. She wanted to reach out and grab it, pulling that life-giving heat around her. Wanted to reach out and grab *him*.

"I'd give anything to change the way things went down tonight. I hate that you had to see her that way," he said huskily, and she trembled in reaction, nearly undone by his words. "And I hate that you had to make a choice between us. I'm so damn sorry about that."

God, did he have any idea how much she

needed him to hold her when he said things like that? When he talked to her as if he cared...as if she meant something to him?

Knowing she was close to running across the room and throwing herself in his arms, she took a deep breath and forced herself to finish answering his question. "So, um, Jessie and I knew Si was having a hard time dealing with what had happened, but we...we never believed she would try something as insane as a partnership with someone like Calder."

He pushed his hands in his pockets, and propped his shoulders against the wall behind him. "What do you think she wants with him? I mean, if she can open a portal into someplace like Meridian, why not open one into hell and go after Mike herself?"

"I don't think she could. It's said that only a powerful source of pure evil can go into the deepest circles of hell and survive."

"So she made a deal with Calder." His voice was low, gritty. "Her help, in exchange for her husband."

"Yes...but he'll never keep his end of the bargain. And I don't think it would work even if he did. If Calder tries to go into hell and bring Mike back for her, he won't...he won't be the same. He won't be the man she fell in love with. She's lost him forever, and now we've lost Si." Her voice cracked at the end, and she buried her face in her hands, her shoulders shaking as she fought to hold back her tears.

And then he was there, standing right in front of her. He didn't give her any time to protest or pull away. He just wrapped her in his arms, holding her against his chest, and she melted into a hot, shivering rush of tears, the overwhelming sorrow inside her too much to contain. She hadn't allowed herself to cry over Sienna in months, too afraid that once she started, she'd never be able to stop. But she felt no fear in Noah's arms. She could lower her guard and give herself a moment to fall apart, because she knew he'd be there to bring her back when she did. Knew he'd lend her some of his incredible strength to pull herself together, if she couldn't quite manage it on her own.

He held her tight until the hard sobs finally quieted, then secured one arm around her waist as he lifted his hand to her face. With the backs of his knuckles, he tilted her chin up so that he could see her expression. She knew she must look frightful, no doubt with a pink nose and tear-splotched eyes, but that wasn't the way he looked at her. He stared down at her with an intense, heavy-lidded gaze, acting as if she were the most beautiful thing he'd ever seen. As if he were trying to memorize every detail of how she looked at that moment. His lips were slightly parted for the sensual rasp of his breath, a flush of color burning along the crests of his cheekbones, his hand almost feverishly hot as he placed it against the side of her face. The texture of his calluses against her damp cheek was so sexy, she wanted to grab his hand and rub it all over her body, needing the sweet burn of pleasure to blot out the pain.

"I always hated to see you cry," he whispered in an aching tone, catching a slow-falling tear with his thumb. "I hate it even more now."

She licked her lips, noticing the way he watched the quick flick of her tongue, and asked him the question that had been looping through her brain all night. "Why did you put yourself between me and that Casus?"

Her hands were pressed against his muscular chest, and she felt his heart jump at the question, its beat heavy and hard beneath her palms. He settled that searing gaze on her mouth and said, "If I had the choice, I'd put myself between you and danger every damn time."

"Why?"

"Because I can't stand the thought of anything ever happening to you."

She groaned, completely undone by those husky words and the breathtaking look in his eyes. Lifting onto her toes, she reached up and grabbed handfuls of his short hair, pulling his head down to hers. And then she kissed him. Kissed him with all the unspent emotion and need that had been building inside her for the past twelve years. He gave a low growl, and sank his tongue into her mouth with a bold, possessive thrust, turning the explicit kiss into something raw and delicious. He wasn't just taking. He was comforting her with his mouth, pouring breathtaking emotion into every lick and stroke, letting her know she wasn't alone. That she could ask him for what she needed, and he'd give it to her.

The kiss went on for long, drugging moments, drowning her senses in pleasure, until he suddenly ripped his mouth from hers, sucking a deep, shuddering breath into his lungs. He pulled his head back, and stared down at her, studying her face...her eyes. He ran his hand over his mouth, as if he was rubbing the taste of her into his skin, and his gaze narrowed until the blue was nothing more than a silver spark of light between his thick lashes. "Will?"

She swallowed, and somehow found her voice. "I'm not asking you to have sex with me," she whispered, settling her hands on his shoulders. "I'm not...ready for that yet. Not after everything that happened. But that doesn't mean we can't make each other feel good tonight. I'd like that, Noah." She took a quick breath, then forced out the rest. "Because I'd really, *really* love to know what it feels like to come with a part of you inside me."

"Goddamn it," he growled, a shudder moving through his hard frame. "You make it so hard to do the right thing, Will."

A grin touched her lips as she said, "Then do me instead." His chest shook with a hard, gritty laugh, and she smiled. "I'm serious, Noah."

"I'm sure I should be thinking about this," he muttered, lowering his head and pressing hot, seeking kisses along the column of her throat, making her burn for more. "But I can't."

She arched her neck to give him better access, her voice breathless and dreamy. "It's okay. I don't think this requires a lot of thinking."

Another deep, husky rumble of laughter, and then he lifted his head and locked his hungry gaze with hers. "I don't know if this is right," he admitted in a low rasp, his dark brows drawn together in a fierce expression.

"I'm a big girl, Noah. I know what I'm doing." She paused suddenly, not liking the unpleasant thought that wormed its way into her brain. "You're not just trying to protect my pride, are you? Maybe the truth is that you just don't want me."

He raised an eyebrow and snorted as he

grabbed her hand, shoving it against his impressive erection. "That feel like I don't want you, Will?"

The thick, rigid length pulsed against the press of her hand, and she couldn't help but curl her fingers over it and squeeze, loving the way he hissed a shaky curse through his teeth. "Then what's the problem?"

"The problem is that I'm not myself. I'm cha—"

She cut him off before he could get started down that road. "And I'm not human, Noah. I can take care of myself, if I have to. You don't scare me."

"I'm not worried about scaring you."

She could read the truth in his eyes. "You won't hurt me, either," she said softly, letting her emotions and her hunger show, so that he would know just how badly she wanted him.

"Jesus," he muttered, shaking his head. "I can't think when you look at me like that."

"Then don't think. Just kiss me again."

And he did.

She could feel the tremor of raw hunger that spread through his body as their lips touched, feel the breathtaking strength he used to hold himself under tight control. Sweet, shivering chills spread over her skin, her heart beating hard and fast, like something trapped inside her chest.

The tenor of the kiss was different from before. No less giving, but he took more. Demanded it. His hands lifted to her head, long fingers spearing through her hair, shaping around her skull so that he could hold her still for the marauding pleasure of his mouth. It was all passion and scalding heat, driving her wild, and she struggled against him, trying to get closer, her hands coasting over his hot skin, unable to get enough of those hard, mouthwatering muscles.

Then he was lifting her off her feet as if she weighed nothing, and Willow found herself lying in the middle of the bed. Noah came down over her, his hard thighs bracketing her hips as he pulled at her clothes, nearly ripping them off her body.

"Noah?"

"I know, no sex. I get it." His voice was ragged, desperate, his chest rising and falling with the heavy force of his breaths. "But I'm getting you under my mouth, Will. I'm spreading you open and getting my fill."

"Oh…" Her mind blanked as he changed position, and she couldn't think of a single thing to say, except for maybe *Hurry,* when he was already going at warp speed. And she was suddenly feeling a little...shy. Odd, since she'd never been shy before. But then, she'd never had Noah Winston kneeling between her legs, his rough hands hot on her skin as he slid them between her trembling thighs and shoved them apart, spreading her wide open, just like he'd said he would do. He made a thick, gravelly sound in the back of his throat as he pressed her knees against the mattress, the explicit position leaving her sex completely exposed. A muscle pulsed in the rigid set of his jaw as he settled his scorching gaze between her legs. She could tell by the dark lust on his face that he liked what he saw. His nostrils flared as he pulled in a deep breath, the low groan on his lips telling her he liked her scent, as well.

She choked back a shaky moan and gripped handfuls of the sheets, struggling to keep still. She wondered if he could tell how nervous she was, if he could feel the tension tightening through her body, because he didn't ravage her in a fit of lust. Instead, he inhaled a slow breath of air, and seemed to force himself to take it slow. To give her a little time to relax.

"I can't get enough of the way you smell," he rasped, taking another slow, deep breath as he stroked those callused hands up her thighs. He ran a thumb through her slick, swollen folds, possessively stroking that most intimate part of her. "Did you know I could smell you in the woods the other day? Before you put that knife to my throat? I knew you were there because I'd picked up your scent. And it made me hard as hell."

She tucked her chin into her chest so that she could get a better look at him. "Really?"

A dimple appeared in his cheek. "Guess it's a good thing I've never been able to stand tucking in my shirts. It covered the evidence," he rumbled, and then, without any warning at all, he licked her. Right *there,* across the soft, drenched folds of her sex. Then he licked her again, slow and deep, taking her taste into his mouth. He pulled pleasure up out of her as if it were his to control, the husky growl on his lips telling her he was enjoying the intimate act as much as she was.

Bracing himself on his elbows, he used his thumbs to hold her open, tasting every slippery part of her, inside and out, his growls of satisfaction getting deeper, darker. She writhed beneath him, feeling the stunning sensations rush and swell, racing through her veins. When he lashed her clit with the flat of his tongue, working it fast and rough, Willow arched her back and screamed like she was dying, shocked by the guttural cry that ripped from her throat as the orgasm swept through her like the devastating blast of an explosion.

"That's it," he growled, rubbing the words into her drenched flesh. "Keep coming for me, Will. I can't get enough of it." He kept going at her, thrusting his wickedly talented tongue inside her clenching sheath, the sounds he made almost more animal than man as he drank her in, demanding everything she had.

She didn't know how much time had passed before she heard him say her name.

"Yeah?" she gasped, wetting her lips.

"I lied."

She blinked as she tucked her chin in again and stared down at him. "About what?"

"I said I was getting my fill," he told her, his voice low and breathless. "But I can't. You taste too good."

He didn't wait for a response, which was good, since she couldn't do anything more than moan when his tongue was pushing inside her like that. Hell, she could barely remember her name. He ate at her with that same mind-blowing intensity until she was tugging on his hair and pumping her sex against his mouth. Until her back was arched, and ragged cries of pleasure were tearing from her throat. Then he kissed his way up her flushed body, licking and nipping with his teeth, until he'd reached her breasts, which were already heavy and aching for his touch. He sucked on each nipple, getting them both wet and red, then lingered, licking her slowly, as if he were lapping at something sweet, the same way he'd licked her between her legs, and she decided the man was freaking diabolical. But in a good melt-your-bones-with-bliss kind of way.

When he finally raised his head, his lips were shiny, those blue eyes darker in color than she'd ever seen them before, but glowing with a warm, provocative fire. He braced himself above her on his powerful arms, the strong lines of muscle and sinew a testament to his incredible strength. The charm that Jessie had given him swung from the length of cord around his neck, and she reached up to touch it with her fingertip. "The Casus didn't take over your body tonight, so I guess this worked."

"Either that, or they had orders not to."

"You should trust Jessie," she said, returning her gaze to his rugged face. "She wouldn't have lied to you."

He nodded as he slid his gaze to the side, a sudden frown on his lips. "What's wrong?" she asked, sensing the sudden change in his mood.

"It's nothing," he muttered, closing his eyes.

"Noah, look at me."

He shook his head, a grimace on his sensual

mouth. "I don't want you reminded of those bastards."

Her lips parted as she realized what was bothering him. "Noah, your eyes are beautiful."

"My eyes look just like theirs," he growled, forcing the words through his clenched teeth. "Like the Casus."

"No, they don't." She laughed and his eyes popped open, as if he needed to see for himself what she found so damn funny.

She reached up and brushed the silky strands of his hair back from his face, then traced the masculine shape of his brows. "You're breathtaking," she told him, hoping he could see the truth in her eyes. "You could never look like one of them, Noah."

And it was true, even though he no longer looked human to her, either. There was something deeper in him. Some dark, dangerous current that ran just beneath his striking surface—but it didn't scare her. If anything, she was seduced by the combination of predator and protector, feeling the rush of danger and the tenderness of care all at once. It was a heady assault on her senses that she was helpless to resist.

"Please," she whispered, wishing she could make him understand how amazing he was.

How much she cared about him. "Please trust me when I say that you could never look like one of them."

CHAPTER TWELVE

NOAH STARED DOWN at the woman beneath him, not knowing how she did it. How could the little witch look into his ice-blue eyes like that, with so much pleasure and trust, and not be disgusted by what she saw?

He'd always envied his brothers, whose eyes were a deep, dark blue. Noah had been one of the few unlucky Winstons to inherit the Casus icy eye color, and he hated it. Had never liked seeing his reflection, his stomach twisting when he'd notice those ice-blue eyes staring back at him.

But Willow didn't look at him with fear or revulsion. She looked at him as if she saw something that was wonderful—something worthy of her—and it blew his mind.

No matter how he examined it, Noah knew this was a mistake. But at that moment, he just didn't care.

He stared her right in the eye as he pressed his hand between her legs, sliding his fingers into her drenched silk...daring her to look away. "Come for me again," he rasped, stroking her, then thrusting two thick fingers into that tight, pink little opening. "I can't get enough of it. I need to feel it again."

She spread her legs wider, opening herself to him, and he groaned as he felt her fall so quickly, the tight convulsions clenching around his fingers as he pressed deep and let her pleasure rush through him, dizzying and sweet. This feeling was so huge inside him, he didn't know what to do with it. How to control it. How to fight it. But he couldn't let go, as if he needed the feel of her in his arms to keep going.

Then he felt the heat in his gums, and he snarled with frustration. *"Shit."*

She jumped at the stark sound. "What? What's wrong?"

"Don't freak," he mumbled, keeping his face turned away as he pulled his fingers from her body. "But I, uh... The damned fangs are back."

"Oh," she said, sounding curious...and maybe even a little bit excited. "Let me see them."

His eyes shot wide as he whipped his head back around. He barely moved his lips as he demanded, "What did you say?"

The smile she gave him was so tender, it made him flinch. "Let me see," she repeated.

What the...?

"Seriously, Noah. I want to see them."

Breathing raggedly, he parted his lips, giving her a glimpse, and her smile turned into a soft, mind-melting look of wonder. "Oh, Noah," she breathed out in a soft voice. "They're really sexy."

"They don't look like...?" He couldn't get the rest of the question out, but she knew what he meant. She shook her head, running her fingertip over the shape of his upper lip, then dared to stroke her finger across one long incisor. He shuddered as if she'd stroked his cock, and she grinned.

"They don't look anything like the Casus," she told him, her gaze lifting back to his. Her eyes were hazy with desire. "They're just incredibly hot."

He jolted, feeling something heavy and sweet roll through him, shaking him apart. He trembled as he lowered his lips to hers, claiming her mouth with an urgent, desperate kiss. "Please," he gasped against her lips, settling his hips between her legs. He could feel the wet, scalding heat of her sex through his jeans, a violent need roaring through him that made him tremble and curse. "Christ, Will. *Please*. I need to be in you," he groaned, rubbing the aching ridge of his cock against those slick, plump folds. "Tell me I can have you. Tell me *now*."

"Sit up," she told him, pushing at his bunched shoulders. He wanted to howl with frustration, until she said, "Sit up and open your jeans. Hurry. I want to see you."

"Whatever you want," he growled, loving the bite of her nails in his shoulders as he quickly kissed his way down her body again, taking another greedy taste of her, his tongue lapping at her pink, wet sex. Then he braced himself on his knees as he ripped open his fly, shucked the jeans below his hips and showed her his body.

"Noah." The longing in her soft voice as she said his name, her dark gaze focused in hard and tight on his hungry cock, made him shudder. Then she sat up and wrapped one of those soft hands around him, and he nearly died.

"You don't fit," she said playfully, unable to close her fingers around his thick width, his cock harder than it'd ever been before. "I mean, I always knew you'd be huge, but...geez. Don't you think this is a bit extreme?"

"I'll fit where it counts," he rasped, unable to keep from rolling his hips when she added her other hand, stroking him in a hard, tight pull that drew a drop of moisture at the flared tip. "You'll take every inch of me, Will."

She bit her lip, looking as if she wanted to lean down and cover him with her mouth, licking him the way he'd licked her—but there was something in her eyes as she looked up that told him he wasn't going to like what came next.

"I want you so badly," she told him, still gripping him in her hands, "but I meant what I said before. We…we can't have intercourse."

Yep. He definitely didn't like it.

"Why?"

She looked away, and he nearly howled for the second time that night. "Damn it, Will. What is it? You know I would never hurt you. If it's the fangs, I promise I can control myself. I won't bite you."

"It's not the fangs," she said, shaking her head.

Frustration burst out of him in a violent, graveled string of curses that had her pulling her hands away and scooting out from under him, her back to the headboard as she pulled her legs to the side. He scrubbed his hands over his face, wondering what the hell was going on, when a hard knock suddenly rapped against the door to their room.

Hanging his head forward, he muttered, "Shit."

"It's Damon," she whispered.

He grunted and she moved off the bed. From the corner of his eye, he watched as she pulled on her clothes, and wanted to fucking cry. Or kill something with his bare hands. Like the demon.

"Well," she said when she was dressed, her

gaze carefully focused on his face, instead of his cock. "Let him in."

Noah ground his jaw as he refastened his jeans and rolled off the bed, thinking the situation seemed fitting.

After all, there was a bloody demon at his door.

And he'd definitely landed in hell.

IF THERE WAS one thing Damon knew, it was how to make someone angry. At least, that's what his ex had said, just before she tried to slit his throat. And judging by the look on Winston's face as he ripped open the door, the human was picturing something right along those lines.

He also looked like a man who'd just been interrupted in the middle of something really…important. Poor bastard. Damon almost felt sorry for the guy.

"Did you get lost?" the human growled. "Because your room is next door."

"I'm not here to sleep," he said in an easy drawl. He was buzzing on so much energy after the hot little redhead that he'd found in the nightclub, he probably wouldn't sleep for a few days. "I came to look at that spell for you."

Noah muttered something creatively foul under his breath, but he did step aside to let

Damon through the doorway. "You have shitty timing, MacCaven."

"So I've been told." He knew better than to wait for an invitation as he strode past the human and into the room. Willow was standing beside the rumpled bed, looking all rosy and mellow, her mouth kiss-swollen, eyes hazy with satisfaction, which explained the sweet scent of pleasure lingering in the air. Good for her. He loved Low and wanted her to be happy. Not many guys had caught her eye over the years, and he'd never seen her watch a man with as much hunger as she did Winston.

The human stalked over to the bag he'd left on the sofa, rummaged around inside and then crossed the room again and handed Damon some folded sheets of paper. "This is a copy of the passage in the journal."

"Okay, let's see what we have," he murmured, taking a seat on the foot of the bed. He recognized the obscure demonic dialect the spell was written in, but only because his mother had forced him to study the ancient demon languages when he was young. She'd been fanatical about history, and though he'd hated the lessons when he'd been a boy, a lot of the things he'd learned from her had served him well as a man.

Willow and Noah paced as he read, their nervous energy vibrating against his highly sensitive skin. Their restless movements would probably have driven him crazy, if he hadn't been so absorbed in what he was reading.

"It's a helluva spell," he said twenty minutes later. Rubbing his jaw, he looked at Noah and asked, "Do you know what it does?"

The human crossed his arms over his bare chest and leaned his back against the door. "Will mentioned to you on the way here that her aunt told us it's a Death-Spell. One of the most powerful she'd ever seen. She said it could kill anything."

Damon nodded. "She was right, to a point. But do you know exactly what it *does?*"

"You mean how it works?" Willow asked, perching her bottom on the edge of the sofa. Some of her rosy flush had faded, but her mouth was still red, her golden curls tumbling over the side of her face, making her look like one of those bombshells in an ad for designer jeans. He hoped Winston knew what a lucky guy he was, then thought about the prophecy that had been read at Willow's birth, as well as the spell he was holding in his hand, and decided that lucky might not be such a great description.

"Damon?" she said, trying to catch his attention.

"Sorry," he rumbled, a crooked smile on his

lips. "I was just thinking about how gorgeous you are."

Her cheeks turned pink, and he didn't have to glance at the human to know that Noah was giving him a deadly glare. There was definitely something powerful going on between these two, and he couldn't help but wonder how this was all going to play out in the end.

For all the hunger blazing between them, he could also sense an underlying current of tension. One he figured was going to get cranked higher, and higher, as the days wore on. It would be interesting to see if Winston could take the pressure. But one way or another, he had a feeling Willow was finally going to know just what the human's feelings for her were.

In Damon's opinion, it was an answer that'd been a long time coming.

It was Noah who spoke next. "Christ, Mac-Caven. Are you going to tell us how the spell works or not?"

Setting the papers to the side, he hunched forward so that he could brace his elbows on his knees, his fingers threaded together in a loose hold. "It sucks the evil out."

"Sucks the evil out?" Willow shook her head and frowned. "What do you mean?"

He slowly arched an eyebrow. "I mean if you have sins you're thinking of confessing, it'd be good to do it before performing this spell. Because it feeds on any life force that is inherently evil and consumes it. All that's left behind is the shell."

"So then it'll work on the Casus, as well as the Death-Walkers?" Noah asked.

"It could," Damon replied, settling his gaze back on the human. "But it isn't the kind of spell you can pull off at the drop of a hat. It's going to require some careful planning." His brows lifted, and he paid close attention to the human's expression as he said, "Plus, the catalyst isn't one that's going to be easy to come by, unless you're carrying a source around with you."

"Was Jessie right about that, as well?" Willow muttered. "About the virgin's blood?"

Damon kept his gaze on Winston as he nodded. "The virgin's blood is the main catalyst, just like Jessie told you. It needs to be placed in a special ritual circle that's pretty fucking complicated to make, but I can manage it. But the virgin's blood isn't the only blood you'll need. You need the blood of the damned to pull off the first part."

The human was back to scowling. "What's the first part? How many parts does this spell have?"

"The first part of the spell will draw the Death-Walkers to the circle and trap them within its power. That only encompasses a certain area, depending on how big you make the circle."

Winston's blue eyes started to glow, and Damon knew the guy liked what he was hearing. He wondered how long that feeling would last, considering he was pretty damn certain that Willow hadn't fessed up yet. Then the human answered his question for him, saying, "So let me see if I've got this right. You're telling me that once we get our hands on some 'damned' blood, we'll be able to use it to pull those bastards to one location, and then use the virgin's blood to kill them all at the same time?"

"Every single one," Damon rasped, wondering just how badly she was going to hurt him when he spilled her secret. Knowing Low, he might not be able to walk for a week.

"And seeing as how Damon is a demon," she murmured, "he'll be able to provide the blood of the damned."

"If you ask sweetly."

Willow slid him a wry smile. "I guess it's a good thing we came after you."

He lifted his shoulders in an easy shrug. "Hey, I'm happy to help."

"WHY?" NOAH ASKED, unsure of the demon's motives. "Exactly why are you so eager to help, MacCaven?"

Damon raised his brows. "Why wouldn't I be?"

"For one, it isn't your war."

"Hey, it's not like I asked to get involved." The demon slanted him a narrow look, clearly insulted by the line of questioning. "But you're the one who told me these Death-Walkers are killing innocent people. The way I see it, that makes it everyone's war."

Christ. Noah couldn't believe it. The demon really did have a conscience.

Willow quickly steered the conversation in a new direction. "Is there anywhere specific that the spell has to be performed?"

Damon shook his head. "We can choose the location, so that's good. If there are as many Death-Walkers running around as you guys think, then we're going to need someplace in the middle of nowhere."

"Kansas," Willow blurted, and they both looked at her. "I worked a case there a few months ago, near a little town called Sampson. The family that hired me owns several acres practically in the middle of nowhere. There's some swanky resort in the area, and a few local farms. But nothing else for miles around. It would be perfect for what we need and I can guarantee that no one will be there. I just talked to the family last week and they were leaving for a month-long trip to Australia."

"I'm thinking this Sampson place sounds like a good idea," Damon rumbled, the streak in his hair once again a bright electric blue, as was the symbol at the side of his throat. His dark eyes glittered with humor. "But you're not getting me in a cowboy hat, Low, no matter how much you beg."

She snorted, and Noah felt like he was missing a private joke.

"And what about the virgin?" he practically growled, feeling stupid for feeling left out. "Do you have any suggestions where we might be able to track one down?"

"Believe it or not, that won't be a problem." A flat smile twisted the corner of the demon's mouth. "We already have someone who can help with that little issue."

"Oh, yeah?" Noah tensed, as if he knew a blow was coming, but didn't know from which direction. "Who?"

"A friend of mine," Damon drawled.

Noah narrowed his eyes. "Call me crazy, but I find it kind of hard to believe that a sex-eater would hang out with a virgin."

"Well, you can believe it, because she's right here." Then the idiot jerked his thumb toward

Will, who looked ready to take the demon's head off.

"You think Will's a virgin?" Noah shook his head and snorted. "I don't think so."

"Yeah?" The demon's chest shook with a breathless laugh. "Tell me, Winston, did she or did she not have sex with you tonight?"

"Damon," she snarled, "not another bloody word, I swear. Or you are going to seriously pay!"

All traces of humor fled the guy's expression as he looked away from Noah, and locked his gaze with Willow's. "I'm sorry, honey. But you were gonna have to come clean with the guy sooner or later. I mean, you *are* what's needed for the ceremony. You think that's just coincidence?"

For a breathless span of seconds, all Noah could do was stare, the past forty-eight hours he'd spent with her slamming through his brain in rapid time. When it all crashed together, he nearly fell on his ass. "A virgin?" he croaked, thankful for the door supporting his back. "I don't believe it."

She closed her eyes and took a few deep breaths. Then she stood, pulled her shoulders back and looked right at him. "I hate to say it, but you can. Believe it, that is."

"Jesus, Will. That doesn't make any goddamn sense!"

"Yeah, well, that's one of the great things about life, Noah. Things don't always make sense. And I don't have to explain a single thing to you. Wonderful, isn't it?"

He could feel his frustration being shaped into something ugly and raw, but there was no stopping it. He crossed the room before he even realized what he was doing, and found himself towering over her. "You can drop the damn sarcasm, Will. I want to know why."

"We all want lots of things, Noah." The quiet words rang with a kind of eerie finality that chilled him. "But most of us never get them."

His pulse raced as he stared down into her pale face, his heart pounding like a bitch. He wanted so badly to argue and shout until she'd given him the explanation he wanted, but he knew she was too stubborn to bend. If she didn't want to tell him, she wouldn't. And nothing he said was going to change that.

Clenching his jaw so tightly it hurt, he turned away from her and went to his bag, took out a shirt and pulled it over his head. Then he shoved his feet into his boots, grabbed his cell phone and the fresh pack of cigarettes he'd bought and stalked toward the door.

"Where are you going?" she asked, just before he slammed out of the room.

He didn't bother to turn around as he said, "I need to let the others know about the spell."

"And then what? Are you going to just leave me here?"

Noah gripped the handle so hard, he was surprised it didn't break. "It'd be better if I did."

"Why?"

He could feel the pain beneath her anger, and hated that she was hurting, even when he was pissed enough to turn her over his knee for keeping something like this from him.

"Because now you know you're not getting laid?"

"You saw what happened tonight." He cut her a dark look over his shoulder. "This is getting too dangerous."

"For who? A virgin?" She pulled in a deep breath, looking like an enraged little goddess, her dark eyes glowing with fury. "I'm still *me*, Noah. I don't need you or any man to take care of me. I can take care of *myself!*"

"And not to butt in or anything," Damon drawled, "but you're kinda gonna need her for the spell. Remember?"

Noah scowled, not even bothering to give the smart-ass a reply.

Willow crossed her arms over her chest and

lifted her chin. "You can't ditch me now, Noah. Even if you want to. We had a deal. I helped you find Damon. Now you're going to help me with my sister."

IT WASN'T LIKE they had anything in writing, but that was the way Willow was choosing to interpret their agreement.

"We'll talk about this later." His rigid expression said that he wanted nothing more than to get the hell out of the room...and away from her. "Right now, I have to make this call."

The second the door closed behind him, Damon looked at Willow and raised his brows. "You sure you know what you're doing with this guy, Low?"

"Don't I always?" she muttered.

Damon laughed as he rubbed two fingers over his stubbled jaw. "Then I guess this should be fun to watch."

"I wouldn't look so thrilled if I were you," she said softly, flicking him a deadly glare from beneath her lashes. "Or did you forget that you're the one with the blabbermouth?"

"You can't hold that against me," he argued, though he at least had the grace to look guilty. "You never would have fessed up, and the man needed to know."

"Why?" she asked, wondering why he couldn't have just stayed the hell out of her business.

Damon rolled his eyes. "Because I don't believe in accidents, that's why. Everything that happens, happens for a reason."

It was impossible to sound anything but snide as she said, "So my virginity is going to be the answer to everybody's prayers? Wow, lucky me."

"Think about it, Low. This is more than just coincidence. It *has* to be. Winston walks back into your life after all this time, and he just so happens to need help with a spell that requires a warrior's virgin blood? What are the odds?"

She'd purposefully avoided thinking about the odds…or the spell…or what it all meant. And she didn't like thinking about it now. She knew how fate worked. It would catch up with her whether she wanted it to or not. There was no sense in trying to run from it.

"Come on," Damon drawled. "You know I won't let anything happen to you. I'll be right there with you the whole time. Hell, it might even be fun."

"I might find that comforting," she shot back, "if not for the fact that your idea of fun is completely warped."

"Well, then, forget about me. Look at it this way. Wouldn't you like to be the girl who saves the world?"

"You know what I'd like?" She pushed her hair back from her face and let out a shaky breath of air. "For once, I'd like to be the girl having a good time. Is that so freaking much to ask?"

Before Damon could respond, Noah came back into the room, his scowl even darker than it had been before. "We need to get back on the road."

"Where are we going?" they asked in unison.

"Kierland thinks this place in Sampson sounds like a good idea, so they're going to meet us there."

Damon shot him a wary glance. "Who's going to meet us there?"

"My friends."

"Would these be your vampire and shape-shifter friends?" Damon asked, sounding less than thrilled.

Crossing his arms over his chest, he said, "One and the same. And we can't forget about Seth, who's human. He used to be a Collective officer, but he's one of us now." Noah narrowed his eyes. "You got a problem with that?"

"Not at all," Damon replied with a grimace. "Sounds like a blast. But I'm not the one you need to worry about."

"Meaning?"

"Meaning your friends aren't going to be too keen on working with a demon."

Noah snorted. "They might hate you for being a pain in the ass, but they're not going to hold that little blue streak in your hair against you."

"Watch your mouth," Damon said with a sharp smile, rolling up off the bed. "There's nothing *little* about my streak."

Willow knew a good time to interrupt when she heard one, so she asked, "If they're traveling there now, do they expect me to take part in the ritual with Damon?"

"No," he grunted, his gaze sliding away as he grabbed his bag. "They might have a lead on a possible candidate in South America. One of the guys is flying down to see if he can locate the woman."

Pushing his hands in his pockets, Damon gave a low whistle. "Guess this means Low might be off the hook."

"I don't care what they find down there," Noah muttered. "Will was never on the hook for this job, and she won't be put on the hook for it, either."

"Really?" Damon raised his eyebrows and rocked back on his heels. "And why's that? You planning on divesting her of her virginity before we get there?"

Willow held her breath as she waited for his

reply. But it never came. He just stood there, staring at the demon, a predatory force of violence pouring off him that made her shiver. Then he turned his head, and the look he gave her shot a wave of heat through her body that was so scalding, she felt the roots of her hair go damp. She wondered what was going through his mind as he dropped that blistering gaze to her mouth, then lower, to the base of her throat, where her pulse was beating a crazy, frantic rhythm.

Then he tore his gaze away, threw his bag over his shoulder and walked out of the room without ever saying a damn thing.

Damon's voice was soft, but she still flinched from the demon's quiet words as he said, "I'm guessing that's a no."

CHAPTER THIRTEEN

NOAH DID HIS BEST to stay focused as they headed
down the highway toward Carterville, a little
town in Illinois where he'd agreed to pick up
Ashe Granger, before making their way over
to Kansas. But it was impossible. He knew he
should send Willow packing. Knew it was the
best thing he could do for her. But…he just
couldn't do it.

Despite how pissed he was at her, she still
made him feel…right. Made him feel, for the
first time in forever, as if he had a chance of
fighting this thing. At the same time, she irritated him more than any other being alive.
Drove him crazy with her smart-ass mouth and
her crooked smiles. With her secrets and her attitude. But he'd never wanted a woman more.

And he didn't know what he was supposed
to do with that knowledge. No matter what happened with Calder and the Casus, he couldn't
deny that he was becoming something that
wasn't completely human. How would she feel

if those changes became more obvious? Would she finally look at him as if he was a monster? And how in God's name would he be able to handle it if that day ever came?

He wouldn't. He'd go out of his friggin' mind.

And he'd be lying if he said he wasn't tempted to drag her little ass into the nearest hotel room he could find and show her just how badly he wanted her. Probably not the brightest idea he'd ever had, but he felt compelled to do everything in his power to forge a connection between them. One that couldn't be broken, no matter how many miles eventually separated them.

And he really did *not* want her to be a virgin. He wanted that issue resolved, so that no one got any more crazy-ass ideas about using her to kill the Death-Walkers. He was being selfish, yeah, but he couldn't help it. Who knew what would happen during the ceremony for the spell? No matter how important it was, he couldn't let her risk her life like that. And that was just another item that could be added to the growing list of things he couldn't do.

Couldn't make her leave.

Couldn't get thoughts of sex out of his head.

Couldn't let her risk her life.

Couldn't think straight for a goddamn minute.

Needing a way to unwind before he stressed

himself into a stroke, he reached into the compartment on the truck door for his cigarettes, then grabbed his lighter.

"Isn't it a little early in the day to be sucking down a cigarette?" Willow's voice was barely more than a whisper, no doubt to keep from waking the demon snoozing in the backseat.

"It's never too early," he rasped, taking an angry drag that burned his lungs.

"You know, if you'd asked," she said, her voice getting a little louder, "I could have told you that I don't care for the smell of smoke."

He rolled his window down, then slid her a dry look. "Better?"

"It'll do," she grumbled, the sunlight that was streaming in through the windshield glinting against the ornate surface of the cross hanging around her neck. After what had happened at the bar, he'd decided that morning to give the Marker to Will, knowing he'd feel better if she was wearing the talisman. She hadn't wanted to wear it, arguing that he needed its protection more than she did, but she'd finally relented after he'd threatened to dump the damn thing in his bag and leave it there.

When he finished his cigarette, he checked the clock on the console and said, "We should be there in about twenty minutes."

"We're making good time," she murmured,

sounding bored with the mundane conversation. Hell, she was probably bored of the long drive. Unlike yesterday, there'd been none of the easy banter or laughter that they'd shared during the trip. Damon's presence was part of the problem, the demon's smart-ass interference making it impossible to have a simple conversation. And the angry frustration simmering just beneath the surface of their relationship, or friendship, or whatever you wanted to call it, wasn't helping, either.

But there were a few things that needed to be said, before they met up with Ashe, so he stopped stalling and got on with it.

"I know you're probably not crazy about working with a vamp, but Ashe is a good guy. I want you to cut him some slack."

She slid him a sideways look through those golden curls and laughed. "Don't worry, Noah. I promise not to pick a fight with your pal."

He popped his jaw, and tried not to scowl. "Don't flirt with him, either."

Her brows lifted so high, they nearly disappeared. "Wow, you must think I'm one complicated chick. You're actually worried I'll want to kill *and* screw him? Who knew I was so bold?" She clucked her tongue. "Or disgusting?"

He rolled his shoulder, refusing to offer an apology. Instead, he stayed on the attack. "You can get angry if you want, Will. But after last night, I'm realizing I don't know you at all."

"Don't be so hard on yourself." She leaned her head back against the seat and gave a breezy sigh that he knew was meant to piss him off. "I mean, the whole virgin thing is hardly an image I work to project."

"And what about the birth control pills?" He'd seen her taking one of the little pink pills the past two mornings. "What's the story with that? I doubt there are many virgins walking around taking the pill."

"What's to explain? I have a dangerous job, Noah. One that puts me in close proximity to some really scummy lowlifes. I know how to take care of myself, but things happen. Mistakes, accidents, just stupid bad luck. Sometimes criminals get the upper hand, and I've always thought it was best to be prepared for the worst."

Under his breath, he said, "Hope for the best, prepare for the worst." At her curious look, he explained. "Just something my mother always said."

"Smart lady."

He grunted, thinking about her job, and knowing damn well this wasn't a train of thought he needed to be following. If he sat there and tortured himself wondering about the dangerous scenarios she'd likely found herself in over the years, he would lose it. It was as simple as that.

Another thought occurred to him, and he asked, "Is your...virginity the reason you never dated Damon?"

"He's a wild child," she said evasively, not really answering his question. "I knew there was no way he could keep it tame."

"Amen to that," Damon murmured from the backseat, obviously no longer asleep.

Willow glared over her shoulder. "Put your damn earphones in and stop eavesdropping!"

The demon gave a gritty laugh. "Yes, ma'am."

"So all that crap about your lovers and past boyfriends was just bullshit?" Noah asked.

She turned her face away from him, staring out the window, but he knew she was rolling her eyes. "Virgin doesn't necessarily mean innocent, Noah."

Yeah, he knew that. There were all kinds of things a man and woman could do without actual penetration. Hell, he and Will had done some of them last night. But he didn't think she'd done them with many men. She'd seemed... He didn't know how to explain it. Not surprised by the things they were doing, but unaccustomed to the pleasure that came from doing them.

But why? God, he couldn't wrap his mind around it. She was the earthiest, sexiest, most responsive woman he'd ever known. What had she been waiting for?

He tried to remember if she'd said anything over the past two days that might give him a clue to her reason, but his brain was too bogged down to figure it out.

A few minutes later, Noah pulled into the parking lot of the little mom-and-pop café where he was supposed to meet Ashe. He cut the engine, but made no move to get out.

Willow looked at him through her curls again. "You waiting for an invitation?"

He let out a sharp sigh, and said, "No matter what happens, you are not to say anything to Ashe."

"ABOUT WHAT?" Willow asked, refusing to make it easy for him.

"I could make a really good guess," Damon offered with a husky laugh.

"I don't want to hear it," she muttered, shooting the demon another warning look over her shoulder. He shot her a sexy smile and winked, so she ignored the idiot and turned back to Noah. "If you're talking about my virginity, it's not something you can keep a secret, Noah. They'll need to know. That search in South America might not turn up anything. And it's really just a waste of their time. I mean, I'm not thrilled about the situation, but I'm already here."

He took the keys out of the ignition and said, "It won't be a waste, because they need to find someone else. You don't fit the requirements." She could practically hear his teeth crunching. "They need someone trained to handle a situation like this."

"You think I can't handle it?"

He slid her a shadowed look from the corner of his eye. "This isn't a game, Willow. These are real monsters who will take you down the first chance they get. Whatever Damon has told you is going to happen during this ceremony, I can assure it's going to get violent and it's going to get ugly. I don't want you anywhere near it."

Pride had her lifting her chin. "I know how to deal with things that are violent and ugly. And my profession *isn't* a game."

"Isn't it?" he rasped, and she wondered if he was trying to piss her off on purpose. Was he trying to make her so angry that she left? Hah! As if it was possible. Didn't the guy know she could give lessons in stubborn?

"I help people, Noah."

He snorted like a complete asshole. "You just like beating up on men, Will. Who knows why? Maybe it has something to do with sexual frustration."

Pain lanced through her like the cutting edge of a knife, and she had to fight the urge to strike out at him. Taking a shaky breath, she said, "You son of a bitch. You *are* just trying to piss me off."

"No trying about it," Damon drawled from the backseat. "He is definitely pissing you off. The question is why are you letting him get to you? What do you care what he says or thinks? He's not your daddy."

"You're right, Damon. He's not. Which means I don't have to listen."

"But you're going to," Noah growled, putting one arm over the back of his seat as he turned to face her.

"Oh, yeah?" She gave him a mean smile. "Make me," she said, glaring at him.

He returned her hostile look, the silence getting thick and heavy, a muscle pulsing in the side of his hard jaw. Finally, Noah scrubbed a hand over his mouth and said, "I don't want you to mention anything to Ashe about Calder's bite, either."

Willow couldn't hide her surprise. "They don't know you were bitten?"

"Yeah, they know about the bite. They were there when it happened. But they don't know about the...other stuff."

"You haven't told them about the changes? Why haven't you confided in them?"

He practically forced his response through gritted teeth. "Because it's not exactly something I want people to know."

She could see the things he wasn't saying. That he was afraid of how they would react. Worried they would judge him or lose their trust in him. It broke her heart that he felt that fear, but she knew he didn't want her pity.

"Fine," she said. "I won't say anything about the bite."

"And the other?"

She knew he was talking about her virginity and the ceremony. "We'll talk about it later."

He clearly didn't like her response, but he didn't press the issue, which was good, since she was still pissed at him for what he'd said. He climbed out of the truck, and started to close the door, then stopped himself and leaned back in, pinning her in place with a dark, glittering stare. "You keep pushing me like this, Will, and I'm going to end up taking this goddamn issue into my own hands," he muttered, before slamming the door shut.

Willow took a few moments to enjoy the view as Noah walked across the parking lot, since the man's ass was too perfect to ignore. Then she unleashed on Damon, warning him to cool it with the asinine comments or she was going to contact his ex and tell the woman exactly where she could find his irritating ass.

Damon winced when she delivered the threat. "Damn. You're a cruel woman, Low."

"I'm not cruel," she snapped. "What I am is tired of dealing with you two idiots!"

"Aw, well, you know I'm a jackass. And you should cut Winston a little slack," he said in an easy drawl, propping his arms on the front seat. "Poor man's head is spinning. I don't think I've ever seen a guy so twisted up about a woman before. That man wants you, Low. A lot."

"Shut up, Damon."

"I'm serious."

"It doesn't mean anything," she argued, picking up the soda Noah had bought her when they'd stopped for gas. "Noah's just one of those guys who always wants what he can't have."

"Bullshit. Winston isn't just screwing with your mind. He's acting like a guy who's found that one thing he wants more than any other. He's just too scared to do anything about it, because he knows damn well where it'll lead."

Setting the soda down again, she asked, "Why are you pushing this, Damon? Are you trying to drive me out of my mind? I mean, you're the one who said there was a reason for my forced virginity!"

"And I still believe there is," he said gently,

reaching out and tucking a wayward curl behind her ear. "But you won't have to stay a virgin forever, Will."

Baffled, she said, "How do you know that?"

A low laugh slid lazily from his lips. "I just know, honey."

There was something he wasn't telling her but she didn't know what it was, and she was too tired to figure it out. Damon knew about the prophecy that had kept her single for so many years. Because of that prophecy, she'd never trusted a man enough to have sex with him. Not even Damon, and the guy had definitely tried before their relationship had settled into that of close friends. But she knew that if it wasn't for the current mess they were in, she'd have been tempted to take that risk for Noah.

She just… She didn't think she could ever risk anything more. Already, she was feeling too hungry for him. Too achy. Desperate. Those breathtaking, pulse-pounding minutes she'd spent with him in that hotel room had been more than she'd bargained for. She'd had no idea just how emotionally destructive it would be. The intimacy, the closeness. They might not have officially done the deed, but he'd broken through her defenses, breaching those parts of her that had always longed for things from this man. Things that weren't meant to be hers.

There was too much risk, because she would never be able to keep things casual with Noah.

It wasn't her maidenly virtue that needed protecting. It was her heart.

The door to the café opened, and Noah headed back outside with the vampire at his side. She knew that vamps could walk in the light if they'd fed on the blood of a species that wasn't sensitive to the sun, which meant this guy had likely downed some human blood in the past few hours. Strangely enough, the thought didn't disturb her nearly as much as it would have a few days ago. She kept remembering how Noah's fangs had looked and how she'd ached to know what it felt like to have them sinking into her flesh.

Shaking off that crazy thought, Willow studied Ashe Granger. He was wearing jeans and a gray T-shirt that matched his silver eyes, with a black backpack slung over one broad shoulder. He was tall, like Noah, with a lean, muscular physique that'd been earned through experience, instead of bought in a gym. He was also gorgeous. Not even the shadows under his eyes or the severe cut of his thick, sable hair could detract from the fact that he was sinfully good-looking.

It was said among the clans that the complex nature of the Deschanel was a delicate balance between the light and dark aspects of the world, and Ashe Granger appeared to be a prime example. He was a thing of outrageous beauty, and yet…she could sense that this was a man who could be ruthlessly violent when necessary. Which made her damn glad he was on their side, and not fighting against them.

From what Noah had told her, she knew that Ashe had flown over with his brother to help out with the latest Infettato attack in Wisconsin, and had been in Cartersville to deliver the personal possessions of a young businessman killed in the attack. He could have mailed the man's belongings to his widow and little boy, or even left them to be tossed out in the trash. She knew how cleanups like the one taking place in the small Wisconsin town were handled. There just wasn't time to deal with the little things. But Ashe had thought this situation deserved his personal attention, which meant he had a good heart, and Willow thought there was a strong chance she was going to like the vamp.

She climbed out of the truck, intending to move to the backseat, so that he could sit in the front with Noah. Somehow, she didn't think the idea of putting the vamp in such close proximity to Damon was a good one—at least until she'd had time to see how they got along. She smiled as Noah and the vampire approached, and Ashe smiled back with a slow, wicked curve of his lips. "So you're Winston's new mystery woman," he said in a low, decadent rumble as he took her hand and pressed a warm kiss to her fingers. "It's a pleasure to meet you."

Noah's voice was little more than a whisper, but the warning in the soft words still gave her chills. "Don't even think about it, Ashe."

The vampire laughed, and seeing a fresh opportunity to be a pain in the ass, Damon couldn't leave well enough alone. Sticking his head out an open window, he said, "I don't know why you're warning off the vamp, Winston. I thought Low was still on the market."

"Leave it alone," Noah muttered, then cut a puzzled look toward Will. "I can't believe you said this bloody jackass reminds you of me."

She shrugged, fighting back a smile. "I think it's an attitude thing."

He snorted, giving her a long, hard look that did nothing to disguise the blatant hunger smoldering in his eyes. He suddenly looked like there were a thousand different things he wanted to say to her, but then he glanced at the vampire and the demon, and changed his mind.

"Let's get the hell out of here," he said, pulling his keys from his pocket and heading around to the driver's side of the truck.

Willow didn't say anything as she climbed

into the backseat, but she couldn't stop thinking about that look Noah had just given her. Damon slid her a knowing smile that said *I told you so,* and she pressed her hand to her chest, where her heart was trying to pound its way through.

Was Damon right about Noah? Did he want her? For more than just sex?

And what the hell was she going to do about it if he did?

CHAPTER FOURTEEN

THEY TOOK TURNS driving through the day, stopping only for gas and drinks. It was late afternoon when they finally crossed into Kansas, still about a hundred miles from the rendezvous point where they were meeting up with the others. After so many hours on the road, they were all eager for a shower and some hot food. The shower would have to wait, but they found a diner to take care of their rumbling stomachs when they stumbled across a picturesque little town off the old county highway they were traveling.

The town seemed unusually silent as they climbed out of the truck and made their way toward the diner's entrance. They were parked on the street, along with several parked cars and a van, but there was no one walking along the sidewalks or pouring out of the quaint Main Street stores.

"Anyone else have a bad feeling about this?" Damon murmured as they headed inside.

Noah glanced around the diner's empty interior, and stated the obvious. "Something's wrong." He took a deep breath and grimaced. "It doesn't smell right in here."

Willow shivered, getting the creeps. "This definitely doesn't have that 'welcome to our little hometown' atmosphere."

"There's still food on the tables," Ashe pointed out, his black backpack slung over his shoulder. "Meals only look half-eaten. Looks like people left in a hurry."

Wearing a serious expression for a change, his broad shoulders hard with tension, Damon said, "We should take a look around. See what we can find."

Noah agreed, saying he would search the back of the diner with Damon, while Willow and Ashe kept watch on things out front. He gave the vamp a speaking glance before walking away, as if warning the guy to keep a close eye on her. Or maybe he was warning Ashe not to try any more flirting. In some ways, the vamp had been as bad as Damon during the trip there, getting a kick out of pressing Noah's buttons as soon as he'd realized just how easy it was.

Noah and Damon were only just heading into the diner's kitchen when Ashe suddenly grabbed Willow's arm and yanked her to the wall beside the front window, practically shoving her into the corner. "We've got a problem," the vampire called out to the others, peering around the edge of the diner's homemade curtains.

"What is it?" Willow and Noah asked at the same time.

Before he could answer, Noah started across the room, but Ashe motioned him back. "Stay down. We've got Death-Walkers out in the street. Hiding behind the van parked near your truck. Looks like they're trying to get a better look at us."

"Shit. How many are there?" Noah growled, moving to the far side of the room, where he'd be out of sight. With a fierce look in his eyes, he started making his way toward Willow, weaving through the maze of tables, with Damon right on his heels.

"Can't tell how many." Ashe shifted his position for a better look. "Maybe around ten."

Noah gave another gritty curse, not liking the number, and looked at Damon. "Can you do that spell thing again with the Marker? Knock them into another county or something?"

Shaking his head, Damon said, "'Fraid not, man. Since we're both from hell, my demon mojo won't work on these assholes."

"What about weapons?" he barked, turning his attention back to Ashe. "I've left my damn flasks out in the truck. You got any on you?"

Willow frowned, wondering what they needed flasks for.

"I've got something better than a flask," the vamp rumbled, reaching into his backpack and pulling out a handgun that looked as if it had undergone some serious modifications. Noah and Damon both leaned closer for a better look. "It's Kellan's latest design."

Willow knew from her conversations with Ashe during the drive that Kellan was some kind of techno-genius who designed weaponry and security gadgets for the unit.

Taking out the clip, Ashe showed them one of the bullets. "You can screw the top off these babies and fill them up. I tried it out when Gid and I were up in Wisconsin and it was damn effective. A single shot to the chest takes one of the Walkers down for about twenty minutes. A head shot even longer."

Willow started to breathe a little easier. "That's plenty of time for us to get out of town. After we shoot them, that is."

"There's just one problem," Ashe told them. "These bullets are all empty."

Noah ran a rough hand over his eyes. "You're shitting me."

"Sorry, man. We got hit hard up in Wisconsin and I used up my stash. This is just an empty clip that I tossed in my bag. I've been keeping my eye out for a place where I can load the rounds."

Scratching his chin, Damon asked, "What do you need to fill them with?"

Despite the danger they were in, Ashe was actually grinning as he glanced at the demon. "Holy water and salt."

Damon's expression registered his surprise, then he shook his head and laughed. "That's classic. A *holy water* water gun. I'm liking you guys more every minute."

Willow frowned as she pushed her hair out of her eyes, thinking the weapon didn't sound all that impressive. "I don't understand. What are holy water and salt going to do to the Death-Walkers?"

"It burns them. The combination is the only thing we've found that will send them running," Noah explained. Then he shook his head and grimaced. "I can't believe I forgot to tell you that before."

"You've just had a lot on your mind," she murmured, glaring at Damon when he snickered.

"If holy water's what we're after, there's a church on the street behind this one," the demon said, jerking his chin toward the back of the diner. "I saw the steeple when we drove into town."

Noah took a saltshaker off one of the tables

and grabbed Willow's hand, saying, "We can go
out the back and make a run for it."

The plan turned out to be a good one, since
they made it to the church without any trouble.
But Willow knew better than to think the danger was over. The Death-Walkers were still out
there, and the monsters would search the town
once they realized their prey was no longer inside the diner. She didn't imagine it would be
long before the hideous creatures sniffed them
out.

While Damon went to see if there was anyone else in the building, Noah and Ashe opened
the bullets and filled them with salt and holy
water from the font just inside the church's front
doors. Left with a moment to herself, Willow
walked a little ways down the center aisle. The
inside of the church was silent and cool, and her
breath caught as she stared up at the breathtaking panels of stained glass that ran the perime-
ter of the nave. She'd always thought there was
something lovely about churches, especially the
older ones, like this. Fresh flowers in shades of
rose and cream lined the aisles and altar, the col-
ors making her wonder if there'd been a wedding planned for that morning. She should have
been trying to help the others, but she couldn't
stop herself from taking a moment to simply

stand there and appreciate the beauty of her surroundings.

Lives had begun and ended in this sundappled room. New chapters, and old ones. A place of birth and death and celebrations, and she wanted her share of it, damn it. She wanted it all.

As she turned and locked her burning gaze on Noah's rugged profile, Willow realized she wanted it with the man she loved.

Her lips parted on a gasp as the realization slammed through her, making her dizzy. She reached out with her hand, anchoring herself on one of the pews as she tried to calm down and just breathe. But this...it was too huge to simply accept with ease. She'd known she loved him once, with a girl's heart. And since he'd walked back into her life, she'd known she felt things for him that she'd never felt for any other man. But she'd let her anger and her bitterness cloud her mind, until they had masked the truth of her feelings. Until she couldn't recognize that the crazy, out of control, terrifying emotion he made her feel was so much more than lust.

It was *love*.

As if he could feel the press of her gaze, he turned his head, a crease forming between his dark brows as she stood there trembling and giving him a watery smile. He probably thought she'd lost her mind. He said something to Ashe, who nodded, his attention focused on the bullets he was loading into the clip, then turned and headed her way. She had no idea what she was going to say to him when he reached her, and was saved from making a complete ass of herself when Damon's deep voice rang out from somewhere in the back of the church.

"You guys need to get back here," he shouted. "I've found something you have to see."

Ashe stood guard near the entrance, while she and Noah followed the direction of Damon's voice. They found him standing in a narrow hallway, his shoulder propped against the wall outside an open door. He was pale, the strain on his face an expression that Willow had rarely seen on the demon. It usually meant that something horrific had happened—something he was powerless to do anything about.

As they made their way down the hallway, Damon jerked his chin toward the open door. "Don't say I didn't warn you," he scraped out, running a shaky hand roughly over his mouth.

With her heart lodged in her throat, Willow peered into the room, her soft gasp drowned out by Noah's guttural curse. Inside were the mutilated bodies of a young bride and groom, their flesh ripped and torn, as if something with powerful jaws had fed on them. The groom had wrapped his bride in his arms, and it was clear he had taken the brunt of the attack.

"He was trying to protect her," she whispered, covering her mouth with her hand. "Those bastards!"

Noah pulled her against his chest, his deep voice soft in her ear. "At least they weren't infected."

She nodded, knowing what he meant. As if the Death-Walkers weren't bad enough on their own, they could use their bites to infect their human victims, turning the humans into the Infettato. The infected humans became little more than walking zombies, living only to consume flesh, and forced to obey the orders of those who'd made them.

Damon shut the door to the room, and Willow pulled herself out of Noah's arms, well aware that he didn't have time to comfort her. Damon told them that he'd found more bodies in a few of the other rooms, and she pressed her hand to her stomach, sickened by the senseless loss of life.

"Do you think there are any Infettato in the town?" she asked, walking beside Noah as they headed back to the nave. She could hear Damon walking behind them.

"I don't know," Noah answered, reaching up with one hand to rub the muscles at the back of his neck. "I think maybe they tore through this place on an eating frenzy. I'll call in the local Watchmen unit and have them contain the area. I'm sure there are a helluva lot more bodies to be found."

Shivering at the thought, she rubbed her eyes, feeling more exhausted than she'd felt in years. Physically. Emotionally. She was drained. And Noah looked the same, the bruise-colored shadows under his eyes darker than ever. She was just about to reach out to brush back the dark strands of hair falling over his brow when the window above the altar shattered, sending stained glass raining down on their heads. She got a quick glimpse of the pale, yellow-eyed creatures, their corpselike bodies covered in festering wounds, as they swarmed in through the broken window—and then she was being shoved into Damon's arms.

"Get her the hell out of here!" Noah roared, and the demon immediately tossed her over his shoulder and started running. She had no idea where he was taking her as they traveled deeper into the long hallway, her mind locked on the sounds of fighting she could hear coming from the nave. Damon carried her into a darkened room that smelled of paper and ink, slammed and locked the door behind them, then set her on her feet and flipped on a light switch.

Blinking against the harsh fluorescent glow, Willow saw that the room was a small office, probably used by the church secretary. Damon stood in front of the door, ready to take down anything that came through, and she stumbled back, in shock, until she came up against the wall. She sank to the floor, arms around her knees, and started to rock. Damon said something to her in a low voice, but she couldn't respond. She was stunned silent, trapped in layers of fear, unable to accept what was happening. That she was on the verge, again, of losing something that mattered to her. Something that mattered more than…well, than anything else. Even more than it had mattered twelve years ago.

If Noah survived the Death-Walker attack, was she really going to let her fear of heartbreak keep her from him?

Was she that much of a coward?

She bit her bottom lip, unable to stop the tears that slipped through her lashes, waiting… and waiting. God, how long would it take Noah and the vampire to shoot those hideous monsters? She wanted to be out there fighting beside him, but knew she'd only be a distraction he didn't need, her fighting skills useless against this enemy. She prayed they would hurry, and couldn't choke back her cry of relief when there was a hard rap on the door followed by the sound

of Noah calling her name. She practically shoved
Damon out of her way as she ran to the door and
tore open the lock, throwing herself into Noah's
arms, holding on as if she never meant to let go.

He pressed a quick kiss to the top of her head,
and she forced herself to release her hold, knowing they needed to get out of there. She swiped
the tears from her eyes as Ashe joined them,
the men keeping a sharp lookout for trouble
as they made their way back to Noah's truck.
They didn't know for certain how many Death-
Walkers were in the town, and Willow knew she
wouldn't be able to take a deep breath until they
were on their way.

Climbing into the backseat, she locked her
door, then shoved her tangled hair out of her
eyes. "Well," she said a little breathlessly, "that
was certainly...eventful."

With a gritty laugh, Ashe said, "I just hope
we can make it to Sampson before any more psy-
chotic assholes come after us."

"I'LL RUN THEM down if they do," Noah muttered,
enjoying the brief smile that touched Willow's
mouth as he turned the key in the ignition. But
she didn't say anything more, and that silence
deepened as the afternoon wore on. She seemed
lost in her thoughts, and from the small crease
between her brows, which he could see every

time he glanced in the rearview mirror, he didn't think they were good ones.

They finally found the secluded resort where they were supposed to meet Kierland and those from the unit who had come with him. The Watchmen had been held up by another Infettato emergency, but Kellan had gotten out ahead of the others and was waiting for them in the private bungalow he'd reserved for the Watchmen. When Noah mentioned to Ashe that it seemed a bizarre location for a luxury resort and spa, Damon had laughed, saying, "This is probably Hollywood's idea of roughing it."

Noah was glad to see that the bungalow was set back from the main building, almost buried in the woods, making it easy for them to get in and out without attracting a lot of attention. Once they were ready to perform the Death-Spell, they could get to the site they'd chosen in about twenty minutes. On their return, the privacy of the bungalow's location meant they wouldn't have to deal with any long explanations if they came back looking like the walking wounded.

He parked in one of the empty spaces beside the Spanish-style cottage, and Kellan opened the door, the excited grin on his face putting a bad feeling in Noah's gut. The Lycan's blue-green eyes were bright with anticipation as Noah introduced him to Will, the idiot probably looking forward to making himself a nuisance.

"It's nice to meet another one of the Watchmen in Noah's unit," Will said to Kellan, "though I probably shouldn't call you Watchmen." With a smile, she asked, "Have you decided on a new name yet?"

"Still no name," Kellan replied as they made their way inside. "I've offered all kinds of great suggestions. Grim Reapers. The Death Dealers and the Ass Kickers. But they shot them down, like all the others." He pushed out a dramatic sigh and shook his head. "I'm telling you they lack imagination."

"Obviously," Willow murmured, stifling a laugh.

Noah slumped down onto one end of a sofa and leaned his head back. Damon took the other end, Ashe sprawled in the chaise and Willow took the chair next to Kellan's. While they waited for the others to get there, Kellan regaled her with stories about Noah. The bastard even blabbed about the incident at the local village back in England a few months ago, which was how Noah had come by the scar on his ribs.

With a groan, Noah said, "Kellan, enough already."

"I'm only just getting started," the Lycan rumbled. "I tried to warn you in my texts that there would be hell to pay. I made it clear that you could either tell me who your mystery babe was, or pay the price in blood, sweat and tears."

Thankfully, the jackass was forced to shut up when Kierland and the others finally arrived, the Watchmen pouring into the bungalow's central sitting room in a stream of grim-looking soldiers. Buried were the lovesick smiles and easy laughter that were common among this group of warriors. These were men who had been through hell together in the past year, and they were ready to end it.

While the others spread about the room, Gideon Granger propped his shoulders against one of the textured walls, waiting until all the introductions had been made, then arched a sable brow at his brother. "You lot look like you've seen some action."

Ashe ran a hand over his short scrub of hair and blew out a rough breath. "We had a run-in with some Walkers on our way here. And like idiots, we got caught without any ammo."

"How'd you get away?" Kierland asked, taking a seat in one of the other chairs.

"We found a church, filled up an empty cartridge of bullets and knocked the bastards out with Kellan's new gun."

The Lycan gave a satisfied smile at the mention of his handiwork. "Sweet."

They talked for a moment about Kellan's gun, and then Kierland got things rolling. "We have news," he said, settling his pale green gaze on Noah. "We got a call on our way here. It was from the unit in California."

Fear gripped his insides and squeezed. "Were they attacked? What happened to my brothers?"

"There was no attack, and Bryce and his family are fine," Kierland explained. "But Jackson is missing."

Noah narrowed his eyes. "What do you mean by missing?"

Kierland's expression was grim. "He messed with the security cameras and snuck out of the compound. Took his bag with him, and stole a few weapons from the unit."

"Are you telling me that he fucking ran?" Noah snarled, unable to believe Jackson could be that stupid. "What was he thinking?"

"I don't know what to say, man." Kellan's voice was sympathetically rough. "Sometimes we younger brothers can be a serious pain in the ass."

"Noah, Jackson's a smart guy," Willow murmured, obviously trying to make him feel better.

He shoved his hair back from his face and made a thick sound in his throat. "Christ, he couldn't be *that* smart. The know-it-all is going to get his ass killed."

"The unit is searching all the surrounding counties," Kierland said. "They're going to keep looking for him. If we're lucky, it won't be long before they pick him up again."

"Why hasn't he called me?" He moved to his feet and started to pace, the panic nearly suffocating him, his throat so tight it felt like choking. "Stupid question," he ground out. "I know why. He doesn't trust me. I'm the one who ordered them into protective custody, and now he doesn't trust me!" He stopped and shoved the heels of his palms against his eyes, terrified he was going to lose everyone who was important to him. Everyone who mattered. "Christ, I screwed up."

"Noah, this isn't your fault," Willow told him. "You did what you thought was right."

"Yeah, that should have been my first clue. Every time I try to do the right thing, it turns to shit." He paused, then slowly locked his gaze on Will. "So maybe I should just say to hell with it and do what I want for a change."

Her lips parted, and he watched her eyes go wide as she felt the savage force of his need slam into her.

"Hold it right there," Damon rasped. "You know that's not gonna happen, Winston."

A low, guttural growl vibrated in Noah's chest. "Stay out of this, demon."

"What's going on?" The question came from

fellow Watchman Aiden Shrader, the tiger-shifter's amber-colored eyes bright with curiosity.

Damon rubbed his jaw as he looked around the room. "I think this is probably a good time to tell you guys the search for a virgin is over. And before any of you say something asinine, it's not me."

"Who the hell is it?" demanded a rumble of male voices.

The demon didn't bother to say anything in response. Instead, he just looked at Will…and smiled.

CHAPTER FIFTEEN

How can a person be this tired?

Sienna leaned against the wall of the motel room that Calder had booked for the night, trying to find an ounce of energy. She needed to organize her thoughts. To find some way to make sense of the nightmare she was in.

How had she gotten to this point? How was it even possible that she had become this destructive, ghostlike crone who caused others pain?

The air in the room, which Calder and his men complained was too warm, seemed cold against her skin, making her bones rattle, her soul more fractured than whole. Despite the bright glow of light from the lamps, she felt lost in darkness. She knew something had to be done; there was no time for weakness. Not when Willow needed her help if she was going to survive. But Sienna was locked into this damn union with Calder, having sworn in blood to carry out her half of the bargain.

At this point, taking her own life would be the best thing she could do for her sister.

The promise of death wouldn't have scared her, had she thought she would be with her baby. Her beautiful little Angie. But there was no doubt she would be going to hell. And once there, she wouldn't even have Mike, the condemned human souls kept separate from those of the clans.

Closing her eyes, she tried to listen in on Calder's conversation with his men, wondering what was being said on the other side of the room. There'd been so much to do since she'd woken up in that field the demon had blasted her to, along with the two Casus, that they'd only just rejoined Calder. As his voice rose in anger, she could hear the Casus leader demanding an explanation for the death of their comrade, and knew her accounting would come next. She also knew it wouldn't be pleasant. Now that Calder had completely regained his strength, he would only push her harder to get him what he wanted.

God, Willow. What am I going to do?

"You failed me, witch."

She gasped at the close sound of Calder's deep voice, and opened her eyes to find him standing only a few feet away. With a hard swallow, she said, "I couldn't have anticipated the interference of the shape-shifters the other night. The entire situation was out of control. To take Winston, I would have had to kill him. And I was under the impression you wanted him alive."

"Don't be smart with me," he warned, coming closer, his foul breath nearly making her gag. "Why didn't you tell me about the demon who's helping him?"

She tilted her head back, holding his stare. "Because I didn't know about him."

Without any warning, he backhanded her so hard the sound echoed through the room, and she felt the hot trickle of blood slipping over her chin. It wasn't the first time he'd struck her, but she vowed it would be the last.

"And your sister?" he demanded.

Pressing the back of her hand to her throbbing lip, Sienna said, "How was I to know she would be with Winston? They haven't seen each other in years."

"From what I hear, they seem to be making up for lost time." He gave her a slow, calculating smile. "Which means he'll care about what happens to her."

Shaking her head, she fisted her hands at her sides. "I am not involving her in this."

The Casus laughed. "She's already involved."

"I won't do it," she rasped, knowing exactly what he would ask of her. "I won't help you hurt her."

Before he could respond, the cell phone in his pocket rang. With a disgusted glance in her direction, he took the call, a satisfied smile spreading across his face as he listened. When he finally returned the phone to his pocket, he looked at her and murmured, "One down, two to go."

Dear God. She knew what that meant. Despite the Watchmen's wholesale destruction of the shades in Meridian, there were many shades who had previously escaped and returned to this world, like the one who'd been killed in that field in Mississippi. Though Calder preferred to keep the ones who'd escaped through the portal by his side, the other Casus were still his to command, and his command had been simple. He wanted them watching the Winstons.

"Where you have failed," he said in a low voice, "others have succeeded, Sienna."

"What happened?" she asked, praying that it wasn't Noah who'd been captured. Praying that her sister was still alive.

"I've had a small group of Casus keeping an eye on the compound where the Watchmen took the other two Winston brothers. This afternoon, the youngest must have decided he'd had enough of their protection. He broke out of the compound and escaped."

She closed her eyes, feeling as if she would be

ill. She knew Jackson. Remembered him as an adorable boy who had blushed every time she'd looked at him. And now she was partly responsible for his death.

Grabbing his jacket from the foot of the bed, Calder pinned her with a chilling glare. "I'm going to meet them. In the meantime, I want you to go after Noah Winston again. And this time, bring your sister, as well."

"I already told you no," she whispered.

His nostrils flared as he drew in a sharp breath. "That isn't a request, Sienna. It's an order."

She swallowed the bile in her throat, and somehow found the strength to say, "I am not one of your Casus, Calder. I don't take orders from you."

"Is that so?" he asked in a silky rasp, carefully laying his jacket back on the bed.

Sienna scraped up every last ounce of courage she could find and lifted her chin. "My sister wasn't part of our bargain."

Calder stalked toward her, his gait slow and easy, as if he had all the time in the world. But the deadly look in his pale eyes told her what was coming. "You're taking a dangerous path," he murmured, lifting his hand to her face. He brushed his thumb across her skeletal cheek, watching her expression twist with revulsion at his touch. "Are you sure this is what you want, Sienna?"

Fear thickened her words. "I will *not* help you hurt my sister."

"Then you're hardly of any use to me now," he offered softly, releasing the long, deadly claws on his right hand. She had only seconds to use the invisibility spell she'd learned, and it wasn't enough time. His claws ripped across her abdomen, digging deep and making her scream, just before the spell took effect.

"Where are you?" he snarled, slashing again as she scrambled away from him. He caught her thigh, ripping into the muscle, and she nearly bit through her tongue to keep from crying out in agony. He kept slashing, trying to find her, but she rolled across the floor, slamming into the far wall. Pressing one hand to her mouth, Sienna huddled into a corner and struggled to hold in her cries, knowing he was listening for any sound that would reveal her location.

He turned over a few pieces of furniture, a heavy television set barely missing her as it crashed to the floor with a thunderous crack of sound. Calder finally gave up the game, laughing when he noticed the slick, red blood that covered his claws. Proof that he'd hit his target.

"What now?" asked one of the Casus.

"If you want something done right," he murmured, sending the Casus a sharp smile, "sometimes you've got to do it yourself."

CHAPTER SIXTEEN

NOAH WAS READY to kill Damon for what he'd done, Willow realized. Literally. Kellan and Kierland, the werewolf brothers, were forced to hold him back, while he shouted and cursed, fighting against their hold. Willow had never seen him so furious.

At least, not until she'd taken a deep breath and told them that she was willing to perform the ceremony. Then he got *really* mad. It took twenty minutes before his friends felt he no longer needed to be restrained. But he was still fuming, pacing the length of the room from one end to the other, his body coiled hard and tight with rage.

She could have explained how she'd come to this decision. That the horrific discovery of that bride and groom had settled her mind about the ritual. She couldn't stand by and do nothing when horrors like that were taking place. Something had happened to her that afternoon. Something life-changing and profound. And it had shaken those last vestiges of anger from her heart, leaving it bleeding and open…and eager for a fresh start. She didn't know what the future would hold. Didn't know if Noah would ever love her the way that she loved him. But she wanted the chance to see what would happen. She wanted the promise of that maybe. She wanted to grab on to that hope with both hands and fight for it, but first she had to put an end to the war.

She had the means. She just had to use them.

She couldn't explain any of that to him, though, because she couldn't get a word in edgewise.

"I'm not going to let her do it," Noah scraped out, a muscle ticking beneath his right eye. "We can wait to hear back from Quinn."

Kierland stood with his back braced against the door, as if he feared Noah might throw her over his shoulder and make a run for it. "Noah, we don't have any time to waste," he said, his expression tight with concern. "Tensions between the clans are already too high, not to mention the risk of exposure and the sheer loss of life."

He wiped the back of his wrist over his mouth and glared at the Lycan. "Would you do it? If it was Morgan?" She knew, from what Noah had told her, that Morgan Cantrell was a female Watchman. She was also Kierland's fiancée.

Kierland worked his jaw, and Noah grunted. "I didn't think so."

It was Gideon who spoke next. "Noah, there's a strong chance that Quinn won't be able to find the woman we were told about. It could days before he even locates her. And with every day that goes by, more people are dying."

"I know that, damn it. But we have no idea what might happen to Will if she sets foot in that circle. Those bastards might rip her to pieces!"

She cleared her throat, and said, "Damon thinks he can—"

He immediately cut her off. "Damon doesn't know what's going to happen out there."

Trying again, she said, "But he thinks he can protect—"

"I don't care what he thinks!" His words punched with crunching force, making her flinch. "I'm not letting you take that risk."

"But he—"

"I don't want to hear it!"

"Damn it, are you ever going to let me say anything?" she screamed, and the room went deathly quiet. They were all staring, wide-eyed and curious, and Willow wondered if any of them were as surprised as she was when she picked up the flower arrangement sitting on one of the end tables. With a husky growl, she hurled the vase at the wall, needing the mindless act of destruction to vent her frustration.

"At least she threw it at the wall," Kellan drawled from his spot by the window. "If I were her, I'd have aimed for Winston's head."

Noah snarled, his hands fisted as he headed toward the Lycan, but Willow reached out and grabbed his arm. She put herself in front of him, tilting her head back so that she could hold his furious gaze. "Noah, please listen. I need to do this."

"We don't have to wait for Quinn," he said in a low voice, his chest rising and falling with his ragged breaths. "We can find someone closer. Damn it, there has to be another choice."

"Come on. You know us adult virgins are in short supply." The corner of her mouth lifted with a wry smile. "I'm a rare breed."

"There will be others," he rasped, pacing away.

"Really?" she asked, lifting her brows. "Grown women aren't exactly known for avoiding pleasure. Especially ones who are trained to fight."

He pinned her with a dark glare. "You did."

"Because of a special circumstance. And in case you don't remember what we went through to get here, I'll take a moment to remind you that we're low on time. They have to be stopped,

Noah." Softly, she added, "I promise you I can do this."

"Damn it, I will not lose you!" he roared. "That is *not* an acceptable option!"

His rage was like a physical force, slamming into the walls of the room. Stark, bleak. He was shaking, his eyes wet, and she could only stare back at him in shock. She'd had no idea that Noah could ever experience this depth of emotion, and the fact that he was losing control because of her left her...stunned.

Then his eyes narrowed with suspicion, and Willow braced herself for what was coming.

"Why are you doing this, Will? What's the real reason?" His voice was harsh, edgy, each word striking against her with bruising force as he stalked toward her, his body moving with a sinuous, predatory grace. He looked like an animal on the prowl, and she flooded with heat.

"Is this all just some stunt to get me to admit that I want you?" he demanded. "If it is, then fine. I do. I always have. And I'm more than ready to deal with your damn virginity right this bloody second. But you are *not* putting yourself in the middle of those monsters."

She opened her mouth, and he slammed his hand against the wall at her back, denting the plaster. She hadn't even realized she'd been retreating from him step for step, part of her trying to flee his anger, while the other part was ready for him to make good on the visceral promise of hunger burning in those ice-blue eyes.

Damon cleared his throat, and said, "Before Winston puts any more holes in the wall and we end up with management up here, I think there's something I need to say."

Noah slowly turned his head toward the demon and glared. "I think you've already said enough, MacCaven."

"I've been thinking," Damon rumbled, pushing a hand through his blue-blond hair, "and I have an idea. A...compromise, of sorts."

Crossing his arms over his chest, Noah turned to face him. "What is it?"

"The more I think about the wording of the spell, the more I think that Willow's blood alone will do the trick. I don't think she actually needs to be there in person."

The shock of those words nearly bent her knees, and she found herself leaning more heavily against the wall. "God, Damon. Why didn't you say something before?"

With a wince, he said, "I'm sorry, Low. I wanted to see what Winston here would do. How far he was willing to go for you. And from the looks of things, I'd say pretty damn far."

"That wasn't your call to make!" she snapped, tired of feeling like she was being tossed around on an emotional roller coaster. "Was this all just some kind of game to you? You were just trying to get Noah to admit to..." Her voice trailed off, and she shook her head. With a breathless laugh, she said, "God, I can't even imagine what you were trying to do."

The demon frowned. "I was just waiting for the guy to step up to the plate, Low. Get him to stop lollygagging around."

"You had no right. I can't bel—"

"You can yell at him later," Kierland cut in, his brusque tone sharp with command. "Right now, we need to take enough blood to try out Damon's theory."

"Take it fast," Noah growled, cutting a dark look toward the Lycan. "Because we're leaving."

"And going where?" Willow choked out, wondering what in God's name he was thinking now.

He looked right at her, and said, "Somewhere with a bed."

"Damn you," she whispered, her eyes suddenly burning with furious tears. "You've just gotten your way, Noah. There's no reason for you to go and sacrifice yourself for the cause. I don't want you touching me out of pity."

"You gonna run scared now, Will?" The low words vibrated with challenge. "I didn't take you for a chicken."

Her nostrils flared. "That isn't fair."

"What isn't fair is having to walk away from something you want so badly it never leaves you in peace. But I did it. For you." He prowled closer. "I'm not doing it again."

She blinked, unable to believe he'd just said that. And in front of a roomful of his friends. "I'm not saying never," she whispered, licking her lips. "I just… I don't understand what the rush is."

He put his hands against the wall on either side of her head, caging her in with the hardness and heat of his body. Then he leaned forward, putting his face close to hers, his eyes still burning like blue chips of fire. "I've waited twelve fucking years, and it's been hell." Each word was ground out, as if being torn from someplace deep inside him. "I've reached my limit, Will. You have twelve more minutes, and that's it."

If she'd reacted to his words alone, she might have slapped his face and told him to go to hell. Or demand he give her more of a reason than lust. But she could see the devastating emotions churning in his heavy-lidded eyes, and she knew this was more to him. She didn't know what he felt for her, or what would come later, but for now, it was enough. It had to be, because she wanted him too badly to react with pride.

Instead, she reacted with her heart.

"Okay," she whispered, reaching up and placing her hand against the side of his face. His skin was fever-warm to the touch, and she could feel the fine tremor of emotion rushing through him. "I'll go with you."

The heat in his eyes blazed, the look he gave her so scorching she was surprised it didn't burn her skin. He turned his face, and his breath curled hotly in her palm. "Give them the blood while I'm gone. I won't be long."

"You're leaving?" she asked, hating the panic in her voice that she couldn't hide.

"I'm coming right back, I swear."

Then he walked away and Willow just stood there, feeling like an idiot. Her throat shook, either with laughter or with tears that were trying to escape. She didn't know which it was, but she fought them back, moving in a daze as Kierland led her to a chair, then drew his blade. Damon held her hand while Kierland pierced her wrist with the tip of his knife, collecting the bright wash of blood in a series of small glass vials that Kellan had taken from their field kit.

And then it was done.

With deft strokes, Kellan bound her wrist, finishing just as Noah came back into the room. She made a small sound, her relief nearly overwhelming. Until he'd walked back through that door, Willow had been terrified he wouldn't return.

Damon slipped the vials of her blood into the

bag of supplies he'd put together. Then he looked at Noah, who was putting her bag over his shoulder, and said, "It shouldn't take me long to get things settled at the site, and then we'll perform the ritual. When it's over, I'll call you. But until then, no sex."

Noah scowled, but Damon didn't back down.

"I mean it, Winston. We'll try it this way and call you if it works. But you wait until you get that call."

"I heard you," he rasped, grabbing her hand and tugging her along behind him.

She carefully avoided Damon's gaze as they left the room, knowing the demon was going to be worried about her. But she didn't want to think about that now. She just wanted to enjoy herself, and soak up every moment of the experience, her heart pounding with excitement as they followed a winding path lit with twinkling lights through the woods. The evening air was cool, and the soft breeze felt good against her warm skin as she asked, "Where are we going?"

He held up his free hand and jiggled a key. "We have our own room."

"Is that where you went?"

He slid her a slow smile over his shoulder. "I thought you might like some privacy."

She took a deep breath, then shakily blew it out, her pulse rushing in her ears like a storm.

"This seems so surreal, doesn't it? I mean...I'm finding it hard to believe that it's really going to happen."

He stopped in his tracks and faced her, the smoldering look in his eyes daring her to back down. "You're mine, Will. I know it. You know it. Don't you think it's about damn time we did something about it?"

"Yes." She licked her top lip, lowered her lashes and decided it was time she lay down a challenge of her own. "I wouldn't miss this for the world, Noah. But you should know that I have some pretty high expectations."

The sexy slant of his mouth as he grinned burned her with heat, and she practically melted on the spot. "I'll do my best not to disappoint."

"Me, too."

His chest shook with a gritty laugh, his color high. "Considering how everything you do turns me on, I don't think we're going to have any problems."

"I know this is crazy, but can you believe I'm nervous?"

The gentleness of his look made her breath catch. "You can trust me, Will."

"I do," she said, squeezing his hand. "But I'm just... I want this so badly, Noah. The wait for that bloody phone call is gonna kill me."

He pulled her into his arms, nuzzling the sensitive spot beneath her ear, and Willow could hear the smile in his voice as he said, "Then I guess I'll just have to keep you busy."

CHAPTER SEVENTEEN

As he locked the door to their private bungalow, the soldier in Noah couldn't believe that
he was choosing sex instead of a fight. Especially a fight that was this important. But then,
it's not like he was just running off and getting
laid. He was going to be making love to Willow.
Touching her. Tasting her. Burying himself in
her sweet little body.

His friends were smart, and God only knew
they could fight dirty. He could trust them to
handle things on their own. He had to. There
wasn't an acceptable alternative.

He took a quick look around the room as he
set their bags down, relieved it was as nice as
the Watchmen's bungalow. Spanish tile covered
the floor, the stucco walls painted a warm yellow. The furniture was dark and rustic, including the sprawling king-size bed that took up the
far wall. The bed was covered in acres of sand-
colored silk, with midnight-blue sheets, and he
couldn't wait to see Willow lying there beneath

him, her pale body spread out across that dark cotton.

"It's going to be a while before they call," she offered a little unsteadily, sounding nervous again. Despite the desire Noah could detect in her mouthwatering scent, she retreated as he prowled toward her, the hunger in his veins one that Noah had always felt for this woman. *Always.*

But at the moment, that familiar hunger seemed anything but human. It was too dark. Too raw. Too demanding.

He needed her now, damn it. And as she backed into the room's dresser, she looked as if she was on the verge of running away from him.

"Just because we're waiting for that call," he said, "doesn't mean we can't enjoy ourselves in the meantime. Right?"

"I...guess not."

Noah stared into her flushed face, saw the worry in her beautiful brown eyes, and realized exactly what she was thinking. Quietly, he said, "You don't have to be so suspicious, Will. If I was only doing this to get you out of taking part in that ceremony, I'd already be making damn sure you were no longer a virgin. We'd be skin-on-skin, and the only thing either of us would be worrying about is how many times I can make you come."

That easily, her worry melted, and her lips twitched with a smile. "Well, I guess that answers that." Her head tilted a little to the side, her gaze curious and warm. "I'm assuming you'd like to skip the condom part, since you mentioned us being skin-on-skin."

Hearing those husky words on her soft lips made Noah so hard he thought he might hurt himself. "I know you're on the pill," he told her, "and I'm clean. I've always worn a condom. Every damn time."

"That's sensible," she murmured, her smile turning wry. "Especially seeing as how there have been so many."

Noah stepped closer, enjoying that crackling energy that always sparked between them. "I'd rather not wear one with you. But I will, if that's what you want."

"What do *you* want?"

"I want them to hurry the hell up with that phone call so I can get inside you," he growled, his muscles coiling as he studied her eyes. Her worry and tension had eased, so he wrapped his arm around her waist and pulled her against his chest, his head dipping low so that he could nuzzle her throat. "I need to touch you," he groaned, "but I can behave. I won't go too far or do anything you don't want me to."

"Well, that's no good," she said with a breathless laugh, arching her neck for him. "I want you to *do* everything, Noah. All of it."

He made a hungry sound in the back of his throat. "I like the sound of that."

"And I want to do things, too."

He pulled his head back, his heavy-lidded gaze locking with hers. "Yeah?"

She smiled when she saw the rise of color burning beneath his skin. "Oh, yeah."

Then she dropped to her knees in front of him, and Noah nearly died. Together, they fought to get his jeans open, the task complicated by the way their hands kept getting in each other's way. He finally just gave up and let her have her way with him, his hands trembling too much to do anything but slow her down. She didn't waste time once the jeans were open, wrenching the denim over his hips along with his boxers, and his cock sprang out with almost embarrassing enthusiasm. If he hadn't been so on edge, he would have laughed at the poor bastard.

She made a kind of husky sound that curled his toes, the warmth of her gaze on his cock making him sweat as she took her time studying him. He was harder, thicker, than he'd ever been before. Unable to wait for her to get started, he took himself in his fist and pressed the swollen head against the center of her lower lip, so turned on he had to grip himself hard to keep from coming. *Not yet, damn it.* He wanted to see this. Wanted to watch his woman taking him in. He had no doubt the sight was one that would blow his mind.

Her breath rushed against the taut, sensitive skin, a small sound like pain breaking from his throat, and he shuddered, the wait nearly killing him. Seed spilled from the tip in a shiny drop, his teeth gritted against the pleasure as she finally opened her mouth a little more and swiped up that glistening bead of fluid with her tongue. "You're killing me," he groaned in a raw voice. "Take me in, Will. *Please.*"

She covered the head with her lips, swirling her tongue over him, then sucked him in, and he nearly fell over. Slamming his hand against the wall beside him, Noah braced himself, thinking she just might be the death of him. His head fell back on his shoulders as the sensations rolled up his spine, making him dizzy. He took a deep breath and lowered his head again, not wanting to miss a single second.

He'd been in this position hundreds of times, with too many women to count. But it had never been like this. He clenched his jaw, fighting the driving urge to come in her mouth. Not this time. He wanted to be buried deep in her lithe little body, feeling her clench around him, pulling him in, soaking him in her heat. But she was making it damn hard for him to keep it together.

"Jesus, Will." He sucked in a deep, shuddering breath, locking his knees to keep his balance. "That feels..."

Damn it, he didn't have words for how it felt, the pleasure indescribable, heightened by the fact this was *Willow* on her knees before him, licking and sucking on his shaft with that sweet, sensual abandon, as if she couldn't get enough.

It terrified him, this power she had over him. This need that was unlike anything he'd ever felt for another woman. He was...hardly a prize for someone like her. But if he kept her coming hard enough, maybe she wouldn't be able to think about how much better she could do.

When he knew he wasn't going to last another second, Noah yanked her into his arms, practically tossing her into the middle of the bed. He ripped his shirt off and came down over her before she'd even stopped bouncing, managing to get her out of her boots and clothes even faster than he had the last time. He couldn't even be bothered with his own boots and jeans, leaving the denim hanging around his thighs.

"Damn it, I can't wait," he groaned, pushing her legs apart and putting his mouth to her. She was already warm and wet, and he growled a sound that was dark and thick as he took her with his tongue, loving the way she tasted. She came for him so quickly, it made him smile, the experience one he was already helplessly addicted to.

He kept at her until the orgasm eventually faded, then braced himself over her body. Soft color burned along her delicate cheekbones, her lowered lashes leaving shadows on her skin. She was impossibly beautiful, both on the inside and out, and before the night was over, she was going to be his. Noah didn't know what he'd done to deserve such an incredible gift, but he was humbled by it just the same. And willing to do whatever it took to keep it.

With a shaky breath on his lips, he said her name.

She licked her lips. "Yeah?"

Noah brushed her hair back from her face, and waited until she opened her eyes. "I just want you to know that I should have done this a long, *long* time ago," he whispered, and as he pressed his mouth to hers, he lowered himself between her legs, rubbing the steely length of his shaft against her tender sex. She was creamy and warm, coating his skin, the breathless anticipation in her eyes so beautiful it made him light-headed.

He knew, with every part of him, that he would remember every detail of this moment for the rest of his life. The way she looked and felt beneath him. The way his heart pounded and his body trembled.

She arched a little, wiggling her hips, as if trying to get him inside her, and Noah scraped out a gritty curse, his lips pulling back over his teeth as he pleaded for mercy. "Damn. You've got to stop that, honey."

"But I want you now," she moaned, rubbing her body against his, her soft hands stroking his sides and back. "I need you inside me, Noah. I don't want to wait."

"I don't either, baby." He caught her hands, lifting them over her head, and pressed them against the bed. "But I promise it'll be worth it. Hell, we haven't even gotten to the good part yet."

"Oh, God," she groaned. "You'll kill me."

They both stilled the moment the words left her lips, but she was the one who moved first, pulling one of her hands from his hold and pressing it to the side of his face. Noah turned his head, pressing a hot kiss against the center of her palm. "I'd never hurt you," he told her, the quiet words as solemn as a vow.

"I know. That's why I'm here. I trust you, Noah."

He believed her, and yet, he could see there was something she wasn't telling him. There were still secrets she was holding close to her chest, and he forced himself to ask, "Are you sure you want this, Will?"

Her eyes went wide, as if she couldn't believe he'd asked that question.

"I need an answer, honey." The words were low and rough. "Before it's too late. Are you sure this is what you want?"

She took a deep breath, curled her hands around the back of his neck and brought his mouth to hers. *"I'm sure."*

WIPING THE BLOOD and sweat from his face, Damon turned in a slow circle, surveying the destruction that spread out around him. Even without the gore and blood from the carnage, the flat patch of land where they'd performed the ceremony only moments before was bleak. No wonder Dorothy had wanted over the fucking rainbow.

It'd taken him a while to get things set up, the intricacies of the ritual circle making his head pound. Damon had used his blood in the initial stage of the spell to pull the Death-Walkers there, the sounds of their rage something he knew would stay with him for a long time. The second step, which used Willow's blood, was even more complicated, taking him longer than he'd expected. The Watchmen had been forced to fight off the Walkers that were being pulled into the power of the circle, the creatures' bodies literally crashing from the sky. Now that the battle was over, the group of warriors looked a little worse for wear. But despite being bloody and bruised, they were smiling and slapping one another on the back as they took a moment to celebrate the fact that they were all still standing.

Then they gathered around Damon, offering him their thanks and congratulations for a job well done, and he realized he actually liked these guys. Liked their style, their humor and their willingness to fight as dirty as they needed to. Not a single one of them had curled their lip at the idea of working with a demon. Not even one who was a sex-eater, though there'd been some good-natured ribbing about keeping him away from their women. It hadn't taken them long to earn Damon's respect, and he was even thinking he might offer to help them out again someday. Maybe hunt down some of the Casus shades still trolling around. Lend his hand in taking out some rogue vamps.

Of course, he'd have to deal with the ex–Mrs. MacCaven first, which wouldn't be easy. She was like a rabid beast on his trail and she needed to be put down. For good.

"Shit," Ashe muttered, sliding a slow look

over the land, where thousands of nonhuman bodies littered the ground. None of them had expected the process of "sucking out the evil" to be quite as gruesome as it had turned out to be. "Cleaning this mess up is going to take for-friggin'-ever," the vamp complained.

"At least it's over," Kierland rumbled, pulling his shirt off so he could use it to clean his blood-smeared face.

Kellan's smile was wide as he looked at his friends. "Guess we've got some weddings to plan now, and I, for one, am done with waiting."

"Screw the planning," Aiden muttered, pressing his hand against a nasty wound that sliced across the top of his shoulder. "When we get home, I'm dragging Liv's little ass down to the village church and making it official. I don't care what she says."

The others laughed, teasing the tattooed tiger-shifter about how easily his woman could twist him around her finger. Aiden was in the process of some good-natured retaliation, pinning Kellan in a headlock, when the Watchmen realized Damon was heading back toward the trucks they'd parked about a half mile away.

"Where the hell are you going?" Ashe called after him. "You helped make this mess, demon. Now you can bloody well help us clean it up!"

"I need to get someplace where I have cell reception so that I can call Noah," he shouted over his shoulder.

Ashe nodded, then narrowed his silver eyes. "You're coming back after that, right?"

Damon didn't bother to respond, knowing this wasn't the time for lengthy explanations. Instead, he kept on walking as he pulled his cell out of his back pocket. He hadn't turned the phone on in weeks, worried the ex might use it to trace him, but he knew that he wouldn't be sticking around Sampson much longer. When the phone finally booted up, Damon lifted it in the air and searched for a signal...wondering if Winston had managed to wait for his call, after all.

WHEN HIS PHONE RANG, Noah reached for it like it was a lifeline. "Yeah?" he barked.

Damon's voice was gritty with exhaustion. "It's done."

"It worked?" he asked, trying to get his mind to focus. Not an easy thing to do when he was braced on one arm over Willow's naked body. "And everyone's all right?"

"Yeah, everything's fine. The monsters are fried and your friends are all okay."

"What happened?" he asked, hoping like hell the demon kept it short. At the moment, all he wanted were the cold hard facts...and then he wanted to be done with this call as quickly as possible.

"You know how it is. Blinding lights, scent of sulfur in the air. More blood and guts than we'd expected, and a shitload of dead bodies left behind."

Noah snorted. "Sounds like fun."

"Yeah, it was a real blast," Damon drawled. "Tell Willow thanks for me."

"I'll tell her after." Noah knew he didn't have to specify after what.

Damon's laugh was low and husky. "Be careful with her...but have fun."

"I intend to," he grunted, disconnecting the call and tossing the phone over his shoulder, not caring where it landed.

"What happ—"

Before Willow could finish her question, Noah pushed the head of his cock inside the tender clasp of her entrance, and she gasped.

"I'm...sorry. Can't wait," he ground out, unable to keep his hips from rocking forward, working himself in deeper. She was warm and slick and so tight he had to grip down hard on his control to keep from losing it. He didn't know how she did this to him. Here he was, with nearly fifteen years' experience on her, and *he* was the one who felt like the bloody virgin, his body shaking with nerves and desperate need as he

worked himself in deeper…and deeper, then finally slid in to the hilt. She was hugging every
thick, rigid inch of him, the clasp of her body
like a tight, wet mouth, and Noah fisted handfuls
of the bedding, the muscles in his arms bulging
as he pulled back, then forced his way inside
again. It was hell on his system, but he forced
himself to take it nice and slow, gritting his teeth
so hard he thought his jaw might crack from the
pressure.

"Oh, God…that's… Wow." She closed her
eyes and smiled, looking as if she was savoring
the feel of him inside her, and it was the sexiest damn thing he'd ever seen. His cock pulsed,
stretching her wider, and she opened her eyes
as she laughed, her warm gaze sparkling with
happiness. "Noah, you feel so…" She arched a
little, trying to get more comfortable, her breath
catching as she said, "You feel incredible."

"You're so…tight." He groaned, the slick,
dragging suction as he nearly pulled out of her
straining his control. He wanted to pound back
into her, giving it to her hard and fast, but knew
she wasn't ready for it.

She just didn't agree with him.

"I want you to go faster," she moaned, stroking her hands down his back and curving them
around his ass.

With a husky laugh, Noah gripped her wrists

and pinned them over her head again, the position stretching him out over her body, her tight nipples rubbing against his chest. "Just do it!" she cried, straining against his hold. "Damn it, I need—"

"Be patient, honey." His ragged breaths rattled between his parted lips. "I said I wasn't going to hurt you and I meant it."

Her voice was hoarse. "But I want you!"

"You're getting me," he growled, squeezing his eyes shut, using everything he had to keep it together. "But you're tiny and tight, and I… Damn it, I'm trying not to screw this up. If I hurt you—"

"Please, Noah." Her breath caught on a sob, and he lifted his lashes, seeing the tears glistening in her eyes. "I've been waiting for you for so long," she whispered. "Don't make me wait anymore."

He gave another low groan, undone by those soft words, knowing damn well that she'd just defeated him. He couldn't have stopped then if his life depended on it. A graveled curse hissed through his teeth as Noah pulled back his hips, paused, then tightened his muscles…and shoved back into her. Hard. Her slim body arched as if she'd been jolted with an electric shock, a keening cry on her lips that was full of pleasure and lust. God, she was incredible.

He watched her from beneath his lashes, unable to look away, his thrusts getting deeper, heavier, and he couldn't hold it...couldn't stop it. He was already coming, the pleasure so intense it almost stopped his heart as he filled her up with thick, scalding streams of heat. It damn near turned him inside out, a guttural cry ripping from his throat that was unlike any sound he'd ever made before. He poured into her until he had nothing left—but he didn't stop. He stayed hard, going at her harder. She was slick with his seed, and he was being too rough, he knew it, but he was lost. She took all of him, taking him all the way to the root, and he shuddered, undone, the feeling so good his eyes damn near rolled back in his head.

"Noah?" she whispered, the pleasure-thick sound of her voice just driving him on. She hadn't come yet...but she was close, her body drawing tight beneath him.

"I'm not done with you," he growled, bracing himself on his knees as he gripped her legs and shoved them wider, opening her to him completely. He watched his cock hammering into her pink, wet sex and nearly exploded with lust. He loved how they looked together, his dark hair meshed with her pale curls, her slick skin stretched impossibly tight around his ruddy shaft. He felt lost, out of control, pushed so far beyond anyplace he'd ever been it was almost frightening.

When she turned her face to the side and caught her lower lip in her teeth, he knew she felt it, too. That blinding, roaring force that was pulling them together. That terrifying loss of self as they merged and changed and became something new. But she was pulling away, afraid. Leaving him there on his own.

With his pulse thrashing in his ears, Noah pushed her legs up higher, leaning over her, grinding his body at an angle that he knew would drive her wild. "Open your eyes, Will."

Her blond curls flew as she shook her head. "I...can't," she panted, biting her lip again.

"Open your damn eyes!" he barked. "If I'm going to fall apart, then you can bloody well come with me."

Her lashes lifted, eyes glassy and bright with tears. "I know it sounds stupid but I'm scared," she whispered.

He thrust into her so hard, it shoved her up the bed, his voice a raw scrape of sound. "You think you don't scare the shit out of me?"

"Hardly." She gave a breathless laugh, wiping the tears from her face with trembling fingers. "You chase the devil, Noah."

He swallowed, and had to force his tight throat to work. "Devil's one thing, Will. He can only kill me. You're the only person in this world who has the power to take me apart."

Her mouth twisted with a smile, but the look in her eyes was sad. "You always were good with words."

"Damn it. I'm not lying to you," he growled, letting go of her legs and covering her with his body. His hands burrowed into her silky curls, shaping around her skull as he held her still for a deep, ravaging kiss. "I'm good with *you*," he said against her soft lips. "Just you, Will."

Noah prayed she'd understand what he meant as he poured everything he felt into the act, taking her hard and deep, making promises with his body that he couldn't put into words. His mouth worked over hers as they climbed higher, their skin sweat-slick and hot, steaming with passion as the pressure built. They kissed as if they were starved. As if they were finally feeding a devastating hunger that'd been burning inside them for too many years. He rubbed breathless, unspoken words into her lips as they strained together, his need for her bordering on violence. But she wasn't afraid anymore. When they crashed over the edge, battered beneath the shattering waves of pleasure, she wrapped him in her arms, holding him close…and trusted him to keep her safe through the storm.

CHAPTER EIGHTEEN

PERFECT. THAT WAS the only word Willow could
think of to describe what had happened between
her and Noah. The experience had been more
intense than she'd ever imagined, but a mind-
blowingly, breathtakingly, scream-because-it-
feels-so-good kind of perfect. She wanted to do
it again…and again. But she enjoyed this part,
as well. Cuddling against Noah's hard, muscular
body, the sound of his heartbeat drifting through
her head as she rested her cheek on his warm
chest, teasing one of his brown nipples with her
fingertip.

Compelled to learn as much as she could
about him, needing answers to all the questions
buzzing through her mind, she asked, "What
was your life like after you left Sacred?"

She could hear the smile in his voice as he
said, "Don't you know? I thought you checked
up on me."

"I know about your bar. But that's all." She
hadn't wanted to tempt herself with more infor-

mation than his career, too afraid she wouldn't be able to resist the temptation of going after him.

He stretched, settling more comfortably into the pillows, and said, "I ran wild once we got to California. I was pissed at my mom for dragging me there. At myself for going. At fate for making it seem like the right thing to do at the time. I drank and got in fights and picked on guys who were a hell of a lot meaner than I was. That's when I started training, figuring I needed to know how to look out for the family and myself."

"When I was talking to Kellan earlier, he said something about how your weapon of choice is a knife. Is that true?"

"Yeah, and it's probably because I've spent so much time training with them. I can handle a gun, but in the world of the clans, sometimes a knife is the best weapon you can have when you aren't sporting your own set of claws." As if in silent agreement, neither of them pointed out the fact that he had a set now.

He lowered his chin and looked at her. "That's why you carry a blade, isn't it?"

She nodded, saying, "Harris taught me how to handle a knife as soon as he thought I was old enough to learn." A wry smile curled her lips.

"But it was Damon who taught me how to fight dirty."

Running his hand down her back, he asked, "Do you hear from Harris very often?"

"No," she murmured, glad that he was finally asking about her brother. She thought Noah might have been purposely avoiding the topic, after the things she'd said that first night about the way he'd turned his back on Harris. Touching her fingertip to the leather pouch Jessie had given him, she went on to say, "He's even worse than Jessie, living in isolation out on the bayou with no phone and no internet."

"What's he do for a living?"

Wanting to be able to see his face while they talked, Willow folded her hands on his chest and rested her chin on them. "If Harris has a job, it's nothing Jessie and I want to know about. She's positive that he's become some kind of mercenary."

He lifted his brows, clearly surprised. "I thought he was planning on going to med school."

"Yeah, well, you know how that goes," she said with a sigh. "Things change."

"I guess they do," he murmured, his gaze locked on hers with a quiet, piercing intensity that told her he was thinking about more than just her brother. That he was thinking about *them*.

Flustered and off balance, she asked her next question before she did something crazy, like admit she was already madly in love with him. "So, you, um, moved to California, ran your bar and seduced hordes of beautiful women. Do I have that right?"

He shook his head, a lopsided smile on his lips. "Not quite. I ran my bar, *dated* women from time to time and I waited."

"Waited for what?"

For you, he thought. But Noah kept those telling words to himself, and simply said, "For this crap to start with the Casus. My mother seemed to know that it was coming in our lifetimes. I don't know how. She just did."

He took a deep breath and lifted his arm, sliding his palm beneath his head. "That night that I left you—it's not an excuse, but my mother had just told me that she believed the Casus would return in our lifetime. I think that's why I lost my control, once I'd gotten you away from Stubb and had made sure you were okay. We were alone, and I knew it would probably be the last time. Knew I was going to need to distance myself from you. That I wasn't going to get to keep you, no matter what happened."

"Why?" she demanded in a soft rasp, her throat tight with emotion.

His laugh was gritty and deep. "Think about

it, Will. How could I build a life with a woman not knowing if I was going to wake up one morning and find a monster living inside me?"

"Your brother did."

"Yeah, but…" His voice trailed off, and she knew what he'd left unsaid.

"But his wife isn't me. She's not a *Chastain* witch. Not from a race known for its prejudices."

His body stiffened beneath her, the muscles under her hands rigid with tension. "That's not what I said."

"But it's what you were thinking." Willow put her hand on the side of his face, rubbing her thumb against the sensual shape of his lower lip. "Noah, how many times do I have to tell you? I don't care about your bloodline. Hell, look at mine. The Broussards are all as crazy as can be."

"Well, I happen to like crazy." He rolled her to her back, coming up on his side beside her, and gave her a deep, melting kiss. Then he pulled his head back and smiled. "And right now, I want to get your crazy little ass in the shower with me."

Willow lifted a self-conscious hand to her hair and winced. "I must look awful."

"You look beautiful," he rumbled, his lips curving in a smile that was slow and wicked. "But I have a whole lot of sexual fantasies saved up about you, and having my way with you in a shower is high on the list."

Willow told him to lead the way, and ten minutes later, she finally understood what was so wonderful about showering with a lover. There was something deliciously erotic about standing together in the warm water, their hands stroking and slipping all over each other's bodies.

"So what now?" she asked, enjoying the feel of Noah's hands lathering soap over her shoulders and arms. "Your mission to save the world has been completed. Are you going to leap tall buildings in a single bound?"

He stared down at her through dark lashes that were beaded with water, his mouth kicked up at one corner in a sexy grin. "I think I'm more of the Batman type."

"Hmm. Dark. Broody. I can see your point." She went up on tiptoe and pressed her mouth to his, kissing him slowly, deeply, loving the way he kissed her back. Loving this slippery, steamy, provocative intimacy that had wrapped around them. She never wanted it to end.

So stop stressing. Just enjoy it...

Breathless from the kiss, she rested her flushed cheek against his chest and tried to follow the good advice. But failed. "Seriously," she rasped, "what's next, Noah?"

"I don't know," he admitted with a shrug.

She pulled back a little and locked her gaze with his. "Well, I've been thinking."

He lifted a worried-looking brow. "And?"

"I could try something. A spell. One that would pull Sienna to me, and hopefully anyone who's with her. Then your friends and I could kill Calder and get it over with. Heck, I bet even Damon would help."

"You don't have that kind of power," he argued. "If you did, you'd have used it when you were searching for Sienna."

"You're right. At the moment, I don't have that kind of power. But I know how to get it. Spells like that fall under the darker side of witchcraft, which I've always steered clear of. But I'd be willing to learn, if it means keeping you safe. All it would take is a little research and a few phone calls."

"No way in hell," he growled. "You're not doing it."

Willow frowned. "Why not?"

"Because I don't want you messing with that crap. It's dangerous. And if it worked, that bastard Calder would find some way to hurt you." His words punched with brutal force, betraying his emotions. Fear. Anger. Panic. "Damn it, Will. That's got to be one of the dumbest ideas I've ever heard."

"Then I guess I'm just too stupid now to know a good idea from a bad one," she said softly, unable to get angry when she could sense how worried he was.

"You're not stupid. I wish," he muttered, a pained expression on his rugged face. "You're too bloody smart for your own good. Not to mention stubborn and brave. It all makes for a pain-in-the-ass combination."

"Come on, admit it. You like me plucky. A doormat of a woman would bore you to tears." Cocking her head a little, she watched him from beneath her lashes. "And speaking of women, I hear you have a hell of a reputation when it comes to the ladies."

"Jesus," he growled. "Don't listen to the shit that Kellan talks."

Willow arched one brow. "You're denying it?"

"Like I said, I've dated," he admitted, an endearing flush of color darkening his cheekbones, as if he was embarrassed. "But never anything serious."

"No one ever tempted you to settle down?"

"They might have tried, but it was a waste of time." One of his hands slipped beneath her hair, curving around the back of her neck, the other settling against the side of her face. "I've always been too hung up on you."

Just like that, he floored her.

"It's true," he told her, reading the shock in

her eyes. "Sex has been fun, but it was never anything like this. Like what we have."

"But I don't even know what I'm doing," she whispered, making his chest rumble with a gritty laugh. "I couldn't have been that good."

"If you were any better," he rasped, "it would have killed me."

Despite the sexy grin on his lips, she could see the shadow of sadness in his eyes. "Why do I get the feeling that this breathtaking confession isn't leading to something good, Noah?"

"Because what I want docsn't matter." He pulled back from her, hands fisting at his sides, and his voice dropped. "Until I deal with Calder, I can't ask you to be a part of my life."

"Then let me try the spell," she pleaded, placing her hands on his chest.

He shook his head, his expression grim. "I'm not letting you get involved in this, Will. I don't want you anywhere near that bastard."

"Then what's your plan?" she demanded, her voice shaking with frustration. "Are you going to lock me up? Hide me away somewhere?"

"I'm going to get you someplace safe," he growled, "and then I'm tracking down Calder and putting an end to this once and for all."

Willow started to tell him that it would be a cold day in hell before she let him run off and face that monster on his own, then changed her mind. Instead, she reached down and took him into her hand.

"What the hell, Will?" He made a rough sound in his throat as she stroked him, his cock responding with a hard pulse. "You gonna try to control me with sex?"

A grin touched her mouth. "Maybe that's exactly what I'm going to try." She ran her thumb over the heavy, swollen head, where a pearly drop of moisture had gathered, enjoying the ragged sound of his groan. "Will it work?"

He grabbed her, lifting her off her feet and quickly pressing her against the wall of the shower, his expression dark and intense, as if he was thinking hard about what he wanted to say. And then he told her to put her legs around his waist, and he worked himself inside her with a thick, breathtaking lunge.

"I've told you why I left that night. But do you know why I've stayed away all these years?" he asked, keeping his hips pressed hard against hers, pinning her to the wall.

She shook her head, her throat burning with emotion as she waited for him to tell her.

He kept his eyes locked on hers. "Because I knew I couldn't stay close to you and not fall harder than I already was. I wouldn't have been able to stop myself from falling completely in love with you. Wouldn't have been able to keep my hands off you. And that scared the living hell out of me."

She opened her mouth, but he placed his fingers over her lips.

"Just listen to me," he told her. "As pissed as I was at Harris that night, his words were true. I didn't have any business messing around with you."

Pushing his hand away, she said, "Why? And before you give me that crap about you being dangerous, you know I don't believe it, Noah. I didn't care about your bloodline."

"It wasn't just that. You were too young."

"I was old enough to know what I wanted."

His quiet laugh was wry, tinged with pain. "Not the way I would have given it to you."

She couldn't help but challenge him. "If it was anything like what you gave me tonight," she said huskily, "I would have been in heaven."

Tiny lines fanned out from the corners of his eyes as he narrowed his gaze on her, and then he quietly said, "I want you to tell me why you were still a virgin." His chest brushed against her sensitive breasts as he pulled in a deep breath. "Did something happen? Did someone try to hurt you?"

"Noah, it's not something I want to talk about."

"Please." He pressed his forehead to hers.

"Please, tell me something, Will. Anything. The not knowing is driving me crazy. Haven't you wanted sex?"

"I've wanted sex," she admitted in a low voice, running her hands over his slippery shoulders, the hot water beating down hard on his back. "I'm a flesh-and-blood woman, and I have needs like everyone else. But...you're the only man I've ever trusted enough to have it with. Who's made me willing to take the risk."

"I don't understand," he grated, lifting his head. "Why's it a risk?"

"Please, just drop it." She tried giving him a teasing grin. "You know, I might be new to this whole sex thing, but shouldn't you be...moving?"

The look on his face said he knew exactly what she was doing, but he let her get away with it. "I'll get to the moving part," he told her. "But you're new to this, and you feel swollen inside. So I'm giving you time to get used to me." He started to kiss her again, then pulled back his head, his pale gaze glittering and sharp. "You know, you could have come after me, Will."

"After what Harris told me?" She gave a soft snort. "I don't think so."

"What did he tell you?" His blue eyes were piercing, demanding an answer.

She let her head fall back against the wall and

answered his question. "He said you told him that I was too inexperienced for you to waste your time on a repeat."

A scowl settled between his dark brows. "I never said that."

"It doesn't matter anymore if you did." She tried to move her hips, wanting him to get on with it, needing that violent rush of pleasure to burn away the pain of this conversation, but he kept her pinned against the wall.

"I'm telling you the truth, Will." He reached up and shoved his hair off his brow, his mouth compressed into a hard line. "Harris must have been trying to protect you."

Willow lifted her hand and touched his face with her fingertips. "But I don't need to be protected from you. Do I, Noah?"

He flinched, his gaze flicking over the scar Calder had left on his arm. "Will, I'll fight this thing till the bitter end, but there's no guarantee that I'll win."

"Noah, there's never a guarantee. All we can do is enjoy what time we have with each other, for as long as we can," she said in a low voice, putting her face close to his, her hands tangled in his hair. Then she kissed him, pouring everything she felt into the touch of her lips against his, lost in the warm silk of his mouth, and he finally lost control, thrusting into her with deep, hammering drives.

"Come," he rasped as he reached between their bodies, stroking her clit with the callused pad of his thumb, and she climaxed within seconds, as if her responses were his to command. The orgasm was lush and tight, bringing tears to her eyes. Emotion washed over her, blissful and surreal, like a dream that she didn't want to end. But his arms were solid and strong, keeping her tight against him, his grip one of greed and possession. It eased her to know that he wanted this as badly as she did. That he needed it.

He kept thrusting, her body accepting him more easily now, and with his mouth at her ear, he told her how she felt to him, the wicked words making her shiver with excitement. She loved the feel of his powerful body pressed tight against hers. Loved the flexing of those strong, rippling muscles as he moved against her…inside her.

She cried out as the second climax tore through her, and it was like having pleasure shot through every cell, her body writhing, pulsing with heat. He rode her through it, his hips moving faster, slamming him into her, and she loved it. Loved the feel of his raw power. Of his primal aggression. And when his head fell back, his masculine throat corded with strain, she loved that she was the one who'd made him shudder and gasp as he exploded inside her. That she was the one who pulled that guttural shout from his chest. The one who held him as he collapsed in her arms.

They stayed braced like that against the wall, locked into that tight, clutching embrace, until the water finally turned cold. Then Noah wrapped her in a towel and carried her back out to the bed, holding her against his body while he used his fingers to carefully work out the tangles in her curls. Willow thought she might have started to doze, her hand resting against his leather charm, when someone knocked on the door, and they both stiffened with surprise.

"Do you think that's Damon?" she asked, pushing up on an elbow.

He shook his head and climbed off the bed. "The demon knows better than to bother us," he said in a low voice, pulling on his jeans. Willow slipped out of the bed and threw her clothes on as he went to the door, a low curse on his lips as he looked through the peephole. "Who is it?" she asked around the knot of dread in her throat.

He sent her a worried look over his shoulder. "It's your sister."

She gasped, and Sienna's voice came through the door. "Please let me in, Willow. I need…I need to talk to you."

"Open the door," she told him, praying she wasn't making a mistake.

Noah's gaze was dark with suspicion as he allowed Sienna to enter the room. She moved in a stiff, shuffling gait, a dark blanket wrapped tight around her shoulders.

Closing the door, Noah asked, "How did you get here?"

"Portal," she gasped, nearly stumbling.

Willow put her arm around Sienna's waist, planning to help her to the sofa, when her sister's body simply crumpled to the floor. Going to her knees beside her, Willow cried, "Si? What's wro—"

"There's blood on the floor," Noah rasped, cutting her off. Willow lifted her head, seeing the smears of blood on the Spanish tiles, the air becoming thick with the scent of it.

"Get that damn blanket off her," he barked, kneeling down on Sienna's other side.

Sienna seemed to have lost consciousness, her eyes closed as they unwrapped the blanket from her frail body. Willow had to choke back a scream when she saw the blood that covered Sienna's torn gown. "Do you think Calder did this?" she asked Noah, who grabbed one of the towels they'd tossed on the foot of the bed and pressed it against Sienna's shredded stomach.

"It looks like the bastard clawed her," he growled, checking the wounds on Sienna's thigh.

Sienna gave a low groan, and he said, "I think she's coming to."

"Si, sweetheart," Willow crooned, keeping her voice soft. "Can you hear me, honey? Can you open your eyes?"

Sienna lifted her lashes, revealing a pain-filled gaze. "Willow, I'm so sorry," she gasped, trying to reach for her. "Was just…trying to do the right thing for my family." She fell back, her face convulsing with pain, while tears leaked from the corners of her eyes. "I needed Calder to go—"

"Shh," she whispered. "It's okay. I know why you made the deal. You don't have to explain."

Sienna clutched Willow's hand. "Once I had Mike back, I knew he'd find a way to get Angie for me. Even if we had to sneak into heaven and steal her away, I knew he'd find a way. Then I'd have them back."

"Oh, Si."

"But I was wrong," she moaned, squeezing her eyes shut. "God, I was so stupid. Mike wouldn't even recognize me now. He'd be so ashamed. He probably hates me."

"Don't," she rasped, brushing the pale strands of hair back from Sienna's brow. "Don't talk like that. Mike has always loved you."

"I just wanted him back," Sienna sobbed, a fresh wash of blood seeping through the towel Noah was holding against her stomach as she was gripped in a violent coughing fit. "I just…"

"Si, you need to calm down," Willow said, keeping her voice firm. "Everything's going to be okay. We're going to get you to a hospital."

"No time." Sienna's eyes popped open, wide with panic. "I have to tell you now, before it's too late."

Willow shook her head. "No more confessions, Si. I love you. Jessie and Harris love you. This is going to be okay."

Sienna sounded frantic, her cold fingers clenching around Willow's hand so tightly it hurt. "Shut up, Willow, and listen to me. There's…there's a dark spell that I've learned."

"From who?"

Sienna shuddered. "You don't want to know. Just listen. I need to tell you how to find Calder. The spell will help."

Another knock came at the door, and Willow looked up, her worried gaze locking with Noah's. After instructing her to keep pressure on the wound, he moved to his feet. She started to tell him to be careful, but he held his finger in front of his lips, signaling her to be quiet.

Noah's steps were silent as he padded to the door and peered through the peephole again, then she heard his low gasp. "What the hell?" he growled. "It's Jackson!"

"Noah!" Sienna called out, trying to warn him. But she was too late. He'd already ripped open the door...and Anthony Calder walked into the room.

Willow knew it was the Casus inside Jackson Winston's body the instant she saw his eyes. They were cold and cruel as they glanced down at Sienna's bleeding body, then settled slowly on Willow's face. "Noah," she whispered, "it's him. It's Calder."

She saw the horrible truth register on his face as Calder turned toward him, and then the Casus lifted his palm toward Noah, and Noah's body flew across the room, slamming against the far wall. He struggled to move, but his arms and legs were locked in place, as if some invisible force was holding him there.

"How are you doing that?" Willow cried, surging to her feet.

The Casus smiled. "Why don't you ask your sister?"

"He forced me to show him my spells," Sienna whispered, blood bubbling on her lips as she struggled to say the words. "He has enough power inside him to fuel the spell, because he's immortal. It's my fault. I'm so...sorry."

Noah shouted Willow's name, his deep voice

vibrating with fury. "Get the fuck out of here! Now!"

A fresh wave of terror gripped her when she realized she couldn't move her arms or legs. It wasn't that she wanted to run. She wasn't leaving Noah alone with this monster. But she'd left the Marker on the bedside table, and she needed it to kill this son of a bitch.

"Willow!" Noah roared. "Get your ass out of here!"

"I can't," she whispered. "It's affecting me, too."

Calder gave a husky laugh as he lowered his arm and crouched down beside Sienna, studying her ghostly face, while Noah and Willow remained locked in place. The fact that he could hold the two of them like this without even putting any effort into it meant he was even more powerful than Willow had feared.

Rage darkened Noah's face, the tendons in his neck straining as he fought to break free. "I thought this spell didn't work against other witches."

"That's only when it's performed with a witch's power," she explained. "He's using Sienna's spell, but he isn't a witch."

Watching Calder with a deadly glare, he snarled, "How the hell did you get inside my brother?"

The Casus looked over his shoulder, flicking his gaze over the leather charm hanging around Noah's neck. Then he smiled, saying, "I'm afraid your baby brother wasn't too impressed with your little protection token. I found it in his bag. He hadn't even bothered to put it on."

"I'm so sorry, Noah." Sienna's voice was barely a thread of sound. "I didn't stop him. I waited too long."

Still looking at Noah, Calder said, "I was going to take you first, but baby brother made it so easy for me when he ran away from his guard dogs."

"Fuck you," Noah snarled.

With another gritty laugh, Calder pushed to his feet and straightened his clothes. "You know," he said conversationally, "now that I'm in this body, I'll probably be able to stroll right into that Watchmen compound in California and take over that other brother of yours next. Save you for last, so that you'll get the chance to see the show. After all, I plan on having a lot of fun with that feisty little wife of his."

"You son of a bitch!" Noah roared, straining against the force of the spell so violently that a blood vessel burst in his eye.

"And when that gets boring," Calder drawled,

"I can always play daddy with his precious baby girl."

"Monster," Sienna rasped, the quiet word barely audible over Noah's shouting. Searing hatred burned in her eyes as she lifted a shaky hand and pointed it at the Casus. "Go to hell, you bastard!"

A blinding light suddenly formed behind the Casus, circular in shape, the violent roar of a windstorm filling the room. A ferocious scowl twisted Calder's face as he fought to move away from the light, but it seemed to be sucking him in, like a giant whirlpool. He snarled, releasing his fangs and claws as he struggled to reach Sienna, who was clearly losing her strength as she fought to control the portal, but the pull of the wind was too powerful. He turned his chilling gaze on Willow, and she screamed as he lunged forward. She could hear Noah's and Sienna's horrified shouts as Calder's clawed fingers wrapped around her wrist, the freezing spell he'd put on her making it impossible for her to fight him. With an evil smile, he yanked her against him, and the portal sucked them in with a deafening, explosive blast of power.

NOAH WAS STILL picking himself up off the floor when Damon kicked down the door and burst into the room. He took one look at Sienna, then cut his dark gaze toward Noah. "I felt...something. Some kind of power surge. What the hell happened?"

"Calder was here," he grated, the aftereffects of the spell and the blast making him nauseous. Or maybe it was just his fear for Willow that was twisting his insides in knots. "Sienna blasted him through one of her portals, but he grabbed on to Will and dragged her through with him."

Damon cursed, his face turning pale with fear.

Noah made it across the room and dropped to his knees beside Sienna. "Si, listen to me," he said, turning her face toward him. "I need to know where you sent him."

"Outer Circle. Use the demon. Find her..." She swallowed, struggling to continue. "If...if something happens, tell her the key to the spell is love."

"What spell?" Noah grunted. "The one to find Calder?"

"No. Another one. The one to save her heart," she whispered, and then she slipped away.

Noah lifted her hand and pressed a hard kiss to the backs of her fingers, then reached down and closed her eyes. "What the hell does Outer Circle mean?" he asked, moving back to his feet. "The outer circle of what?"

"Of hell," Damon rasped, scrubbing his hands down his face.

He froze as the meaning of those chilling words sank in.

"Why would she send him there?"

"Because she knows the fucker won't be able to escape." Damon lowered his hands and looked at Noah, his blue eyes burning with fury. "And she knows I'll be able to get there."

"How?" he demanded.

Damon gave him a sharp smile. "I'm a demon, man. Getting in and out of hell is what I do."

A flicker of hope started to burn in his gut, but he was still wary. "If that's true, then why didn't Sienna just come to you for help? Why bother with Calder?"

"Her husband was human," the demon explained. "His soul, if it's even there, would have been kept in one of the lowest parts of the pit. No one goes there unless they have a death wish."

The spark of hope flared into a roaring blaze, fueled by fierce determination. "Every second we waste is a second Willow's trapped there with him," Noah growled. "We need to go *now*."

Damon's eyes went wide. "Are you serious? You're planning on coming?"

Noah locked his jaw and the demon ran his tongue over his teeth. "Shit, I can see that you are," Damon grumbled, blowing out a rough breath. "Noah, you know what's going to happen. If you show up there, Calder's going to find a way to take you over. He'll use Willow for leverage against you. You should just let me go on my own, man."

"And if he kills you? She'll be trapped there with him."

"He isn't going to kill me."

"He'd better not, because I need you to get her out of there once he turns his attention on me." Noah grabbed the Marker off the bedside table and handed it to the demon. "When it happens, you know what to do."

Damon's stare was deep and measuring. "You sure you're willing to give up your life for hers? Because that's really gonna piss her off. She'd want you to stay here."

Noah narrowed his eyes. "You leave me behind, demon, and I *will* kill you."

Damon's tone was wry. "Believe it or not, I hear that a lot." Then he reached down, grabbed Noah's arm and everything went black.

CHAPTER NINETEEN

WILLOW COULDN'T BELIEVE her eyes.

"No," she croaked, a scream of frustration rumbling in her throat as she spotted Noah and Damon walking toward her, while the barren landscape of the Outer Circle spread out for miles behind them.

"I knew Winston would come for you. It was only a matter of time," Calder purred in her ear. He held her locked against the front of his body, one arm wrapped across her torso, just beneath her breasts, the other around her throat. Her hands were trapped behind her back, bound with a length of cord he'd taken from his pocket, her wrists already worn raw from where she'd struggled to break free.

Considering she was literally in hell, the place wasn't nearly as horrific as Willow had imagined it would be. But then, this was just the Outer Circle, and she knew the deeper in you traveled, the more hellish it became.

But here, there were no monsters. Except for the one standing at her back.

The setting reminded her of the desert, only with a sky that was bloodred instead of blue. Beneath her bare feet, the ground was covered in blisteringly hot sand, and there were huge outcroppings of red, jagged rock dotting the landscape for as far as the eye could see. Willow had been staring across that rugged landscape since she and Calder had arrived, filled with fear, but thankful for the fact that Sienna had found a way to save Noah.

And then he'd suddenly appeared, about forty feet away, standing beside Damon, and she'd known that she was truly in hell. Her heart pounded harder with each step that brought the two men closer, her throat burning with the need to rant and scream. Didn't Noah know that she would have gladly given up her life to save his? That if she'd had her choice, he would have remained back in their world...and left her to fate?

Didn't he know that when Calder took his body, it wasn't only going to kill him, but her, as well?

"Sienna?" she rasped when Noah came to a stop a few yards away from where she stood trapped in Calder's evil embrace, Damon lingering a little farther back. Noah shook his head in response to her question, and tears spilled from the corners of her eyes. "You shouldn't have come here," she whispered, her voice cracking at the end.

Calder pulled her tighter against his body and smiled. "But then he would have missed all the fun," the Casus murmured. "And we can't have that. After all, he's the whole reason for this little drama."

Noah's gaze burned with a cold, murderous rage as he looked at the Casus. "You won't get out of here, Calder. You're trapped in this shithole forever."

A low laugh rumbled in the Casus's chest. "I wouldn't be so sure about that, Winston. I've found that where there's a will, there's a way."

Jerking his chin toward her, Noah said, "Let the witch go and we'll talk about what you want."

"Ahhh, but you already know what I want." Calder released the claws on his right hand with a sibilant hiss of sound and trailed them down the center of Willow's body. "So take off that bloody charm hanging around your neck, or I'll kill her right now."

Keeping his eyes on the Casus, Noah curled one hand around the charm, and Willow shouted, "No! He's going to kill me no matter what you do! Damn it, Noah, look at me! Don't you dare take off that charm!"

But he did it anyway, pulling the charm over

his head and dropping it to the sandy ground. Willow's horrified scream echoed through her head as she watched the leather pouch slip from his fingers, its slow descent toward the ground seeming to take an endless forever. She didn't stop screaming as Calder shoved her away from him, his maniacal laughter full of triumph and satisfaction.

She must have stumbled and fallen, because the next thing she knew, Damon was yanking her off the ground and setting her on her feet. He used his talons to quickly slice through the cord that bound her wrists, then shoved her behind him, as if he meant to protect her with his body. Desperate to get to Noah, Willow tried to get around the demon, but Damon fisted his hand in her shirt and she only made it as far as his side.

She sucked in an outraged breath, ready to demand her release so that she could run to Noah, when Damon looked at Calder and said, "So what now, Casus? That body you're in needs to die before you can hop into Winston. You planning on having us kill you? Or are you gonna do the deed yourself?"

The Casus smiled. "I don't need to die, demon. Thanks to one of Sienna's spells, I can slip from this body to his before you can even reach me."

Until that point, Noah had kept his gaze focused on Calder, ignoring Willow's pleas for him to look at her. But he turned his head toward her now, his beautiful eyes dark with regret. He moved that devastating gaze slowly over her face, touching upon her features one by one, as if he wanted to imprint them on his memory, knowing this was the end.

"I can't believe you came for me," she whispered, her voice ravaged by pain, and his gaze lifted from her mouth, locking with hers. It seemed they held that stare for long, heart-wrenching moments, though in reality it was no more than a handful of seconds. Noah's throat worked, and he parted his lips, but whatever he was about to say was lost on a breathless gasp as his body suddenly shuddered and jerked, his arms and jaws spread wide as a dark vapor poured into his open mouth. She knew it was Calder, Jackson's body now lying lifeless on the ground, and she gave a hoarse cry, the back of her hand pressed to her trembling mouth as tears poured down her face.

The experience of claiming a new body was obviously taxing for the Casus. He was hunched forward, with one hand braced against an outcropping of rock, while the other clutched his stomach, his chest heaving with hard, rasping breaths. Then he finally lifted his head, and slid Willow a slow smile. "I think the poor man was about to tell you he loved you." The smile spread like a stain. "I couldn't have timed that better if I'd planned for it."

"You bastard!" she cried, filling her hands with fire, wanting to burn the Casus to a crisp. But he was in Noah's body...which meant she couldn't hurt him. Not without giving up hope that she could get back the man she loved, and she refused to do that.

"Come on," Damon growled. "I'm getting you out of here."

"No, I'm not leaving him!"

Damon's voice was hard, but gentle. "He's gone, Low. That's it."

"No, goddamn it. That is not it." She spun toward Damon in a rage of fury and grief, beating her fists against his broad chest. "Noah's still in there. I know it!"

"I wouldn't count on it," Calder rasped. She turned her head and watched him coming toward her, and he looked like Noah. Like the man that she'd loved. But he wasn't. The walk was all wrong. The cruel expression. The cold, deadly look in his eyes. The idea flashed through her head that this might be how the prophecy came true. That she would die by Calder's hand while he was living inside Noah's body.

With a sharp smile, the Casus lifted his arms,

blasting a wave of power at Damon that was meant to freeze the demon in place. But it didn't work.

As Damon stepped away from Willow, his chest shook with a gritty laugh. "Sorry, big guy. You're on my turf now. Those spells of yours aren't going to do a goddamn thing against me here."

With a snarl, Calder launched himself at the demon, swiping at him with his claws, and as the battle started, Willow wondered if the Casus knew what he was getting into. Damon was one of the meanest fighters she'd ever seen. Amazing...and deadly. She cringed every time he landed a crushing blow against Noah's body, hoping he couldn't feel the pain. But Calder had finally gotten the strength he wanted, because he wasn't going down. He was fighting back, coming at Damon hard and fast, striking out with his claws again, and again. But he couldn't take the demon down.

Roaring with furious frustration, Calder began to take his true Casus form, Noah's handsome face transforming into that of a muzzled monster—but Damon wasn't having it. With a crushing blow to the Casus's jaw, Damon sent the monster sprawling to the ground. Kicking him to his front, the demon placed his knee in the center of Calder's back and grabbed his wrists, pressing them against the Casus's spine at a painful angle, while chanting a demonic spell. As Calder regained consciousness, he pulled at his arms, trying to move them, but he was bound in place.

"You can't break the spell," Damon drawled, "so don't even try."

"What have you done to me?" the Casus snarled, struggling to pull his legs beneath him, but Damon kept him pinned in place.

"We're in hell, you bastard. You have no idea what I can do here."

While Calder continued to fight to break free of the invisible bonds, screaming obscenities, Damon reached into his back pocket and pulled out the Dark Marker.

"No!" Willow shouted as she ran toward the demon. "What the hell are you doing? You can't kill him!"

Keeping a firm grip on the cross as she tried to rip it out of his hand, Damon said, "Low, if the shit hit the fan, this is what Noah wanted."

"What are you talking about?" she cried, refusing to believe him.

"Noah gave me the Marker. He knew Calder would want him in exchange for you. That's why he gave me the cross. He wants me to end it, so that bastard can't ever come after you again."

"Well, that's too damn bad," she growled.

"Because I'm not letting the son of a bitch take him away from me!"

"Then what do you want me to do?" he barked, the gritty words edged with frustration.

The idea that shot into Willow's brain was so brilliant, she almost smiled. "Do you have any of my blood left?" she asked in a breathless rush.

"What?"

"The blood that you took earlier. The virgin blood. Do you have any left?"

Damon reached in his pocket and pulled out a small vial that was only half-full. "Just this. I gave the rest to Kierland, in case those guys need it for another ritual."

"It'll have to be enough," she said, praying it would work. "You can perform the Death-Spell from the journal, and it'll suck that evil bastard right out of him!"

"I can try," Damon told her, his tone lacking any real enthusiasm. "But, honey, there might be nothing left when Calder's gone. Noah might not be in there anymore."

"He'll be there," she snapped, refusing to give up on him. "Noah's strong. I bet he's ripping that asshole to pieces on the inside. We have to help him."

She didn't know if Damon believed her, but he didn't argue or call her crazy. Instead, he did what any good friend would do, and he helped her fight for the man she loved.

Placing another binding spell across Calder's shoulders and legs, Damon moved to his feet, then picked up one of the jagged rocks that were scattered over the ground. Standing several yards away from the Casus, he knelt down and started drawing an intricate circle in the sand with the rock. When he was done, he squinted up at Willow and said, "I don't know how this is gonna go down, Low. You might not want to look. The scene with the Death-Walkers was bloody as hell."

"That's because they were pure evil to begin with," she argued, wondering if she sounded crazy. And not caring if she did. "Noah isn't. He just needs that monster ripped out of him." She jerked her chin toward the vial of blood that Damon was holding, and said, "Now do the damn spell."

Since the body he wanted to perform the ritual on was already there, Damon didn't have to carry out the first part of the ceremony, and was able to go straight to the second. Kneeling in the center of the circle he'd drawn in the sand, the demon chanted in a low, guttural voice as he poured some of the blood in his hand, then smeared the blood around the edges of the circle. He repeated the process a second time, chanting louder, and a hot, powerful wind began to surge around them, knocking Willow to her knees. Calder, who hadn't stopped his snarling and cursing, suddenly fell silent, his body shuddering with violent convulsions. Then there was a blinding, deafening explosion of light that sent a shockwave over the land, and when it was gone, Noah's body lay on the ground with a deathly, silent stillness.

"Oh, God," Willow cried, scrambling on her knees to reach him. She shoved him to his back, then pressed her ear to his chest. "His heart isn't beating!"

Damon's voice was soft as he knelt by her side. "Maybe he's gone, honey."

"No!" she growled, pushing Noah's hair back from his face. "He isn't gone and he isn't evil! The spell wouldn't have killed him. Just Calder."

"Okay, Low. If your man's still in there, then it's up to you to get him back."

Willow jerked her gaze to the demon. "What are you talking about?"

"Before she died, Sienna said to tell you that the key to the spell that would save your heart is love. I think she was talking about the Life-Spell."

She blinked hot tears from her eyes, her lips trembling with shock. "But the Life-Spell is something that only the most powerful spell-makers can complete successfully. I'm a fighter, Damon. I'm not… I don't know how to…"

He placed a comforting hand across the back of her neck. "Si believed you could do it, Low. And so do I."

"Oh, God." She swiped at the tears streaming down her cheeks. "Okay. I'll do it. But I need my knife," she said, patting her jeans. "Where the hell is my knife?"

Damon grabbed her hand, turned it over and laid his knife across her palm. "Use mine."

"Thanks." She stared down at the shiny steel of the blade…hating what she was about to do with it. "I'm going to kill him for putting me through this," she muttered under her breath.

Damon gave a rough laugh. "Uh, honey, I already did. Now just do your thing and bring him back."

"I'm scared," she whispered, staring down at Noah's beloved face. "I don't know if I can do this, Damon."

"You love him?"

"More than anything," she answered without hesitation.

"Then it's gonna be fine."

Knowing she couldn't wait any longer, Willow wrapped both hands around the hilt of the knife and closed her eyes, reciting the words of the ancient spell that all young *Chastain* witches were forced to memorize. When she'd finished, she opened her eyes and lifted the knife, plunging the blade straight into his heart. A sob broke from her throat as she closed her eyes again and kept reciting the chant, praying with everything she had that it would work. The seconds ticked by, heavy and slow, but she refused to give up hope, her hands gripping the hilt of the knife so tightly they started to tingle. But then she felt a surge of warmth coming from the knife, and she realized the tingle was from the slight vibration moving up through the blade.

Opening her eyes, Willow's breath caught on a gasp as she found the knife glowing with a white, vibrant light. When she released her hold on the hilt, the knife began lifting out of Noah's chest, rising higher and higher, until it hovered nearly a foot in the air above his body. Suddenly, a powerful stream of light shot from the tip of the vibrating blade, straight into Noah's chest, the beam glowing increasingly brighter until she had to lift her hand to shield her eyes.

Then the vibrating stopped, the knife fell on its side against Noah's chest and he jerked into an upright position with a sharp gasp. "Where's Calder?" he croaked, his eyes wild with panic as he grabbed her arm.

"It's okay," Willow told him, trying to curve her trembling lips into a smile. "He's dead."

Noah's brow furrowed, as if he was trying to remember something important, and she said, "Damon killed him with the Death-Spell." His eyes went wide, and she explained how the demon had still had some of her blood in his pocket.

Damon pulled out the vial and jiggled it in the air. "There's still a little left. I'm thinking of maybe tracking down the ex and handling her once and for all," he drawled, and Willow gave a watery laugh.

Rubbing at the center of his blood-covered chest, Noah stared up at the demon. "If you pulled Calder out with the spell, then why do I remember having a knife plunged into my chest?" He tucked in his chin and glanced down. "There's blood, but no wound."

Willow was still explaining why she'd had to stab him, and how the spell had healed the wound, when Damon looked at the watch on his wrist and whistled. "Hey, Low. Guess what? The prophecy didn't come true."

STILL FEELING AS if he'd had the crap beaten out of him, Noah slanted the demon a piercing look, wondering what the hell he was talking about. "What prophecy?"

Damon held up his hands and shook his head.

"Ask Low. I'm not touching that one for love or money."

Noah looked at her, intending to do just that, but she sidetracked him with a smile.

"You came for me," she whispered, staring at him with tear-drenched eyes. "Even knowing what that bastard would do to you, you came for me."

"Always," he said in a low voice, wanting to take her into his arms, but knowing it wasn't the time. His body ached as he got to his feet, but he choked down the pain and reached for her hand to help her up, enjoying the way she melted into his side. Looking at the demon, he said, "Thanks for your help."

"How did the two of you get here so fast?" Willow asked.

It was Damon who answered her question, saying, "I was on my way up to your bungalow to check on you, when I felt the power surge from Sienna's portal spell."

Again, Noah had that feeling there was something going on he didn't know about. "Why were you checking on Willow?"

"Don't worry about that now," she murmured, squeezing his hand. Her precious face was drawn with grief and exhaustion, and he forced himself to let it go. For the moment. But once they were alone, Noah planned to sit her ass down and finally get an answer.

"Come on," Damon rumbled. "Let me get you guys out of here."

Noah looked over his shoulder, a low curse on his lips when he saw where Jackson's body had fallen after Calder had left it. He couldn't just leave him there, damn it.

Damon's hand settled heavily on his shoulder. "Don't worry about him," the demon said in a low voice. "Let me get you guys back to the others, and then I'll come back for your brother."

"Thanks," Noah rasped, wondering if the demon realized he'd just earned himself a friend. For life.

CHAPTER TWENTY

Six days later

STANDING ON A Broussard's doorstep was always a stressful place for a man to find himself, and this time wasn't any different. Except for the fact that Noah was getting ready to pledge undying love to the woman he couldn't live without. That was sure as hell something he'd never done before.

It'd been almost a week since he'd gone into hell after Willow, and he missed her. He'd hated spending that time apart from her, but if things turned out well for him today, he'd promised himself that he'd never be apart from her again.

Before leaving California, he'd talked with the guys from his unit, who'd made it back to England, and the conversation had been a good one. Aiden had dragged Olivia down to the village church and gotten married. Now that the war they'd been fighting for the past year was officially over, Noah figured all the guys would be hitched by the time August rolled around. Which meant there were going to be lots of weddings and celebrations going on back in England, and he didn't plan on suffering through them alone. He wanted his woman at his side, sharing in the laughter and the smiles. He wanted Willow. Forever.

Coming to the decision had been easy.

The hard part was what came next.

Noah imagined it would entail a lot of groveling and saying he was sorry, but he was ready. Hell, he'd been born for this. For taking care of her. Making a life with her. Loving her. Worshipping her. He just had to convince the gorgeous little witch that he was in this for the long haul, which was something he'd never let himself admit when he'd had the threat of Calder hanging over his head.

Ashe had told him to just open his heart and tell her how he felt.

Kellan had suggested he soften her up with some mind-blowing orgasms first, and spring a proposal on her while she was still dazed with pleasure.

Noah figured he would start with the first idea, and if things weren't going well, then he'd slide right into the second.

Finally working up the courage to knock, he held his breath as he waited for Willow to answer the door. She lived in Baton Rouge, in a pretty little white house with dark green shutters, and a front garden that was damn near overflowing with flowers. The morning was warm, the Louisiana sun beating down on the back of his neck as he waited on her front porch. He was just getting ready to knock again, when the door finally opened, the sight of her standing there in the sexy cutoffs and halter top damn near stopping his heart.

She blinked as she pushed a handful of those golden curls out of her face, looking surprised to see him. "How did you find me?"

Soaking in the sight of her with hungry eyes, he said, "Damon gave me a call, and I begged him for your address." The demon had phoned Noah to let him know that his help was available if he ever needed it, saying he'd be happy to give the Watchmen a hand tracking down the remaining Casus, including those assholes who had come through Sienna's portal with Calder during the battle in Meridian. He just had to sort out the situation with his ex, and then he said he'd be in touch. Noah had actually thanked him…and told him he was looking forward to working with him. Then he'd gotten right to the begging part.

Leaning a smooth shoulder against the door frame, Willow crossed her arms under her breasts, her dark eyes shining with humor. "I can't believe Damon gave it to you, seeing as how he was sworn to secrecy."

Noah grinned. "Yeah, well, before you're too hard on him, I had to promise to worship the ground you walk on and listen to some colorful warnings about what will happen to me if I ever hurt you. But he finally shut up and gave me the damn address."

The look in her eyes turned warm and soft. "I can't believe you're here," she whispered.

"And I still can't believe you left the way you did." He knew damn well she could hear the hurt in the low words. The fear he couldn't shake that she'd left because she didn't want him.

Once Damon had brought them back to their bungalow at the resort, Noah had gone down to talk to Kierland about what had happened, and to let his friends know that he would be taking his brother's body back to California. When he'd come back to the room, Willow was gone. It hadn't taken long to figure out that Damon had borrowed one of the unit's rented trucks to drive her back home, and they'd taken Sienna's body with them.

Clearing his throat, he said, "You didn't even tell me goodbye, Will."

IT WAS TAKING everything Willow had not to throw herself into Noah's arms, but she knew she had to do this right. Knew there were things that needed to be said.

She wet her lips and tried to keep her voice steady. "I'm sorry I left like that, Noah. I just... I knew I had to get out of there. If I didn't, I was going to fling myself at you and beg."

He stepped closer, and the wicked slant of his mouth made her shiver. "I wouldn't mind a little begging from you."

Willow bit back a smile. "I figured your ego was already big enough."

The look in his eyes got brighter. "And now?"

She moved out of the doorway so that he could come inside the house, and closed the door behind him. Then she leaned her back against the door, soaking up the sight of him in the faded jeans and T-shirt, completely undone by the fact that he'd come after her. She didn't know how it was possible, but he was even more gorgeous than she remembered. Hard and dark and dangerously beautiful, with that lean, ripped body and rugged face. She was breathless with excitement, her heart pounding to such a wild rhythm she could feel the vibrations shuddering through her body.

"Will?"

She gave herself a little shake, locking her gaze with his hot stare, and finally said, "I spent a lot of the time we were together last week wondering how people could stand to take the risk of falling in love. I mean, there's so much potential for pain. Heartache. But then, after those Death-Walkers came after us in the church, I got over being scared. I just didn't get the chance to tell you."

"To tell me what?" he asked.

She took a deep breath, and explained. "That day, I figured out that love is what gives us the strength to take the risk. To open ourselves up and let the one we love inside. To give them everything that we are, both the good parts and the bad. To embrace all the wild chaos of emotion that comes with falling in love and build something solid out of it. Something beautiful. So I'm ready to fling my heart at you, Noah Winston. If you want it, it's all yours. Actually," she said a little unsteadily, "it's yours no matter what. I can't stop loving you."

"Oh, I want." His voice was a deep, dark drawl that sounded like sin. "I definitely *want*."

The corner of Willow's mouth twisted with a grin, and she rubbed her damp palms on her shorts. "That's good to hear. Because I was tired of waiting."

He stepped closer, vibing his hot sexual energy at her. "Is that why your bag is packed?" he asked.

Willow flicked a quick glance at the bag she'd

set beside the door that morning, and nodded. "I got tired of waiting, so I was coming after you," she confessed, tucking a strand of hair behind her ear as she looked into his beautiful eyes. "You know. To do that whole flashy flinging myself at your feet thing."

"I think I would have liked that," he said with another sexy smile. Then the smile fell, and he said, "I'm sorry I didn't get here sooner, Will. There was a lot to get settled with my family, and honestly, I told myself that you needed the time to think about what you wanted." He rubbed his jaw, then blew out a rough breath. "But I think I was just scared of what you would say. That's why I didn't call. Figured if I was here in person, it'd be harder for you to turn me down."

Her tone was wry. "I can't imagine you've *ever* been turned down."

"Not for sex," he rasped, the look in his eyes turning molten, melting her down. "But I'm going after something more this time."

"You don't want sex?" she asked with a soft laugh, teasing him. Her chest felt so light, she was amazed she didn't just float away, the happiness surging through her veins making her light-headed. "Man, I'm crushed."

"Oh, I want the sex," he drawled. "You're standing there breathing, which means I want sex. But I'm going for the ultimate prize. I want it all."

The pounding of her heart got faster. "All?"

"I want forever, Will." A corner of his mouth kicked up. *"And* the sex."

"You can stop going on about the sex," she said, rolling her eyes. "The sex is a given, buddy."

His voice lowered. "And what about the rest?"

She crossed her arms again and lifted her chin. "Before we talk about the rest, you need to know that I won't let you walk away from me again."

His expression tightened, and he took a step closer, bringing that hot, mouthwatering male scent with him. "I'm an idiot, Will. I know it sucks, but you're just going to have to live with it because I can't live without you. I had thought I was making the biggest mistake of my life by coming back to Sacred, but it turns out I'd already made it. The biggest mistake of my life was walking away from you all those years ago, and if you'll give me the chance, I promise that I'll never do anything that stupid again."

He didn't wait for her response. He just pulled her close, holding her in his strong arms, and pressed his forehead to hers. "I know I'll make mistakes, but I will work my ass off to be the best damn thing that ever happened to you," he told her, his deep voice rough with emotion.

"Because that's what you are to me—the best, most beautiful, amazing person I've ever known. Because I want to spend my life making you happy." He lifted his head, and stared into her eyes. "I want you shining with it, Will. I want everyone in the world to know how much I love you."

"That's what you were going to say, isn't it?" she whispered, a salty rush of tears burning at the back of her throat. "Before Calder took you over."

"Yeah." He lifted his hand, pushing her curls back from her face. "It killed me that I didn't get the chance to tell you how I felt."

She gave him a watery smile. "You've told me now. And I loved hearing it."

"Actually, I'm glad you brought that bastard up, because I need to…" He struggled for the right words. "Will, you know what's been going on with me. The fangs, the claws. There's no guarantee where this is headed."

"I don't care."

"You sure about that? Because it's a helluva weight to pack on your shoulders."

"I love you, Noah. Whatever the future brings, we'll handle it together. I promise I'll be right there with you."

Then she took his hand and led him back to her bedroom, until they were standing beside her lace-covered bed with its colorful mound of pillows. Noah was the first man she'd ever taken into her bedroom, and she loved the way he looked there. So hard and masculine and tough, surrounded by her feminine things.

His big hands were warm on the bare skin of her lower back as he looked down at her and said, "I want you to tell me about that prophecy, Will."

"We can talk about that later," she murmured, more concerned at the moment with getting him out of his clothes.

"We'll talk about it now."

She could tell from his tone that he wasn't going to let it go. With a sigh, she said, "The prophecy said that I would be killed by the man who took my virginity within four hours of the deed or deflowering or whatever you want to call it."

It was clear, from his expression, that she'd stunned him. "Jesus. Are you serious?"

Willow shrugged. "I know it sounds crazy, but it's true. Jessie told me after she found us together that night. She said that the prophecy had been told at my birth, but she'd just been waiting for the right time to tell me."

He made a rough sound in his throat. "And you slept with me, anyway?"

He sounded so shocked she couldn't help but smile. "Like I said at the time, I trust you."

Willow could see him thinking it through. "And that's why Damon was coming to check on you, isn't it?"

"I think he wanted to be close by, in case I needed him."

He shook his head. "It was a helluva chance you took with me."

"Not really," she told him, pushing his T-shirt up over his abdomen, wanting to get to his hot bare skin. He got the hint, pulling the shirt over his head for her. "I had faith in love over fate. And I felt like I was going to die, anyway, if I didn't get you inside me."

"And now?" he asked.

She smiled as she wrapped her arms around his neck. "I'm still feeling that way."

He took her face in his hands, and her emotions overflowed as he said, "I know you spent a long time having to be careful, Will." He leaned forward and pressed his forehead to hers again, his voice breathless and low. "But you don't have to be careful anymore. I love you, and I would never do anything to hurt you."

NOAH KISSED THE tears at the corners of her eyes, and his deep voice vibrated with the force of his feelings as he spoke. "I wish I were a Lycan or a vamp. Wish that I could put my claim on you. Mark you in some way, so that every other man in the world would know you belong to me. But I can bind us with something that's just as real, Will. With something that will be as strong as any clan bond could ever be. With something that will last forever."

"God, I need you," she groaned, the husky words shredding the last of his control.

He swallowed as he tried to calm his heart and take it slow, but it was a wasted effort. He was too desperate to do anything but rip those sexy clothes off her even sexier little body and fall on her like a madman. They ended up sprawled across the bed, her soft laughter spilling through the sunlit room as he struggled to get his stubborn jeans off. When he was finally free of the boots and denim, Noah pinned her beneath him and lowered his head, eager to take her smiling mouth with a hungry kiss, when a burning pain filled his gums, and he knew his goddamn fangs had released.

"Are you tempted, when they come out like that?" she murmured, twining her arms around his shoulders.

Warily, he asked, "Tempted to what?"

"To bite me?" she asked, her eyes clear and bright, without any trace of fear. "To have the taste of my blood in your mouth?"

"I would never risk you like that," he said, the gritty words edgy and raw. "So don't even talk about it."

"If you want this to work," she said in a soft voice, drifting her fingers through his hair, "then you have to be willing to trust yourself, Noah."

He forced his response from a tight throat. "It's not that simple."

"I never said it would be. But whatever gave you the impression I wanted simple?"

He could feel the heavy weight of temptation beating down on him, his pulse roaring in his ears. "Damn it, Will. I could hurt you."

"Noah, you might not trust yourself," she whispered, "but for what it's worth, I do. So why don't we see where this goes? Who knows? You might not even like it."

His chest shook with a sharp, breathless laugh. "Not likely. Everything about you drives me wild. Your blood isn't going to be any different."

"Then let's give it a try."

He couldn't believe this was happening. "You're crazy, you know that?"

She just smiled, her eyes shining with emotion. "Not crazy. Just in love." She reached up, rubbing her fingertip between his brows. "I don't want that look of worry in your eyes for the rest of our lives," she told him. "I'd rather see satisfaction there. Need. For me."

"Where?"

She blinked back at him. "Where, what?"

He ran his tongue over one sharp tooth, knowing exactly what he wanted. "Where am I allowed to bite you?"

She shivered, and he could tell from her scent and the provocative look in her eyes that it was from excitement, and not fear. "Wherever you want to, Noah."

He parted his lips, figuring he should tell her thank-you, or make more promises that he wouldn't hurt her, but he couldn't get a goddamn word out. All he could do was lower his mouth to her chest, nuzzling the soft weight of her breasts, so desperate to sink his fangs into her it was like a physical pain in his gut. He wanted her blood. Wanted the feel and the warmth of it sitting in his mouth. Against his tongue.

"Spread your legs wider," he told her, the words thick and graveled with need as he reached down and positioned his cock against her tender opening. She was already warm and wet, and with a feral growl rumbling on his lips, Noah drove himself into her, thrusting deep and hard...and bit into her breast. She gave a husky cry as her flesh closed in tight around his fangs, the rich taste of her blood spilling over his tongue, sizzling and sweet, and he jerked from the violent rush of pleasure, his eyes nearly rolling back in his head.

Her back arched as he pounded into her, her arms clasped tight around his head, holding him to her. He was too far gone for anything but this rough, hammering rhythm, the bed banging against the wall as his powerful thrusts shoved her across the mattress. She came hard and fast, drenching him in scalding heat, and he took another long, greedy pull at her breast, before forcing himself to stop, worried he'd take too much.

Noah stared at the small punctures in her pale flesh with hot, burning eyes, then lifted his gaze…and she said, "I love you." And that was all it took, those three little words hurtling him into the most violent, explosive orgasm he'd ever known, the dark, crashing pleasure ripping through him with so much force he had to clench his teeth, his eyes going hot and damp as he poured himself into her.

When it was finally over, Noah gave a low groan, collapsing beside her, and pulled her into his arms. She cuddled against his chest, pressing soft kisses to the hammering pulse at the base of his throat, and he told her, in a rough, pleasure-wrecked voice, just how madly in love with her he was. And he thanked her for coming back into his life. Then he thanked her for saving him.

THEY SPENT THE day in bed, lounging together in a tangle of limbs, watching the sun work its way through the sky, making love and talking about the future. Wondering how he was going to take the news, Willow eventually said, "Just so you know, I'm probably going to make you marry me."

"Hold that thought," he told her, reaching over the side of the bed for his jeans. When he turned back to her, he was holding a beautiful diamond wedding band, and he slipped it onto her finger.

"There's no probably about it," he said with one of those warm, wicked smiles that never failed to curl her toes. "We are definitely getting married. As far as I'm concerned, it's a wedding that's going to be twelve years overdue."

"I want traditional vows," she whispered, holding the sheet against her breasts as she sat up. She held out her hand to admire the ring, then looked at Noah, who was lying against her pillows, looking too sexy and gorgeous to be real. "Fidelity and eternal love, till death do us part."

He put his hand against the side of her face, rubbing his thumb across the corner of her mouth. "The two things you won't ever have to worry about are my faithfulness and my love. My body and my heart belong to you, Will. There's nothing that could ever change that."

And she could see the truth of those breathtaking words burning in his eyes.

Flicking her tongue across her lower lip, she said the first thing that popped into her mind. "You are going to look *so* delicious in a tux."

He pulled her against his chest as it rumbled with laughter. "I'll wear the monkey suit, if that's what you want. But you're just going to end up ripping it off me the first chance you get."

Willow shrugged. "We can sneak away at the reception for a quickie, then you can put it back on for me. Problem solved."

"Whatever makes you happy," he drawled, rolling her under him and working his way back inside her, which seemed to be where he liked to spend most of his time. Not that she was complaining.

"You know, this was always my idea of a perfect day," she told him. "Sunshine and sex with the sexiest guy I've ever known."

He snorted. "Glad you think so."

"What's yours?"

"My idea of a perfect day?"

"Yeah," she whispered, stroking her fingertips down the masculine line of his spine, loving the way his muscles jumped at her touch.

He cocked his head a little to the side as he stared down at her, a tender smile on his lips as he said, "It's always been the same thing, ever since that first kiss."

"And?" she asked, her breath catching as he started to move in a slow, sensual rhythm. She was sore from the day's excesses, but too hungry for him to care. "I want to know what it is."

"Okay." His smile turned wicked. "My idea of a perfect day is fucking you until we're both too sore to ever move again."

Her chest shook with breathless laughter and she swatted him on the shoulder. "You're so romantic!"

"Hey, I try." He grabbed her wrists, stretching her arms over her head as he came down over her, putting his face close to hers. "But, honestly, my perfect day is just being close to you, Will. Holding you in my arms. Hearing you say 'I love you' when I'm buried deep inside you. It doesn't get any more perfect than that."

"Then get ready for a perfect life," she told him, hoping he could see the love shining in her eyes. "Because you can have that every day."

"I don't need perfect," he whispered against her mouth. "I just need you."

CHAPTER TWENTY-ONE

FOR THE PAST WEEK, Willow and Noah had stayed holed up in her little house in Baton Rouge, and it'd been the best week of her life. But there was a wedding to organize, and they'd been asked to come down to Jessie's so that they could start making plans for the big day. They'd parked Noah's truck back at the bar, and as they made their way along the path where Willow had first pulled her knife on him, she couldn't help but smile. It was a familiar expression, since she found herself smiling a lot these days.

They'd both lost something important to them because of Anthony Calder, but they'd found something, too. Something they'd both been waiting for a long, long time, and they couldn't help but cherish it.

When they reached Jessie's door, Willow started to lift her hand to knock, but the door was suddenly ripped open with an audible whoosh. "Well, get your ass in here," Jessie snapped, shooing them in. "I can't stand this anymore.

It's driving me batty." Jessie's dark gaze glittered with emotion. "And bad things happen when I go batty."

From the corner of her eye, Willow watched Noah give a hard swallow, his Adam's apple bobbing in his throat. He looked nervous, but she couldn't tease him. She'd never seen Jessie this wound up and she was feeling pretty nervous herself.

They followed Jessie into the cabin's small dining room, and Willow was surprised to find Harris already seated at the table. Her brother looked even more dangerous than he had the last time she'd seen him, as if he could break a man apart with his bare hands. He rose from his chair to give her a hug and to shake hands with Noah, and Willow was relieved that they seemed genuinely happy to see each other. Maybe that was another old wound that could be healed, and she sent up a silent prayer that the two would become friends again.

"Let's get this over with," Jessie said, taking a seat beside Harris, while Willow and Noah took seats on the other side of the table. Jessie folded her hands into a tight knot on the tabletop, her white brows drawn into a deep crease beneath Rufus's furry chin. "This isn't easy for me to say. But I know it's something I need to tell you."

Willow felt like her heart had just lodged itself in her throat. "Jessie, please. Just spit it out."

"You're right. I'm sorry." Jessie looked slowly from one to the other, then finally said, "I lied about the prophecy. I created it for the specific purpose of keeping the two of you separated."

Noah took a sharp breath, and Willow put her hand to her forehead, feeling like she'd just been smacked in the face. "What are you saying?" she whispered.

Jessie's gaze almost looked teary as she said, "I knew Noah was the one who would hold your heart, Willow, and that he would feel the same way. I knew it from the first moment the two of you ever set eyes on each other. But I also knew that you needed to stay a virgin."

"How did you know?" Noah asked, taking hold of Willow's trembling hand.

Jessie looked at Noah and explained. "The voices. They told me she would be needed for a purpose one day, and that it was necessary for her to remain untouched." Returning her bright gaze to Willow, she said, "I'd been planning on telling you before you got much older, but it wasn't…easy. And then you were found with Noah that night, and everything changed. I knew I had to do something to keep you from going after him."

"So you made up the prophecy to separate us," she whispered, the soft words full of pain.

Jessie frowned. "The voices have never lied to me before, so I did what had to be done. But only because it was necessary."

"Why?" she demanded. "I mean, why separate us? You could have just told us the truth. Warned me to stay celibate."

Jessie snorted. "That never would have worked. The way he looked at you—it was only a matter of time before he would have gotten in your pants."

Harris winced, looking as if he was in pain. "Jessie, seriously. Think about what you're saying. I don't want to hear crap like that about my baby sister."

"Anyway, I couldn't take that risk." Her aunt's voice was firm with conviction. "Not when your virginity was going to be so important. The second I read that spell that Noah brought me, I suspected it would be you. And I was right."

"You should have told us," Noah rasped. "You had no right to keep this a secret for so many years."

Jessie lifted her brows. "And would you have been able to keep your hands off her if I had?"

He started to say something, then stopped, and Jessie laughed.

"I didn't think so." She reached up and adjusted Rufus, then took a deep breath. "I know you're both angry, but the lie served its purpose, keeping Willow's virginity intact until she was needed for that spell."

Noah braced his hands on the table and leaned forward. "She's always been needed," he growled. "I needed her!"

Completely unfazed by his anger, Jessie reached across the table and patted the top of his hand. "And now you have her, Noah. For the rest of your life. And you're smart enough to appreciate what you've got."

He cursed something foul under his breath, but sat back down, and Willow took his hand again, giving it a little squeeze, since she doubted he was going to like her next question for Jessie. "You managed to keep me away from Noah, but didn't you ever worry I might hook up with another man?"

Shaking her head, Jessie said, "Once I told you about your death, I knew no other man would have the ability to tempt you. He was the only one."

"Oh, God," she groaned, sliding a wry look toward Noah, whose angry mouth was already curving with a gloating smile. "I think I can actually see your head getting bigger."

Noah and Harris laughed, and then Jessie said, "I know this has all come as quite a shock to you both, but I'd like to make it up to you, if you'll let me."

"How?" Willow asked with a heavy dose of suspicion.

Jessie gave her a hopeful smile. "How about a honeymoon on a private island in the Caribbean?"

Willow arched one eyebrow. "You know the owner?"

"You could say that." Jessie's smile grew wider. "I *am* the owner."

"An island?" Harris croaked, his dark eyes going wide with shock. "How the hell did you manage that?"

Her aunt shrugged. "Let's just say that a recent client wished to show me his gratitude with a profound gesture of generosity. I told him some flowers would be fine, but he insisted on giving me the island."

While Willow gaped at Jessie, Noah rubbed a hand over his eyes. "I don't even want to know," he muttered under his breath, and Willow stifled a laugh. He was no doubt thinking the same thing she was, wondering just what kind of spell her aunt had performed for this mystery client. God only knew what the woman had been up to this time.

"It's a beautiful place," Jessie added, obviously intent on tempting them to accept her offer.

"White sand beaches and crystal-blue waters. I think there's even a waterfall. It would be incredibly romantic."

"We'll think about it," Willow murmured, unwilling to let Jessie off the hook that easily. Pushing her chair back from the table, she asked, "Any other bombshells you want to drop on us before we go?"

Jessie settled her warm stare on Noah. "Only something that the voices have been telling me about this young man here."

"About me? Oh, God," he muttered.

"Don't look so worried, Noah. This is a good thing. It's about the changes you've been going through."

He tensed, looking a little green, and Willow gave his hand a comforting squeeze.

"They assure me that your worries about becoming a monster are unfounded. You'll remain human. Because of your Casus bloodline, Calder's bite has simply provided you with some...interesting extras. Perks, if you like, without any of the disastrous consequences."

"See?" Willow whispered, a soft smile on her lips as she pressed a quick kiss to the top of his head. "I told you there was nothing to worry about."

Moving to his feet beside her, Noah cleared

his throat and said, "Thanks, Jessie. I appreciate you telling me."

"Anything for family," Jessie replied, and Willow choked back a laugh at the way he turned
that interesting shade of green again.

They made their way to the front door, with
Jessie and Harris walking behind them, and Willow caught her brother's gaze before following Noah outside. "You planning on staying in
touch?"

His mouth twitched with something that could
have almost passed for a smile. "I have to be here
to give you away, don't I?"

"You will if you know what's good for you,"
she warned with a husky laugh, and then her
expression turned serious. "I hope you'll come
around more, Harris. I miss knowing my brother."

He shoved a hand through his wavy hair and
winced. "I'm sorry about that, Willow. I just…
Things have been pretty crazy for me lately. But
I, uh, promise I'll be better about making time
to see you."

"I'll hold you to that." She started to turn
away, ready to join Noah outside, but Harris
reached out and grabbed her arm. Willow took
in his strained expression, and waited for him
to say what was on his mind.

"I'm sorry I wasn't here to help you with Si.
And I'm sorry I interfered between you and

Noah all those years ago," he forced out in a low rasp. "I should've kept my nose out of it, but I was…I was just worried about you."

"I know," she told him, pressing her hand over his. "I don't blame you, Harris. It wasn't your fault."

Relief filled his gaze. "You forgive me?"

"Only if you promise to spend next Christmas with us," she told him, thinking how wonderful it would be to have a traditional family holiday, complete with turkey and a tree and all the people she loved.

Harris looked uncertain, but…touched. "You serious?"

Her response was swift. "As a heartbeat."

His tension eased, and his mouth finally curved with a warm smile. "Then I'll be there."

INSTEAD OF HEADING back to the truck, Noah asked Willow if she'd mind walking for a while through the woods with him. There were plenty of paths for them to follow, and he wanted to give her a little time to relax before they drove into town and spent the day at various meetings, making plans for the wedding.

For his own part, he was angry with Jessie for what she'd done, meddling in their lives in such a way that it had cost them twelve years—but he was also relieved by the things those little voices had told her about the effects of Calder's bite. He hoped Will understood how much it meant to him that she'd given him her love when they still didn't know what the future held. He would never forget that trust on her part. And he sure as hell would never betray it.

As he watched her from the corner of his eye, Noah wondered if she had any idea how devoted he was to her. With a smile, he realized he had a lifetime to show her, and he looked forward to every moment of it.

"It's beautiful," he rumbled, enjoying the fresh air and the dappled warmth of sunlight as it floated through the trees. There was just enough of a breeze to make the heat comfortable, but he could sense Willow's tension. "Just take a deep breath and try to relax, honey."

"I know. I'm sorry. But I'm so mad I could strangle her," she growled, taking her aggression out on an unsuspecting tree as she kicked its wide trunk with her boot.

His grin was wry. "Uh, yeah, I can see that from the flagrant tree abuse."

She gave a choked laugh and stopped kicking, her pale hair falling over the side of her face as she turned and slumped against the tree, her right side pressed against its moss-covered bark. "It's not fair, Noah. Why did we have to lose all that time?"

"I don't know," he said, walking over and pulling her into his arms. "All I know is that you're mine now. And there's nothing on the face of this earth, in heaven or in hell, that can ever change that."

She put her arms around his neck, and that easily, he could feel her anger melting. "I can't stay mad when you're holding me," she told him. "I love you too much."

"God, Will. I'll never get tired of hearing that. And I'm so damn sorry it took me so long to come back to you." He kissed her between the fervent words, each touch of his lips a promise of what was to come. Of the love he had to give to her, that would always be hers. "I'm sorry I missed all those years with you."

"Being without you for so long, it sucked big-time, Noah. But you know what?"

"What?" he rasped, staring deep into her eyes.

She smiled and went up on her tiptoes, her lips soft against his ear.

"You were worth the wait."

The husky words shot through him like a jolt of lightning, and he grinned as he held her tighter, crushing her against his chest. "I'm glad you think so."

"Oh, I know so," she whispered, letting her head fall back as he pressed his mouth against the base of her throat. "I doubt you noticed, but we're not far from where you parked your car the night you found me with Stubb."

He lifted his head and looked around. "You're right."

"I have a secret," she murmured.

He arched one eyebrow as he brought his gaze back to hers. "Yeah?"

She took a deep breath, then said, "I only went out with Johnny because I had this crazy dream of making you jealous."

Shock skittered through his system. "You sneaky little witch."

Rolling her eyes, she said, "Well, yeah." Then she started to smile. "You can't believe how surprised I was when the dream actually came true."

"I should put you over my knee for doing something so foolish," he rumbled, curving one hand over her sweet little ass.

"Actually," she drawled, giving him a sultry look through her long lashes, "I was thinking you should just finish what you started that night."

Damn, but he loved the way she thought.

"We don't have a car for me to lay you down on, but I can improvise." Noah lifted her off the ground and pressed her against the moss-covered trunk of the tree.

"Mmm," she moaned, wrapping her beautiful legs around his waist. "I've always wanted to have sex in a forest."

"Only with me," he growled, sounding like a possessive beast. But there was no help for it. When it came to Will, he *was* a possessive beast, ready to pound his chest and fight to the death against any man who tried to take her away from him.

Her soft laugh was proof she was on to him. "That's a given."

He brushed his lips against the side of her throat, so much blood rushing south to his groin he felt light-headed. "You gonna let me bite you again?" he groaned, his fangs slipping from his gums in a scalding rush of heat, his pulse roaring in his ears.

"You want to?" The hushed words trembled with excitement, her hardened nipples pressing into his chest, begging for the touch of his hand.

"The taste of you is still hot in my mouth." His voice was thick, rough with need, the raw, predatory edge impossible to disguise. "I can't get it out of my head."

"Then go for it. You know how much I love it," she whispered, pulling him tighter to her as he cupped her breast through the soft cotton of her shirt, a searing wave of heat traveling up his spine as he stroked his thumb over the swollen tip.

"Tell me you love me again." He gasped against her soft lips, his chest aching from the violent force of his breaths.

"I love you, Noah."

"I love you, too," he growled, beyond thankful that she was wearing a light, flowing skirt as he wrenched the gauzy fabric out of his way. Then he tore the gusset out of her panties and pressed his shaking hand against the slick, plump folds of her sex, making sure she was ready for him. "So much it makes me crazy."

"You've always been crazy," she teased, reaching between them and attacking the buttons on his fly. She ripped them open, taking a firm grip on his granite-hard cock as she added, "That's why we're so perfect for each other."

Noah's chest shook with a gritty laugh as he pushed the blunt head of his shaft into her warm, cushiony sheath, the pleasure somehow more intense each time he took her, blowing his mind. He didn't know if it was like this for everyone who was in love, but he considered himself one lucky son of a bitch to have found this kind of happiness.

Her head tilted back, eyes drifting closed as a satisfied smiled played softly over her beautiful mouth. "I can't wait for you to be my husband, Noah. For you to belong to me, body and soul."

"I always have," he whispered, his deep voice rough with emotion. "You just didn't know it."

"I know it now." She gasped, her lush body arching against him as he lost the battle with his control and shoved inside her with a thick, powerful thrust, going all the way to the hilt.

As her sweet, scalding heat surrounded him, making him shudder with ecstasy, Noah lowered his head, scraped his fangs against the tender column of her throat and vowed, "I'll never let you forget it."

EPILOGUE

The Lake District, England

IT WAS, WITHOUT DOUBT, the biggest wedding celebration Willow had ever heard of. In the past month, seven other couples from Noah's Watchmen unit had exchanged vows, and now they were throwing a huge bash in honor of the auspicious occasions. The party was being held in the gardens of Harrow House, the magnificent estate the unit was currently using as headquarters. A jazz band played from one of the upper balconies, the crowded dance floor surrounded by linen-covered tables with stunning floral centerpieces. The caterer had outdone herself with a sumptuous array of dishes, while the open bar provided an endless supply of wine and champagne and other tempting libations.

Everywhere she looked, people were smiling and laughing, and Willow's head was spinning as she tried to keep track of all the new faces and names. She'd met most of the other Watchmen in Noah's unit the week before, when they'd come over to the States for their own wedding, and she liked them all. The men were rugged, gorgeous alpha types who knew how to play as hard as they worked, and their women had been so welcoming, Willow knew it wouldn't be long before she'd make some lasting friendships. A first for her, since she'd never been able to make any close female friends; but she was looking forward to the shopping trip she and the other women had planned in a few days, as well as the spa day Kellan's wife, Chloe, had scheduled for the group.

As the jazz band began to play "Someone to Watch Over Me," Noah took Willow's hand, pulled her away from their chattering table, where they'd just finished a mouthwatering chocolate soufflé, and led her onto the dance floor. As he pulled her into his arms he gave her one of those wickedly sexy smiles that always melted her, then spun her into a move that left her breathless with laughter, her feet practically floating over the ground as they swayed among the other couples.

Resting her cheek against his strong shoulder, Willow closed her eyes and smiled as she thought of the weddings they had attended during the past week. "They were beautiful ceremonies," she said in a dreamy voice. "I've never been to so many fairy-tale weddings. It was like magic."

"Not as magical as ours," he murmured, nuzzling her temple, his big hands pressed possessively against her back, which was bared by the sexy black dress she'd picked up in New Orleans before they'd flown over. She gave a blissful sigh, remembering how incredible their wedding day had been. Damon had shown up to serve as Noah's best man, which the demon had gotten a kick out of. And Harris had stuck around to give her away, just as he'd promised, looking sinfully handsome in his tux.

After the ceremony, the reception had been held at Broussards, and she knew the whole parish would be talking about it for years to come. At one point, Kellan and Damon had danced shirtless on one of the tables and nearly sent the older ladies into a swoon, while their friends had all laughed so hard there'd been tears in their eyes.

And true to his word, Noah had let her pull him away from the fun to sneak off to one of the refurbished cabins, where she had her wicked way with him. Of course, he'd demanded to have his with her as well, devastating her senses with pleasure until her throat had been raw from her husky cries. By the time they'd made it back to the reception, she was rosy and flushed from the mind-shattering orgasms, and it had been time to cut the cake.

They'd postponed their honeymoon so that they could attend the rest of the weddings in England. But they would be leaving for Jessie's private Caribbean island the week after next, and would be staying for three weeks. They'd invited Bryce and his family to come and stay with them the last week they were there, and Willow was looking forward to getting to know them better. Bryce had offered to buy Noah's bar back in San Francisco, and he'd been happy to agree, saying he wanted to spend his time working with the Watchmen and helping Willow with her cases, since he didn't plan on letting her out of his sight.

It still brought tears to her eyes whenever she thought about the depth of Noah's devotion to her; a miracle that at times she feared was simply too good to be true. Of course, whenever she asked him to pinch her, to prove that she wasn't dreaming, he would smile that sexy crooked smile of his, toss her over his broad shoulder and carry her away to their room. Then, once behind closed doors, he would spend hours showing her in devastating, explicit detail just how real he was.

"I've had a wonderful time tonight," she told him, lacing her fingers behind his neck as she lifted her head from his shoulder. "Your friends are great."

He grinned. "They're a bunch of smart-asses most of the time, but they're a good group of guys."

"Get your facts straight," Kellan drawled, a huge grin on the Lycan's face as he swirled by with a laughing Chloe in his arms. "We're not good, Winston. We're the *best*."

Noah laughed at the jackass, then lowered his mouth to Willow's ear. "Not that this isn't fun," he rasped, giving a playful nip to her earlobe, "but I'm dying to get you alone."

"Me, too," she whispered, trembling with desire. "I think I'm addicted to you, Mr. Winston."

Willow could feel him smile against her temple. "You've got it all backwards, baby. I'm the one who's addicted to you."

Her breath caught as he pulled her closer, dancing her into the jasmine-scented shadows at the edge of the dance floor. A pale shaft of light from one of the flickering sconces illuminated his gorgeous face as he stared into her eyes, and she shivered under the raw force of his gaze. Then he tilted his head down, moving his mouth over hers, and she lost herself in the breathtaking depths of his kiss, his tongue stroking hers. The kiss became deeper, more urgent, heat layering upon heat until she couldn't hear anything but the frenzied racing of her heart.

She pressed one hand to the center of his chest, against the soft linen of his shirt, wanting to feel his own pounding heartbeat. Jessie's leather pouch pressed against her palm, and she experienced a sharp pang of relief at the fact that he was still wearing the charm. It had been decided that both Winston brothers should continue to wear the charmed pouches, until they were certain all the Casus had been destroyed. Noah and his friends didn't believe the Casus shades that had escaped with Calder would be able to switch their hosts as easily as Calder had, but they weren't taking any chances.

The band took a break and Noah reluctantly ended the kiss, his dark whisper in her ear promising untold hours of erotic pleasure once they'd headed up to their room. Then he took her hand, leading her from the dance floor. She stifled a giggle as she caught sight of the proper-looking jazz band heading toward the bar, wondering how they would react if they suspected they were playing to a crowd that consisted of far more clansmen and women than it did humans. There were even a few vampires in attendance, thanks to Seth McConnell's beautiful wife, Raine. But the Granger brothers were missing out on the fun, having been forced to leave that morning in order to deal with some mysterious family emergency, and Willow knew their friends missed them.

When she and Noah rejoined their table, they were just in time for a fresh round of champagne. As the bubbling glasses were passed around, Molly Buchanan, who Willow noticed had been drinking iced water all evening, suddenly said, "Ian's had another dream."

From what Noah had told her, Willow knew that the dark-haired, blue-eyed Ian Buchanan could see visions of the future in his dreams. And from the sparkling look of happiness in his wife's pretty eyes, his latest dream had undoubtedly been a good one.

Glancing at her friends' expectant faces, Molly grinned and said, "We're going to have a baby!"

"Holy shit!" someone blurted with excitement, while one of the others slapped Ian on the shoulder and said, "Congratulations, man. That's so freaking cool."

"More like bloody terrifying," Ian rumbled, looking a little pale.

Molly rolled her eyes. "He's already worrying himself sick, but I'm going to be perfectly fine." She leaned over, placing a tender kiss against her husband's grim mouth. "I promise."

Ian pulled her closer, whispering something

in her ear that made the petite blonde blush, and Willow couldn't help but smile. She loved watching all these gorgeous males fawning over their women. They obviously weren't afraid of public displays of affection, but then neither was Noah.

Kierland moved his chair back and stood up on the far side of the table, drawing everyone's attention. "I'd like to make a toast," the Lycan called out, a smile on his handsome face as he gave his lovely wife a sexy wink, then looked around the table and lifted his glass of champagne. "To new friends, new beginnings and a future we can all look forward to!"

They all lifted their glasses, clinking them together for good luck, then tossed back the cold champagne. As the flutes were set back on the table, Ian cleared his throat and said, "I, uh, had another dream, as well."

"What was this one about?" Aiden drawled, his brawny arms wrapped possessively around his wife's narrow waist as she sat perched on his lap.

Ian rubbed a hand across his hard jaw. "I know what name is going to be chosen for the new organization after the votes come in next week from the other units."

When Noah and several of the others asked what it was, their deep voices overlapping, Ian took a deep breath and told them what he'd seen in the dream. "We're going to be collectively referred to as the *Specialized Teams for a Unified Defense*. Or, if you make it an acronym, S.T.U.D."

There were several gasps, a few colorful curses, and all of their eyes went wide with disbelief.

"Shit," Noah grunted. "You're making that up, Buchanan."

With a heavy sigh, Ian said, "Trust me, man, I wish I was. But that's the name."

While the others groaned, Kellan threw back his head and howled with laughter, the husky sound echoing loudly through the warm summer night. For a moment Willow worried that the mood of the party had been spoiled, but one by one, the Watchmen's frowns gave way to wry, lopsided grins. Then one of them gave a gruff bark of laughter, followed by another, and before long they were all laughing as hard as Kellan.

With Noah's long arm wrapped around her shoulders, Willow looked around the group and smiled. She knew that life with the Watchmen would often be difficult, not to mention dangerous. At times even deadly. But as she listened to them laugh and rib each other with good-natured humor, she also knew it was going to be a heck of a lot of fun.

And as Noah suddenly pulled her onto his lap,

kissing her as if he'd die without the taste of her lips against his, there was only one way Willow could think of to describe the future....

Breathtakingly, mind-blowingly *perfect*.

* * * * *

GLOSSARY OF TERMS
for the Primal Instinct Series

The Ancient Clans: Nonhuman races whose existence has been kept secret from the majority of humans for thousands of years; their abilities differing as widely as their physiology. Some only partially alter when in their primal forms, like the Merrick. Others fully transform, able to take the shape of an animal, similar to those who compose the Watchmen.

These are but a few of the various ancient clans that remain in existence today:

The Merrick: One of the most powerful of the ancient clans, the Merrick were forced to mate with humans after years of war against the Casus had decimated their numbers. Their bloodlines eventually became dormant, dwelling within their human descendants, until the return of the Casus and the time of their awakening. In order to feed the primal parts of their nature, the newly awakened Merrick must consume blood while having sex. Characteristics: When in Merrick form, the males have fangs, talons, flattened noses and massive, heavily muscled physiques. The females have fangs and talons.

The Awakenings: Each time a Casus shade returns to this world, it causes the primal blood within one of the Merrick descendants to rise within them, or awaken, so that they might battle against their ancient enemy.

The Buchanans: One of the strongest Merrick bloodlines, the Buchanans were not only the first of the Merrick to awaken, but they also each possess an unusual power or "gift." Ian has a strange sense of premonition that comes to him in dreams, Saige can "hear" things from physical objects when she touches them and Riley's telekinetic powers enable him to control physical objects with his mind.

The Casus: Meaning *violent death,* the Casus are an immortal race of preternatural monsters who were imprisoned by the Merrick and the Consortium more than a thousand years ago for their mindless killing sprees. Recently, however, they have begun escaping from their holding ground, returning to this world and taking over the bodies of "human hosts" who have dormant Casus blood running through their veins. The escaped Casus now prey upon the newly awakened Merrick, feeding on their flesh for power, as well as revenge. Characteristics: When in Casus form, they have muzzled faces, wolf-shaped heads, leathery gray skin, ridged backs and long, curved claws. The males have ice-blue eyes, while the females have eyes that are pale green.

Meridian: The metaphysical holding ground where the Casus were imprisoned for their crimes against the other clans…as well as humanity. Although it was created by the original Consortium, no one knows how to find it until the ancient archives reveal that the Dark Markers are not only the keys that will open the gate to Meridian, but that they will also form a map that leads to the prison's hidden location.

Shades: Because of their immortality, the Casus can't die in Meridian. They have simply wasted away to "shades" of the powerful creatures they once were, which is why they're forced to take human hosts when they return to this world.

The Deschanel: Also known as vampires, the Deschanel are one of the most powerful of the ancient clans, rivaling the strength of the Merrick and the shape-shifters. Although duality is a common feature among many of the clans, the trait is especially strong within the Deschanel, whose very natures are a dichotomy of opposites—of both darkness and light—which makes them complex friends...and dangerous enemies. Characteristics: Pale, pure gray eyes that glow after they've taken a blood feeding. Despite their power and strength, they move with a smooth, effortless grace that is uncommon among human males of their size. They also have incredibly long life-spans, until such time as they finally take a mate.

The Burning: The body of an unmated Deschanel male runs cold until he finds his mate. The phenomenon is referred to as being "in heat" or "burning," since his body begins warming from the moment he finds her.

The **Förmyndares:** As the Protectors of the Deschanel, it is the duty of these warriors to destroy any threats to the vampire clans.

Nesting Grounds: Ancient, sprawling castlelike communities where Deschanel family units, or nests, live for security; they are protected by powerful magic that keeps them hidden from the outside world. The grounds are located throughout Scandinavia and other parts of Europe.

A **Sangra** *Bond:* A bond that can be formed between a human male and a Deschanel female, enabling the male to track her over long distances.

The Alacea: A powerful, eclectic clan of psychics who have varying degrees of powers. Most can see into the past or the future, with a few having the ability to read another's thoughts in the present—but usually only one form of sight is given. Characteristics: Dark, sky-blue eyes.

Aldori Trance: A deep trance state that an Alacea with mature powers can enter, but there are often serious consequences.

Transsis: Light trance states that the Alacea use when they need to rest, but don't want to go into a deep sleep.

The Witches: Although there are many witch clans still in existence, their powers vary greatly from one clan to another. Characteristics: Physical traits vary according to the specific clan of witch.

The **Chastain:** One of the most powerful castes of witches who can train to be either spell-makers, healers or warriors.

The Boudreaux: A carefree clan of witches whose specialty is beauty spells.

The Mallory: A powerful clan of witches whose diverse powers were bound by a curse. Because of the centuries-old curse, they magnified the emotions of those in their presence to extreme levels—but the curse is now coming to an end.

The Reavess: A clan of witches who can communicate mentally with those in their families. They access their considerable power through the use of spells, and will bond their true loves to them through sex. They are also able to assume the traits possessed by their mates during "joining."

The Saville: A snobbish clan of witches who have little power.

The Regan: An aggressive clan responsible for hunting several rival clans to near extinction. Characteristics: Long noses, pointed ears and deeply cleft chins.

The Kenly: A mountain-dwelling clan nearly hunted to extinction by the Regan. Characteristics: Short statures and large, doelike eyes.

The Feardacha: One of several ancient clans that reside in Ireland. They are extremely superstitious, believing that the dead should never go unchecked. As a precaution, they tattoo pagan symbols on their hands and arms, believing the symbols will draw to them any evil souls that manage to escape from hell, so that they might kill them once again. Characteristics: Tattoos, mocha-colored skin and pale green eyes.

The Vassayre: One of the more reclusive clans, they seldom come out of the underground caves where they dwell. Characteristics: Dark markings around their sunken eyes.

The Deuchar: One of the most violent of the ancient clans, they are the mortal enemy of the Shaevan.

The Shaevan: One of several ancient clans that reside in France.

The Shape-shifters: A richly diverse, powerful collection of clans whose members can take either the complete or partial shape of a beast.

The Prime Predators: Consisting of the most dangerous, predatory animal species, they are the most aggressive breeds of shape-shifters, well-known for their legendary sex drives and their unquestionable devotion to their mates. In order to claim a mate, a Prime must bite the one who holds their heart, marking them with their fangs while taking their blood into their bodies. They are also known for their incomparable skill as warriors and their strong healing abilities. Examples: The tigers, jaguars and lycanthropes.

The Lycanthropes: Also known as werewolves, they are formidable warriors who can actually change humans to their species with the power of their bite if they are in wolf form. However, in order to mark their mates, they must make a bite with their fangs while still in human form.

The Raptors: One of the rarest breeds of shifters, the Raptors are known for being ruthless warriors and possessive, utterly devoted lovers. Although they do not completely shift form, they are able to release powerful wings from their backs that enable them to fly, as well as sharp talons from their fingertips for fighting.

The Charteris: Dragon shape-shifters who possess the ability to control fire, and whose bodies burn with a dangerous heat when making love to a woman who holds their heart. It is believed that no pure-blooded Charteris are still in existence.

The Archives: The records that belonged to the original Consortium that are believed to hold vital information about the ancient clans. Though the new Consortium spent years searching for them, the archives were eventually found by the Collective Army, then taken by the Watchmen.

The Death Journal: A journal found with the ancient archives that explains how to kill a variety of clan species, many of which are no longer even in existence. There is a passage in the journal written in an archaic language that the Watchmen can't decipher, but which they believe will explain how to kill the Death-Walkers who have escaped from hell.

The Collective Army: A militant organization of human mercenaries devoted to purging the world of all preternatural life. In an ironic twist, the Collective Army now finds itself partnered with the Kraven and the Casus, in exchange for information that they believe will enable them to exterminate the remaining nonhuman species.

The Consortium: A body of officials comprised of representatives from each of the remaining ancient clans, the Consortium is a sort of preternatural United Nations. Their purpose is to settle disputes and keep peace among the differing species, while working to hide the existence of the remaining clans from the human world. More than a thousand years ago, the original Consortium helped the Merrick imprison the Casus, after the Casuses' relentless killing of humans threatened to expose the existence of the nonhuman races. The council fashioned the Dark Markers in order to destroy the immortal killers, only to be murdered by the newly created Collective Army before they could complete the task. Years later, the Consortium re-formed, but by then its original archives had been lost... all traces of the Dark Markers supposedly destroyed during the Collective's merciless raids, which nearly led to the destruction of the clans.

The Dark Markers: Twelve metal crosses of enormous power that were mysteriously created by the original Consortium, they are the only known weapons capable of killing a Casus, sending its soul directly to hell. They also work as a talisman for those who wear them, offering protection from the Casus. Although the Dark Markers were hidden in order to keep them safe, there is a set of encrypted maps that lead to their locations. The Watchmen and the Buchanans are using these maps to help them find the Markers before they fall into enemy hands.

"Arm of Fire": Weapon mode for a Dark Marker. When held against the palm, a Dark Marker holds the power to change one's arm into an "Arm of Fire." When the cross is placed against the back of a Casus's neck, the flame-covered arm will sink into the monster's body, burning it from the inside out.

The Encrypted Maps: When Saige Buchanan discovered the first Dark Marker in Italy, she found a set of encrypted maps buried alongside the cross. The maps, which lead to the hidden locations of the Dark Markers, had been wrapped in oilcloth and preserved by some kind of spell.

The Death-Walkers: The demented souls of clansmen and women who were sent to hell for their sadistic crimes, and who are now managing to return to our world. It is unknown how to kill them, but they can be burned by a combination of holy water and salt. Driven mad by their time in hell, they are a formidable force of evil, seeking to create chaos and war among the remaining clans simply because they want to watch the world bleed. Characteristics: Although they retain certain traits from their original species, each of the Death-Walkers has cadaverously white skin and small horns that protrude from their temples, as well as deadly fangs and claws.

"The Eve Effect": A phenomenon that affects various breeds of shape-shifters, causing them to be drawn to certain females who touch the primal hungers of both the man and the beast. If a male falls in love with one of these females and bites her, she will be bonded to him as his mate for the rest of their lives.

The Infettato: Humans who have been infected by the bite of a Death-Walker. Once turned, they become the "walking dead" and it is impossible for them to regain their humanity. They live only to consume flesh, tracking their prey by scent and blindly obeying the orders of those who made them. As they feed, they become stronger, and they can only be killed when their hearts are removed from their chests and burned. Characteristics: Mottled, yellowish skin, gaunt faces and sunken eyes. Black skin that looks as if it has been burned surrounds their eyes and mouths.

The Kraven: The descendants of female Deschanel vampires who were raped by Casus males prior to their imprisonment. Treated little better than slaves and considered an embarrassing symbol of weakness, the Kraven have been such a closely guarded secret within the Deschanel clan that the Watchmen have only recently become aware of their existence. Hoping to improve their circumstances and become more powerful, the Kraven are working to facilitate the return of the Casus. Characteristics: They are believed to have long life-spans, and their fangs can be released only at night, causing their eyes to glow a deep, bloodred crimson. They can also easily pass for human, but can only be killed when a wooden stake is driven through their heart.

The Wasteland: A cold, desolate, dangerous region that was created by powerful magic, where exiled Deschanel "nests," or family units, are forced to live once the Consortium has passed judgment against them. Protected by spells that make it invisible to humans, this vast region "shares" physical space with the Scandinavian forests surrounding it.

The Watchmen: An organization of shapeshifters whose job it is to watch over the remaining ancient clans, they are considered the "eyes and ears" of the Consortium. They monitor the various nonhuman species, as well as the bloodlines of those clans that have become dormant. Prior to the recent Merrick awakenings, the most powerful Merrick bloodlines had been under Watchmen supervision. There are Watchmen compounds situated around the world, with each unit consisting of four to six warriors. Characteristics: Physical traits vary according to the specific breed of shape-shifter.

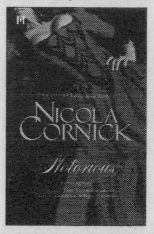

REQUEST YOUR FREE BOOKS!

2 FREE NOVELS FROM THE PARANORMAL ROMANCE COLLECTION PLUS 2 FREE GIFTS!

YES! Please send me 2 FREE novels from the Paranormal Romance Collection and my 2 FREE gifts (gifts are worth about $10). After receiving them, if I don't wish to receive any more books, I can return the shipping statement marked "cancel." If I don't cancel, I will receive 4 brand-new novels every month and be billed just $21.42 in the U.S. or $23.46 in Canada. That's a saving of at least 21% off the cover price of all 4 books. It's quite a bargain! Shipping and handling is just 50¢ per book in the U.S. and 75¢ per book in Canada.* I understand that accepting the 2 free books and gifts places me under no obligation to buy anything. I can always return a shipment and cancel at any time. Even if I never buy another book, the two free books and gifts are mine to keep forever.

237/337 HDN FEL2

Name	(PLEASE PRINT)	

Address		Apt. #

City	State/Prov.	Zip/Postal Code

Signature (if under 18, a parent or guardian must sign)

Mail to the **Reader Service**:
IN U.S.A.: P.O. Box 1867, Buffalo, NY 14240-1867
IN CANADA: P.O. Box 609, Fort Erie, Ontario L2A 5X3

Not valid for current subscribers to the Paranormal Romance Collection
or Harlequin® Nocturne™ books.

**Want to try two free books from another line?
Call 1-800-873-8635 or visit www.ReaderService.com.**

* Terms and prices subject to change without notice. Prices do not include applicable taxes. Sales tax applicable in N.Y. Canadian residents will be charged applicable taxes. Offer not valid in Quebec. This offer is limited to one order per household. All orders subject to credit approval. Credit or debit balances in a customer's account(s) may be offset by any other outstanding balance owed by or to the customer. Please allow 4 to 6 weeks for delivery. Offer available while quantities last.

Your Privacy—The Reader Service is committed to protecting your privacy. Our Privacy Policy is available online at www.ReaderService.com or upon request from the Reader Service.

We make a portion of our mailing list available to reputable third parties that offer products we believe may interest you. If you prefer that we not exchange your name with third parties, or if you wish to clarify or modify your communication preferences, please visit us at www.ReaderService.com/consumerchoice or write to us at Reader Service Preference Service, P.O. Box 9062, Buffalo, NY 14269. Include your complete name and address.

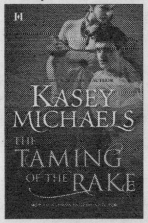

RHYANNON BYRD

77558	RUSH OF DARKNESS	___ $7.99 U.S.	___ $9.99 CAN.
77479	TOUCH OF TEMPTATION	___ $7.99 U.S.	___ $9.99 CAN.
77464	TOUCH OF SURRENDER	___ $7.99 U.S.	___ $9.99 CAN.
77448	TOUCH OF SEDUCTION	___ $7.99 U.S.	___ $9.99 CAN.

(limited quantities available)

TOTAL AMOUNT $ _____
POSTAGE & HANDLING $ _____
($1.00 FOR 1 BOOK, 50¢ for each additional)
APPLICABLE TAXES* $ _____
TOTAL PAYABLE $ _____

(check or money order—please do not send cash)

To order, complete this form and send it, along with a check or money order for the total above, payable to HQN Books, to: **In the U.S.:** 3010 Walden Avenue, P.O. Box 9077, Buffalo, NY 14269-9077; **In Canada:** P.O. Box 636, Fort Erie, Ontario, L2A 5X3.

Name: _____
Address: _____ City: _____
State/Prov.: _____ Zip/Postal Code: _____
Account Number (if applicable): _____

075 CSAS

*New York residents remit applicable sales taxes.
*Canadian residents remit applicable GST and provincial taxes.

PHRB0811BL